INNOCENT SPOUSE

by

Leonard Getz

A Conservatarian Press Publication

ISBN: 978-1-957586-17-5

Innocent Spouse

Conservatarian
Press

Acknowledgements

I am indebted to my wise and discerning editors Susan Goldberg and Jamie Wilson, whose thoughtful recommendations helped fine-tune the characters, tighten the chapters, and enhance the drama.

I am grateful to the fiction writing workshops led by Maria Cefaratti at the Main Line Night School in Radner PA (the workshop met at 10 in the morning). I benefited a great deal from the participants' feedback and used their suggestions in my revisions.

A big thank you to former law enforcement officers and novelists John French and Maria Watson for their expertise and explanations of what takes place at a crime scene, the roles and responsibilities of police officers, detectives and crime scene investigators.

I am blessed to have two intuitive readers, my wife Susan and daughter Sharona who made suggestions that sharpened the narrative.

A heartfelt thank you to David Swindle for first taking on my novel when he was editor of Liberty Island Publishing.

Dedication

To my loving and supportive family: wife Susan, son Philip, and daughters Sharona and Ariella

Chapter One

Taking in the breadth of Broad Street from the window of Doubletree Hotel's penthouse suite, journalist Sandra Wolf fixed her eyes on the bronze statue of William Penn atop castle-like City Hall, silhouetted against the twilight sky, hoping for a sign, for an answer to how to play her next move. Then she remembered William Penn was a religious man and dismissed that hope. He would certainly frown on her behavior.

Resting against the bare chest of her boss, Alexander Anderson, Sandra looked slightly southward and stopped at the venerated Academy of Music where she had attended "The Rascals" concert and wrote a review, even though at the time of their popularity she was barely a toddler. Two blocks down, the conventional Kimmel Center and the risk-taking Wilma Theatre duked it out for center stage.

Brushing her boss's goatee with her signature fluffy black and frosted hair, she turned her attention further south, as far as her eyes let her see, where lately most of her investigative journalism had taken her. It also put her in the crosshairs of her boss, so much so that after secretly meeting him in this hotel room every Tuesday for more than a year, leaning against his chest was like lying on a cushion of crystal nails.

Between her slim fingers she balanced Virginia Slims, her choice of smokes since high school when everyone else puffed Marlboros, and edged her full red-lipsticked mouth into a smile.

"When my article comes out tomorrow, Alex," she said taking a deep, healthy drag, "no one will ever again lump the *Philadelphia Times* into that irritating category, 'liberal media'."

She waited for Alex to take the bait but only felt his chest heave. She had witnessed him lash out against less biting comments. He has been at the helm of the *Times* for over thirty years, writing editorials that defined the paper's opinions, *his* paper and defended it fearlessly. Why was he silent? What was on his mind? Ah, of course she knew what was on his mind. What was on his mind every Tuesday night. He didn't want an argument to spoil it.

"Not only that," Sandra persisted, blowing smoke rings in the direction of south Philly. "We're going to be sending a shock wave through the city. The *Philadelphia Chronicle* won't know what hit them."

She felt him breath with emphasis, like an explanation point.

"Shock waves? Is that what you think we're about? Shock waves sputter and dissipate. And why do you think I give a rat's ass about the *Chronicle*? We're the award-winning newspaper in this city. They're nothing."

"And that's why our readers will listen when we tell them something they don't expect to hear from us. Because they trust us." His arms were around her waist, so she put her hand over his, feeling his wedding band. "I know you care about trust."

She tapped her ash into the black ashtray with the word "Doubletree" in the center. The penthouse suite was the only one where smoking was allowed, and Sandra took full advantage.

"To be honest, right now, I'll show you what I care most about."

Alex leaned over to get his shirt he had thrown on the bed and took a marijuana joint from the pocket.

Sandra eyed it with reluctance. "Oh, of course that. You wouldn't forget that."

Alex licked the stick and, like a dental hygienist, placed it gently between Sandra's barely opened mouth. She let him take her hand holding the cigarette and light the joint with the ember.

"You're going to love this," he said.

She closed her eyes and dragged fully. If love meant inhaling into her lungs all the vexation she had for him at that moment, wishing this simple, decadent act could somehow emasculate him, dissolve his power, then yes, she loved it. But she inhaled too much and coughed. Alex slipped the joint from her mouth and put it in his own, closed his eyes and inhaled. For him it was fuel to refurbish his soul.

"We've been losing circulation for months," she said with another little cough. "Ads too. But all that's going to change." She pointed her cigarette centimeters from igniting his chest hairs.

Alex took another toke. "You think you're telling me something I don't know?"

"I'll tell you what I know. I know when people read about the extremism going on in our city, they're going to want to know more about it. And we'll give them more. Circulation will grow. Ads will come back."

The joint dangled in Alex's mouth like a plank. The mixed aromas of cigarette, weed and Sandra's Kilian fragrance swirled in the room. "I've won 11 Pulitzer Prizes. That should tell you I know what our readers want. What makes you think you know more than me?"

Sandra cocked her head and gave her lips a playful twist. "I see. Well, I don't care much for prizes. Unless you want to give me one."

"It's in that bag on the dresser."

"What is?"

"Your prize."

"My prize? I was just kidding."

Sandra spied a white shopping bag with black ropes peering from behind the flat screen Samsung and wondered how she'd missed it. Her mind must have been shifting gears when she walked into the room; decompressing from meeting a defiant union leader, then gearing up to what could be a defining moment in her career.

From the shopping bag Sandra pulled out a box from Victoria's Secret. She pulled out black garters, black panties, and a black see-through bra.

"I feel like that scene in Annie Hall when Diane Keaton says to Woody Allen, 'this is more like a present for you.'"

He grinned and took another toke. "Now that you mention it, you do look a little like Keaton."

"You went to Victoria's Secret?"

"Not a chance. I had it delivered here."

"That was clever." Strands of frosted locks draped over her delicate forehead. "Well, I'll tell you what. You wait right here."

"Nowhere else I'd rather be." Toke. "Than right here, right now, with you. Just like the song says."

"Yeah, just like the song," She unclipped her halter top and headed to the bathroom, giving Alex a glimpse of the blue ash leaf tattoo he got for her at a shop on South Street, the same place Alex got his, a scorpion.

* * *

Alex turned on CNN, lit another joint, and looked at himself in the Ben Franklin shaped mirror. Just a few strands left of his famous wavy hair, now gray. None of his current colleagues had known him when he was in college. Back then, his hair bounced over his shoulders, and once was pulled by a policeman when Alex was in the course of resisting arrest for instigated campus riots. That got assaulting an officer added to the list. The charge didn't stick. He claimed he was just flailing his arms in surprise when the officer grabbed him by the hair, and hitting him was an accident. He remembered chuckling to himself when the charges were dropped, thinking, I should have hit him harder.

He flexed his muscles, glad they were still hard enough from years of pumping. Maybe not as pronounced as when he wore his tank top on the beach. His legs, still sturdy and enduring after weekly five-mile jogs, cramped up now and then, forcing him to pull over when driving to massage away the pain.

He took note of how the suite had changed over the years. The clunky TV that had once rested on a stand was now a flat screen jutting out from the wall; the three-drawer wooden dresser was replaced with a wardrobe that opened to a small closet and three small drawers. The state-of-the-art coffee maker was a disappointment. The old Sunbeam had a warming plate and a glass beaker that filled two ceramic cups to the brim. The oddity that took its place had no beaker, no hot plate. A foamy coffee packet needed to be rolled into a ball and stuffed into a plastic shell, and a cellophane wrapper needed to be torn away from a Styrofoam cup. With luck, you'd get a cupful that wasn't weak. No lingering in the shower, lest the coffee gets cold. So much for modern hotel coffee.

Sandra stepped out of the bathroom, her hair wet and matted close to her scalp. She stood with her hands on her hips wearing a white terrycloth bathrobe with "Doubletree" embroidered on the front. She let the robe fall and stood there in Alex's gifts.

"Hi, Woody," Sandra said with a smile, glancing downward.

Alex approached and ran his hands from her cheeks to her dark shoulders. They came to rest on the bra covering her firm breasts. She looked up at him and kissed him.

"Just curious," Sandra said. "What title did you give it?"

"What are you talking about?"

"My article, silly. I want to know what you came up with. What title did you give it?" She held his hands and kissed him softly on the lips.

"I don't remember." He kissed her back hard and moved his hands to her ass as if doing so would make her forget the question.

"Oh, come on. How can you not remember?"

"Really, I don't remember."

"Alex, you always have the last word on headlines. You can't not remember." She removed his hands and held them.

Alex pursed his lips. "Listen, I meant to tell you. I needed to push it back a couple of days."

Sandra let go of his hands and stepped back.

"You did what?" She shook her head in quick succession as if doing so will erase what she just heard. "You did fucking what?"

"We had some last-minute switching to do. We had other pieces we needed to go with that couldn't wait. It'll be in on Thursday."

"Bullshit! You killed it!" She picked up the robe. "I knew it!"

"Yeah, don't get all bent out of shape. I just told you it'll be in on Thursday. No big deal."

"What's more important than our worst enemy living next door?"

"Well, if he lives next door, he's not going anywhere so what's the damn rush?"

"You know, Alex, there's something about you, I don't know, something always told me…"

"What? What is it about me? Maybe it's about you. You used to be so level-headed. You wrote for a small-time newspaper in Blue Ash, Ohio, and I gave you a job in one of the most prestigious newspapers in the country. Now you practically accuse an icon of Philadelphia of being a terrorist and you expect me to run with it without being absolutely sure?"

"What aren't you sure about? I told you the whole story."

"Sure about everything. I'm not going to put the city in panic mode. That would be irresponsible, don't you think? It's not just your article, it's the reputation of the *Times*. My reputation. I'm having Evan do some fact checking. That's all. If it all checks out it'll be in on Thursday."

"So you don't trust me."

"Of course I do. This is not about trust. It's about…it's about confirmation. What are you doing?"

"What does it look like?" Sandra slipped up her skirt and reached for her pink sweater.

"Oh, come on. You're blowing this all out of whack. I told you, it'll be in Thursday's edition. That's a promise. We're just checking a few things. I didn't tell you because I knew you'd get all bent out of shape about it, and I was right. Look at you. Wednesday, Thursday, what's the difference? There is no difference."

"What few things?"

Alex stared at her.

"I knew it."

"Don't get so damn dramatic. Hey, look what else I got you. Wait." Alex opened his gym bag and pulled out a bottle of Brunello di Montalcino. "I wanted to surprise you with your favorite wine. Another prize for you. Guess how I got it?"

She continued getting dressed.

"I bid on this bottle for you online and won. And I made sure we had fine wine glasses brought up. Look there on the table."

He took the corkscrew, placed the point in the center of the cork and twisted. "We have the whole night. And the night is young."

Sandra straightened her pink sweater over her new Victoria's Secret undergarments and slipped into her black pointed shoes.

"That's right, Alex. The night is young. I'm young. But you're not. You're still in Woodstock. You still have that delusional pothead leftist mentality. I'm done with that. Since 9/11, my eyes are open. You don't even know how to open yours. And if you did, you'd refuse to believe what you're looking at. Over and over, I watched those planes plowing into the Twin Towers, turning solid concrete and metal into smoke, chards, dust, pulp. The evil of those terrorists turned two innocent passenger planes into mad bullets, and the more I listened to the mendacity of their apologists, the more my view of the world turned. I want our readers to turn with me. I want the *Times* to turn and look at the world for what it is. But as long as you, Alex, the master of our masthead, remains blind and dumb, so will the *Times'* readership. And so will the other journalists if they continue to follow you, which they probably will because they don't know any better. I don't know whether I feel sorrier for you or for your readership. No, I do know. It's not for you."

Sandra opened the door, turned to him, and said, "You should just go home to your wife."

She slammed the door, breaking the silence of the thick, gold carpeted hallway. She pressed the elevator button but didn't have the patience to wait. She took off her shoes and ran down the 23 flights of stairs.

* * *

Alex lay in bed, smoked another joint, watched CNN. He checked his watch. It was midnight. He concluded she wasn't coming back. He decided to head home.

But as he left the hotel garage, he changed his mind. Still high, he drove his Mercedes to South Pine Street, where the city did its best to make the street reminiscent of 17th century America with a cobbled stoned pavement and old gas-style streetlamps with modern bulbs. He parked across the street from Sandra's house.

He had a key but decided that might not be his best move. Better to ring her bell and be let in. He would tell her the piece will be published online first thing in the morning.

He opened his car door, almost knocking over a young, husky, multi-tattooed bicycle rider.

"Fucksamatter witt' chu?" the man said, swerving to avoid a collision. He continued pedaling but looked backward, expecting a response or maybe a fight. Alex ignored him and headed straight to the brick steps that led up to Sandra's front door.

"Asshole." The man gave Alex the finger and pedaled on.

Chapter Two

Ever since Congress decided to take pity on the wives of tax cheats, IRS agent Ivan Rand Samuels's job had become a disaster. Take, for example the audit he did of racketeer Ed Malano, a mob boss from South Philadelphia who gambled away most of his ill-gotten gains. Never paid a dime of tax on the illegal income until Ivan slapped him with a tax bill quadruple the value of his Drexel Hill home, where he lived with his college student daughter Liz. Malano wouldn't, or more correctly couldn't, pay the bill, nor much of anything else, as he strolled the greens of Allenwood, the country club of Pennsylvania prisons, where he would be living for the next twenty years. He wasn't sent there because he didn't pay his taxes—only devout tax cheats get thrown in jail. Malano was there because of his more colorful illegalities: extortion, drug smuggling, gambling and prostitution.

His wife Stephanie had no choice but to go to work to provide for their three kids. Six months later, her paycheck was garnished by the IRS. She, along with millions of other spouses with deadbeat husbands, was shocked to learn that when she said "I do" under the canopy, it also meant "I will pay" the taxes with my lawful wedded husband in sickness, and in health, and incarceration. For wives with absentee husbands, the law firm of Dyckman and Sirrato specialized in combatting agents like Ivan, finding creative ways to argue that their clients did not know and had no reason to know anything about their husbands' unreported income. Clients showed up adorned with Tiffany jewelry, draped in Neiman Marcus garb, and perfected with Dr. Nose surgery, yet Alice Dyckman and Geraldine Sirrato managed to pull off magic.

This May morning Ivan rode the SEPTA rail, grateful its annual strike threat was averted after midnight negotiations. His destination was the Federal Court House on Market Street, where he would face Alice Dyckman defending her diamond-studded client, Stephanie Malano. Losing to Alice was not only a loss for the government; it also meant Ivan would be picking up the dinner tab on their usual Friday night date. He glanced over the top of the *Philadelphia Chronicle*, eyeballing the people who rode the train every morning for years. He went back to his article about the Phillies loss last night, but not before quickly glancing at the article his daughter wanted him to read.

His morning had begun like always, a few moments watching his girl sleep curled up in a tight ball, arms around the feather pillow printed with pictures of willow trees and cumulus clouds. It was her security, one of the few constants in her life. Not her hair; that had gone from long to short, to frizzy to straight, from red to green to blue; her make-up had gone from rich red lipstick and eye shadow mystique to deep dark gothic, and now minimalism. Her emotional state since losing the woman they both loved, her mother and his wife, to breast cancer five years ago had been a spiraling roller-coaster ride filled with pain, anxiety, inwardness; renewal, independence, and at last focus. Nobody could explain, least of all Ivan, why Nancy, who had never missed an opportunity to extend a helping hand to the sick and the elderly, was forced to endure a painful slippage from life, her family helplessly surrounding her. Ivan's questions were the same as those of others dealt unexplainable blows of life, leaving those who survive no other option than to accept and go on. This was all he could tell his young daughter, shaken and afraid to tiptoe back into the world without her mother's embrace. Now she would have to step into the mine field of life by herself.

His daughter stirred, just before her alarm went off. It was safe to talk.

"Love watching you sleep."

Liz opened her eyes and rolled over. "I need a few more minutes."

"What are your plans today?"

"Journalism class," Liz mumbled in her pillow.

"How's that going?"

Liz turned her rolling over into a sit up. "Great. Sandra offered to take me along as an intern to do investigative reporting."

"Investigating what?"

"Don't know." Liz rubbed her eyes. "But she said it would be an eye-opener."

"Is that going to be your gig? When you're all grown up?" Ivan said, realizing after he spoke that it was a tactical slip up. Way to go, reminding Liz of her mother who would not be there.

"Yeah, when I'm all grown up."

"Wish I knew what I want to be when I'm all grown up," Ivan said, trying to lighten up the conversation.

"Hey wanna see something freaky?" Suddenly refreshed Liz reached for her iPhone on the pinewood night table. She hovered over the little gadget as if she was sending a message to the control tower in Nevada. Ivan was still a flip-phone guy, but Liz "needed" this latest device or life would be downright dysfunctional. She needed real time contact with her friends, or to keep up on the crisis in Kandahar. All in the space of the palm he remembered holding as they walked through the Philadelphia Zoo, stopping to stare at the chimpanzees.

"I mean you may not think so but I think it's weird. Something is going on."

"Peace broke out in the Congo?"

"Just wait a sec. Okay, look."

Liz held the iPhone to her father's face, but all Ivan could make out were dots that reminded him of vanilla beans in Breyers ice cream.

"What am I supposed to be reading?"

"Oh, sorry, I'll make the font bigger."

Liz swished her thumb and pointing finger across the screen, then handed the iPhone back to her dad with a smile confident that Ivan had to be able to read this.

"Be Wary of Thy Neighbor…?"

"The article is scary enough but there's more. The story is by Sandra Wolf. You know, my journalism instructor at Temple I just told you about."

"She found out her neighbor is a drug dealer?"

"Worse. Maybe a terrorist. But that's not even the weird part. The weird part is that the article is in the *Philadelphia Chronicle*. She works for the *Philadelphia Times*."

"Maybe she was traded like Bobby Abreu."

"Yeah, that would be like laser fast since she was working for the *Times* when I spoke to her yesterday. She didn't say anything about leaving the *Times* or working for the *Chronicle*."

"Are you that close she would disclose that to you? Changing jobs is not something one discusses until it's a sure thing. And certainly not to a student."

"Yeah, but I don't know. There would've been a hint somewhere."

"The more you know about people the more you realize you really don't know them," Ivan pulled up a sock that had somehow slid down into his arch.

"I guess I'll find out tonight when I see her in class."

"What time did that article come out?"

Liz took the iPhone from her father and scrolled down. "Looks like six fifteen this morning."

"She must have gotten it to the *Chronicle* late last night or really early this morning," Ivan noted.

"I'll let you know. Anyway, I still need a little more sleep."

"But you're wide awake."

"No I'm not."

* * *

The plan was for Ivan to meet the IRS attorney Jerry Flowers outside the courtroom to get their ducks in a row. It would be Jerry's first trial. Although his colleagues and the assistant chief counsel would be in the courtroom watching him sweat before Judge Whitney's logical daggers known for pushing IRS attorneys off balance, and the tall, intimidating, equally sharp stilettos of the unbeaten Alice Dykman, Jerry's only real lifeline would be Ivan, the agent who proposed the tax assessment in the first place. But Jerry was not there. Ivan opened the courtroom door and saw him sitting up front, shuffling papers, hands and forehead already damp from perspiration. Sitting across the aisle was Alice Dykman, her shapely black-stockinged legs crossed, arm stretched and relaxed on the top of the wooden seat to her right. On her left sat her client Stephanie Malano, who strained to look calm while fiddling with the white synthetic strap of her straw purse.

"What happened to meeting outside the courtroom?" Ivan asked, taking a seat next to Jerry. The lawyer's tall, lanky frame seemed shapeless, draped in a dark blue suit a tad too big. Ivan thought someone must have told him blue means power and size doesn't matter.

"I'm sorry, Ivan. I forgot. I just wanted to make sure I have everything."

"Do you?"

"I do. And I'm ready. Got my folders here, my list of cross-examination questions there, just as you suggested."

"Okay, then."

Jerry had graduated from Villanova law school where, for practice, he defended taxpayers against the IRS. If he got any taxes reduced it was mainly because they were entitled to the reduction anyway, but it made Jerry look like a hero. Jerry didn't look much like a hero now. In fact in a few moments, he would look like minced meat after Alice chewed him up, spit him out and stepped on him with the sharp-heeled boots Ivan had bought for her at Macy's during a summer sale.

"All rise," said the bailiff as Judge Whitney strode in. Before she even sat down at the bench, the judge said, "Let's get started..

"Tell the court, Stephanie," Alice said to her client sitting in the witness box, "what you now do for a living."

Ivan had never seen Stephanie wear less than three bracelets on each wrist, diamond earrings, and a pearl necklace perfectly matched to pastel designer dresses and Jimmy Choo heels, hair and makeup model-perfect. Today, she wore a pants suit probably purchased at Ross Dress for Less next door to Strawbridges, flat shoes, no jewelry. Her hair was limp and pulled back in a ponytail. It was clear Alice coached her client to appear as if she was barely getting by. Ivan pulled at his own ponytail, longer than Stephanie's and grayer.

"I'm just a saleslady at Strawbridges. I do perfume," she said clearly.

"And how long have you worked there?"

"Like maybe a few months."

"And before that what did you do?"

"Me? I was just a housewife, just taking care of the kids and all."

"So you never worked outside the home before you started the job at Straw-bridges. Is that right?"

"Well if you don't count working at a pizza shop back in high school, no. But that was like a million years ago."

"Ok, so how long have you been married, Stephanie?"

"Fifteen years."

"And during these fifteen years your husband supported you and the kids, is that right?"

"Right."

"Who did the household shopping?"

"You mean like for food and clothes and toys and stuff for the kids?

"That's right."

"I did."

"And how did you pay for your shopping?"

"Eddie gave me money."

"Eddie Malano your husband," Alice clarified.

"Yeah, Eddie."

"Ok, now I need to get a little personal here because we need some more details on how your husband gave you money and how much."

"Hey, I got nothing to hide. I ain't a dishonest person."

"Nobody is saying that, Stephanie. We just need to understand how things worked a little more. So for example, did your husband gave you money every week or how did it work?"

"Yeah, every week, five hundred bucks."

"And that would pay for groceries, clothes…?"

"Yeah, everything I needed to buy. Going to the doctor, haircuts, school supplies, stuff like that. For the kids mostly. And groceries. And if I needed more, I'd tell Eddie like maybe for a suit for Joey 'cause he wasn't fitting in his suit at the time because he was in a growing spurt you know? Like that and he would give me more."

"Did you keep track of what he gave you every week?"

"Na ah."

"Ok, so now I'm going to ask you some questions about the tax return you filed with your husband."

"Yeah."

"You did file joint tax returns with your husband all these years, is that right?"

"Yeah, I did, I guess."

"Did you look at the tax returns before you signed them?

"Not a lot. I saw what we was making a lot of money. I mean he was. He just told me where to sign and I signed."

"When you say "a lot of money" how much are you talking about?"

"I'd say in the six figures range."

"What business was your husband in?"

"Well, like I told you before. I didn't know a lot about what my husband did except that it was a family business and they owned property all over Philadelphia is all I know or any of us know."

"When you say "any of us" who do you mean?"

"I mean like my sister-in-laws and the cousins. That's just the way it is. They make the money, we take care of the kids and house and all that."

"So just so the court understands," Alice said, narrowing in to her point. "You knew your husband was making a lot of money because you saw large amounts on the tax return. But let me ask you this. If your husband, for some reason, did not include all his income on this tax return would you have any way of knowing that?"

"I wouldn't have the foggiest idea. I wouldn't know that for nuthin."

"Okay, Stephanie, that's all the questions I have for the moment. Now Mr. Flowers is going to ask you some questions."

"Okay. Yeah." Stephanie shifted in her seat as if trying to make herself uncomfortable.

Ivan had seen that shift movement before: when he was sitting at their rosewood dining room table with their accountant, Ogden Dimitri, going through their bank accounts and expense receipts from Robbins 8th and Walnut, to Nina Bucci's Brazilian workout pants purchased at the Reward Project, to Bettye Muller's Tartan Rita shoes bought at Benjamin Lovell at Rittenhouse Square. All paid in cash and a receipt for every purchase. Ivan spent a week totaling three years' worth of purchases. This, plus Eddie's compounding gambling losses, and the income from his criminal activity, when Ivan compared it all with what the Malanos reported on their tax returns, came to an under-reporting of taxable income in the millions. Ivan saw that Stephanie was getting wind of this as she nervously listened from the kitchen, pretending to be preoccupied making cannoli.

The other times he noticed her shift was when she stood outside Strawbridges, defying the cold with fellow smoking co-workers. He passed her on his way to the Reading Terminal to pick up a sandwich. Some days she eyed him with disdain, some days she turned away, some days she would nod hi.

Jerry approached the witness box and Stephanie crossed her legs twice. "Ok, I do have some questions for you as Mrs. Dyckman mentioned."

"Ms. Dyckman," Alice corrected without looking up from her writing pad.

Judge Cynthia Whitney looked down at her. She had been a tax court judge for over twenty years, presiding over numerous innocent spouse cases. Even though she taunted IRS attorneys, her record showed she held for the government as often as she held for the spouse. Her reputation was one of seeing the facts, but also of reading the quirks in people and getting them right. She was not often corrected by an attorney.

"Is that really necessary?" Judge Whitney said to Alice.

"Your honor, in an innocent spouse case I think it's important to establish that a "Mrs" is a married woman, frequently a victim of her husband's tax shenanigans, as we have here."

Judge Whitney was about to respond with what Ivan thought would be a mild admonishment, but a befuddled Jerry beat her to the punch.

"Sorry. Ms. Dyckman."

He turned now to Stephanie who looked ready for whatever Jerry dished out.

"You had mentioned that your husband gave you five hundred dollars a week, is that right?"

"Yeah."

"And if you needed more money, you would ask him for more and he would give it to you, is that right?"

"Yeah."

"I see here in our records you purchased a lot of clothes for yourself, rather expensive clothes."

"What do you mean expensive?"

"Well, I see here you purchased a beaver mink coat for two thousand dollars."

"That was a birthday present."

"And here a designer pocketbook for six hundred and fifty dollars."

"Objection!" Alice stood up. "Is the counsel from the IRS actually saying that because Stephanie bought a decent purse, she's responsible for her husband's unpaid tax of over three point five million dollars plus penalties and interest?"

Judge Whitney looked down at Jerry. "Is that what you're saying?"

"What I'm trying to establish is that although Mrs. Malano may not know what her husband did for a living, Stephanie did benefit from his income."

"Your honor," Alice said. "The petitioner is not disagreeing that her husband provided for her needs, bought her gifts occasionally and put a roof over her head. We contend that Stephanie did not know or have reason to know that not all her husband's income was reported on their tax return or that Stephanie knew she was benefiting from income that would not be reported on the tax return. In order to do that, the government would have to establish that Stephanie knew the money used to purchase the pocketbook was not reported on the return. I would request the court to ask the government to establish that connection."

"Can you do that, Mr. Flowers? Establish the connection between the unreported income and the mink coat and pocketbook?" Judge Whitney asked with a look that told Ivan she knew he could not.

"Not exactly. But we can show that the Malanos spent much more during the years in question than they actually reported on their tax return and, since they lived in the same household as husband and wife, each benefited from the entire income. Therefore, Stephanie is just as responsible as Mr. Malano."

"Again, if I may, your honor" Alice said, getting up again, "the petitioner is not disagreeing with the government's determination that there is unreported taxable income, and we are not disputing the tax liability. What the petitioner is arguing is that under the IRS Section 6015(f) Stephanie did not know nor have reason to know of the underpayment of tax attributable to her husband's unreported income and therefore she is not personally liable for the understatement. She's not disputing that numerous items were purchased for her or that she even purchased them herself. What we think the government needs to do is prove that Stephanie knew when these items were purchased that it was coming from income that was not reported on the tax return."

"I agree," said Judge Whitney. "Can you do that, Mr. Flowers?"

"I will. Yes. That is what I intend to do, yes."

Ivan thought about how much his Friday dinner date with Alice would cost him.

"Then please continue."

Jerry walked over to his table frantically searching for something in his pile of papers.

"What do you need Jerry?' Ivan offered.

"I'm looking for the gambling winnings," Jerry whispered as if he was about to pull out his secret weapon.

"Don't sweat it. I have a copy right here for you." Ivan's thick fingers flipped through his orderly binder and pulled out a folder labeled "Malano's Gambling Winnings."

"Great! Thanks!" Jerry whispered and twisted into a full turn like Ivan remembered learning how to do in his fourth-grade gym class.

"Mrs. Malano, the record shows that you and Mr. Malano frequented the casinos in Atlantic City. Would you agree with that?"

"Yeah."

"In fact, during the summers of the years in question before this court, you frequented the Tropicana, the Trump, Taj Mahal, Caesars, Harrahs, Ballys, and Resorts Casino."

"And?" Stephanie said.

Jerry looked up. "Oh, there's more? Oh, ok, could you please tell the court what others?"

"No, I mean, and what's your question?" Stephanie looked up at the judge apologetically. "I'm sorry."

"No apology necessary," said Judge Whitney.

"I'm coming to that," Jerry said. "According to these records you and your husband had winnings at each of these hotels reported to you or your husband on a Form 1099G totaling, let's see, 75 thousand in one year, 120 thousand in another year, 85 thousand in another year. Here, let me show you."

Jerry marched over to Stephanie with outstretched arms holding out the folder. Before Jerry could reach her, Stephanie held up her palm like a traffic cop. "You don't need to show me. I believe you."

Jerry stopped in his tracks. "Ok, fine." Then, turning to Alice he said, "I have a copy for you, I know I should have given it to you beforehand."

"Don't bother. We have copies," Alice said.

"Oh, great. So, I'll go on. Mrs.—Ms.—Malano, you remember frequenting these casinos with your husband, is that correct?"

"Correct."

"And do you remember seeing or witnessing or even perhaps participating in these numerous winnings at these casinos?"

"Yes."

"Ok, great. Now, I also have here receipts from shops located on the premises of these casino hotels and on the boardwalk. Receipts for purchases of expensive woman's clothing, and accessories and jewelry. Would you like to see them?"

"Not really."

"Ok, so you were aware of the gambling winnings, and you were aware of the purchases you made while you frequented these casinos. But I want to show you something."

Jerry quickly walked back to his desk where Ivan was already with his arm out handing Jerry a folder.

"These are the tax returns, right?" he asked Ivan.

"Yes, they are, Jerry."

"Mrs. Malano I want you to take a look at these tax returns which bear your signature. Do you see your signature?"

Stephanie glanced at the spot Jerry was pointing to.

"I do."

"Now I want to point something out to you. Here on this line is where you're supposed to report your gambling winnings. Do you see any gambling winnings reported on that line?"

"No."

"Did you perhaps look over the tax return to make sure the gambling winnings were reported somewhere on the return?"

"I sure didn't."

"Right. So you knew you had gambling winnings, yet you signed a tax return, in fact three tax returns, knowing you had gambling winnings and knowing that they weren't reported.

"Your honor, I think this proves that Mrs. Malano knew and had reason to know that taxable income was not reported on their joint tax return for which she and he husband are jointly and severally liable for, and therefore she does not meet the requirement under Internal Revenue Code Sixty Fifteen b."

Jerry had made his point.

"Your honor," Alice calmly stood up. "I have here documentation of numerous gambling losses that the Malanos incurred that weren't reported either. We have all the records and copies for Mr. Flowers." Alice handed two copies to the bailiff, one for Jerry, one for the judge. "You'll see that the losses more than offset the winnings, your honor. I would also like to point out that the bulk of the unreported income that the government found is really not attributable to these gambling winnings but to the racketeering, extortion, drug money, prostitution and web porn that Eddie Malano was engaged in, operations that Mrs. Malano hadn't the foggiest clue about, as she has already testified. She believed her husband was in the real estate business, and in fact real estate was part of his business, the part that he did report on the tax returns in question – which was in the six figures."

Jerry flipped the pages, absorbing them carefully as Alice spoke. Ivan wrote "inadmissible" on a piece of paper and slid it over to Jerry. Jerry nodded appreciatively. as Ivan felt his cell phone vibrate. It was his supervisor. He ignored it; now was not the time.

"Yes, your honor, these documents, these receipts for alleged losses, they're inadmissible. If Mrs. Malano – or Mr. Malano for that matter wanted the government to consider these so-called losses, they had 90 days to do so prior to the actual assessment of the additional tax. But they did not do so. So I would ask that these documents be ruled inadmissible."

Alice again slowly rose. "We are not asking for a redetermination of the tax at this time. But if the tax deficiency was ever going to be paid, we could file a claim for refund for the taxes that these losses would offset. All we're asking for here is that we just cut to the chase and take these losses into consideration in the matter of Stephanie being innocent of her husband's wrongdoings."

"I will take both your arguments under advisement," said Judge Whitney. "Do you have any more questions for Mrs. Malano, Mr. Flowers?"

"Yes. Yes I do. In your claim, you say you would suffer economic hardship if you were not granted relief."

"Yeah. I mean, I work at Strawbridges doing perfume. I take home maybe four hundred or five hundred a week depending how I do on sales. There's no way I could pay the millions of taxes and penalties and interest or whatever. Then you guys keep on adding interest so you're punishing me because I can't pay in the first place. And I got kids at home, like I said. They cost a fortune. So I don't know, I mean, yeah, it's a hardship, it's a damn hardship. Oh, excuse me I didn't mean to say that, your honor."

"I've heard worse," Judge Whitney said.

"I see you live on a house in Plymouth Meeting that was appraised at one point five million dollars. Is that correct?"

"I didn't know about what it was appraised at. If you say so, then I guess that's what it is."

"Your honor, if I could interject, I believe the government is suggesting that Mrs. Malano either sell her house or take a loan against the equity in the house, is that correct?"

Jerry was quick to respond. "It has not been shown that those options are not available, and in any case I would have to point out that I would hardly call Mrs. Malano a hardship situation while living in home valued at over a million dollars."

"So she sells the house. Where would Stephanie and her children live? Anything she could afford on a $30,000 a year salary would put her in a hardship situation." Alice shuffled through some papers. "And as far as a loan, here are applications for a home equity loan and lines of credit Stephanie recently applied for. All denied."

"Your honor, the government is not asking Mrs. Malano to sell her house nor does the government have any plans at this time to seize the house, even though the government does have a lien against the house. What we are saying is that Mrs. Malano benefited from all the money, legal or otherwise, that Mr. Malano received. He consistently gave her cash, and she didn't care where it was coming from. Real estate deals are paid by check. So the cash had to come from someplace else. She chose to turn a blind eye to its source. Again, she never inquired, nor did it seem she cared where it was coming from. All she knew is that it continued to flow, so she didn't ask questions. She could have asked. And since there is no record of spousal abuse, there's no reason why she could not have asked her husband when she signed the return, if all the income, all the cash, all the gambling winnings were reported on the tax return."

"So you're saying I would be better off tax-wise if my husband beat me?" Stephanie piped up.

"Well, in a way, yes. It's just one of the factors we look at to determine if innocent spouse relief should be granted. In your case, it's not."

"I see, I guess."

Ivan scribbled something down on piece of paper and handed it to Jerry. "Now is the time."

"Yes, yes," Jerry said to himself but loud enough to let everyone in the court know he's not finished. And at that moment Ivan again felt his cell phone vibrate. Again, he ignored it.

"Mrs. Malano, you said you've been married to Eddie for fifteen years, is that right?"

"That's right, yeah."

"When exactly did you meet?"

"We met in high school."

"When you were a freshman in high school?"

"Actually, I was a sophomore when we met and he was a junior. And we got married after I graduated. I was nineteen almost twenty."

"Ok, so you met him when you were about sixteen and he was about seventeen, is that about right?"

"Yeah, I guess that sounds about right."

"I want to show you some newspaper clipping and some police reports."

Ivan pulled them out of his folder, including a copy for Alice and the judge.

Stephanie looked at the documents with apprehension. She looked up to Alice searching for help. Alice looked over the clippings and it was clear she was seeing this for the first time. She did not rise.

"These are old newspaper clippings and police reports about your husband's arrest for burglary and auto theft and drug dealing. He was arrested when he was eighteen and nineteen years old, during the time you and he were dating or perhaps even engaged.

Stephanie remained silent.

"Is that right, Mrs. Malano?"

"I guess. I suppose."

"Mrs. Malano, could you please now look up from the documents and look at me?" said Jerry, taking a giant step towards taking control of these proceedings.

Stephanie looked up.

"Mrs. Malano, isn't it true that you knew Eddie Malano was involved in illegal activity when you first met him, while you were engaged with him and even after you married him?"

"I love my husband. I don't judge him. That's for others to do. Like you guys."

"Very noble. And by marrying him and sticking with him, knowing his history of involvement in illegal activity, you chose to go along for the ride, wherever that ride would take you." Jerry found his groove and slid into home.

Stephanie looked pleadingly at Alice for help.

"Objection!" Alice bellowed. "What Stephanie did when she was an innocent, naïve, starry-eyed teenager has no bearing on this case."

Peering over her reading glasses perched on the tip of her nose, Judge Whitney looked straight and sternly into Alice's eyes and said, "I think it does. Overruled."

"No further questions, your honor." Ivan nodded to Jerry, oblivious to his smiling colleagues several rows behind him.

Ivan's phone vibrated again and this time he answered. "Court just adjorned."

"You need to get over here right away A new case just came in and I'm assigning it to you. The *Philadelphia Times*."

Chapter Three

Ivan took the elevator from the fifth-floor courtroom down to the first-floor lobby decorated with paintings of national revolutionary luminaries. The painted figures' watchful eyes followed him through the connecting corridor between the courthouse and the federal building. The federal building side was not as spacious, nor were the folks dressed in smart suits like at the courthouse. Blue jeans and sweatshirts were typical attire.

"How was your day in court?" asked Hector one cubicle over from Ivan. He wore blue jeans and a sweatshirt. "Another damsel in distress of domestic tax delinquency?"

Ivan noted the red blinking light on this desk phone. A file thick as a brick that wasn't there when he left work last night squatted in his inbox. "Right as usual, Hector."

"Did Alice get her off the hook? As usual?"

"Maybe not."

"What's this? You said something to wow Judge Whitney that the wife knew it all and spent it all?"

"Whether she's deemed innocent or not doesn't really matter, does it? The tax will never get paid."

"I hear ya. We're all just going through the system, through the motions. Just like life itself. Life is just one big innocent spouse case."

"Don't you have work to do, Hector?'

"I'm talking to you. That takes work. By the way, the boss lady stopped by twice for you."

Ivan gave the thick file on his desk a quick flip. "And she said if I saw you, to tell you to stop by her office right away, "very important" and I quote. So consider yourself quoted."

Ivan listened to his phone messages.

"Ivan, it's Dad. I decided to take a trip. Call me for the details." And a click as he hung up.

Ivan was dumbfounded. His father never made quick decisions let alone one that entailed an itinerary. That only meant one thing. He dialed his father's number.

"Hello hello, damn phone, who's this?" Ivan heard Harold fumbling and talking in the wrong end of his cell phone.

"It's Ivan. What's this about a trip? A trip where?"

"Ivan, yeah, I'm going on a trip. With Diana. In case you're trying to call me and I don't pick up, that's the reason why."

"A trip to where?" His father's obtuseness, deliberate or not, forced Ivan to pull information out of him like well-rooted weeds.

"To the Caribbean. We're going on a cruise. The Norwegian. Balcony ocean view we're getting."

"Her idea or yours?"

"Hers obviously. And her friends Dotty and Martinez. You know them, right?'

"I don't know them. I heard you mention them once or twice."

"They did this cruise thing before and had a great time. They want me to have a good time too. They said I would love it. Don't have to worry about nothing. The cruise takes care of it all; food, everything, entertainment, everything, and shows too. And it's reasonable, the cost. Everything's included. Except for the extras, whatever the hell that means. But I don't think I'll need extras. There's already plenty. So there you have it."

"What does your doctor say?"

A moment of silence on the other end. "About what?"

"What does she think about you being in the middle of the Caribbean with a heart condition?"

"What difference does it make where I am? They have doctors everywhere. Besides, I'm taking care of it. I'm taking the medicine and doing the exercise. There's a pool and exercise room on the ship, Diana tells me. So everything is taken care of. But no, I didn't tell her nothing. Everything I do is not her business."

Reason, Ivan realized, was no competition for the vivacious, young and solicitous Diana and her fun-loving friends Dotty and Martinez. No matter that the other three were 20 years younger than Harold; no matter that Diana, divorced with two unemployed twenty-something-year old kids, could never afford this trip without Harold, or that she had everything to gain and nothing to lose by persuading him to take her on this gratuitous excursion so she can drink and laugh with her friends. She came over, cooked delicious meals in his condo, re-decorated his 15th floor inlet view that his mother Sarah had decorated with her simple taste and charm. Harold was not one to hold onto charm; he held on to memories. Ivan tried to tell his father he needed to be careful. As good as he looked from the outside, Harold smoked all his life and never watched what he ate. Now he was getting conflicting recommendations; one opinion, go for surgery; another, go on a strict diet, exercise regularly and take Crestor. Hearing that the surgical recovery period would be long and arduous, Harold chose the latter and Diana pushed him forward, up the ramp to a balcony ocean view on the Norwegian.

At that moment, Sabrina Hughes, appeared. "When you're off, I need to see you."

Ivan nodded.

"You'll have your cell phone with you?" Ivan asked.

"Yeah, but don't call me because they'll charge me an arm and a leg out there on the ocean. Emergency only. But I don't expect none so there's no need to call. I'll just call you when I get home."

"When will that be?"

"In a week."

"When are you leaving?"

"Manyana."

"Don't forget your pills."

"What pills? Just kidding. Don't worry so damn much!"

"You're going to be out in the middle of nowhere with people who are basically strangers." Ivan heard silence on the other end of the phone. "Are you still there?"

"I'm here but you didn't say nothing."

"Any chance of you changing your mind?"

"Why should I do that?"

Ivan sighed. 'Call me as soon as you get back."

"You got it."

His father hung up, but Ivan held the phone as if it was his father's arm, pulling him away from the ship, away from these strangers. He thought about calling his father's doctor but that would be over the top. He put the receiver down reluctantly and walked out of the cubicles.

Sabrina's office window looked out over the traffic on Arch Street and the Federal Reserve building across the street. He closed the door and took a seat as his thoughts about his dad sank into the ocean, for now at least.

Sabrina looked up sharply. "How did the trial go?"

"Better than I thought. Flowers was nervous at first, but eventually found his groove and made his points."

Sabrina sat tall in her swivel chair. She had smooth cocoa skin and long brown hair with a gray side bang that Ivan remembered her having when they trained together over 25 years ago.

"I see Malano was represented by your favorite," Sabrina said with a head tilt and knowing smile.

"More like I'm their favorite."

"I assume you saw that big case on your desk?"

"*Philadelphia Times*. One of the oldest newspapers in the country and the biggest in this city. I don't get it."

"They asked me to assign it to a seasoned agent."

"It's Spring. I'm a Fall guy."

"Ha! Nah, you're a man for all seasons. You know that, right? I mean, you were in management, you were my manager, you left it. You did what you wanted to do. I've learned a lot from you. You teach me every day."

"And now they want you to assign this case to me?"

"No, I'm assigning it to you."

"Why not Hector? I do innocent spouses."

"You used to do large cases. This is one of the biggest. Don't you want to go back to doing something big, something important?"

"Speaking about big, how is it that the file already needs a crane to lift it when the case hasn't even started? How did all those bank statements, copies of checks, and signature cards get in there? I didn't see any copies of a bank summons. Was somebody else working this case before me?"

"The FBI."

Ivan sat back, tapped his fingers on the armrest. "Oh, really? The FBI is investigating the biggest newspaper in Philadelphia? Why?"

"They didn't tell me, but they suspect something. I don't know what. Maybe it's better that way. They want us to look hard at everything, expenses and income. And they want us to audit the last three tax years."

Ivan looked up at the ceiling, rubbed his chin.

"Why didn't they go to the Criminal Investigation Division?"

"They decided the best route to take is through us. And no one is supposed to know the FBI is involved. My boss knows and the director but that's it. You will treat it like a routine audit—but it's not routine. They want us to dig, get to the bottom of everything. How are they spending their money, how are they getting all their income. Can't all be from subscriptions and ads and corner boxes. Is there unreported income? They suspect something. I don't know what. I don't know if the director knows any more than me and I'm not asking. That's why I chose you. I remember how you found the Eddie Malano illegal casino in the basement of that Levittown restaurant. So I thought, well if you could find that you can find anything. Make you a hero again."

Ivan sighed. He had lost before walking into this office. "Have we sent out our sweepstakes letter?"

"Yes. So they're expecting your call. They know your name. But hey, if you need assistance, Keisha, the new hire is available. It'll be good experience for her. She's in today."

"Wasn't she in the new revenue agent class I just taught? The young lady asking all the questions?"

"That's the one." Sabrina shifted in her chair to look through the glass wall of her office. "She's there at her desk now. See her?"

Ivan turned around. "No, I don't."

"Yes you do. You just don't recognize her. I'll let you go but keep me posted if you see anything unusual going on at the *Times*."

"Like unbiased reporting?" Ivan said still trying to spot her.

"Ha! Go talk to her. I'll see you later."

Ivan walked by the cubicles Sabrina indicated but didn't find her. He retraced his step, thinking maybe he overlooked her.

"Oh Ivan, hey, looking for me?" Keisha, sitting in her cubicle, picked her head up from looking at her iPhone, her champagne lips giving him a bright smile. Ivan did a double take. He remembered her voice from class. He remembered her hair in cornrows spread wide around her head like a thatched tent and tinted light brown bangs that brushed her eyebrows. Maybe her hair was the same, but Ivan couldn't see it. It was hidden under an imperial pink hijab, an item of apparel she hadn't worn in class.

"Hey, hi, how you been? Sabrina told me you'd be coming by. So I'm going to be working with you, right?

"Could be, Keisha," Ivan answered trying not to look surprised at her different appearance. "I see you have the same iPhone as my daughter."

"Oh yeah? I just got this."

"What are you reading there?"

"Me? Oh, just this article in the *Philadelphia Chronicle* that my friend to told me to read."

"I see. Did Sabrina tell you about our case?"

"Yeah, the *Philadelphia Times*. Crazy, right?

"Do you want a cup of coffee?"

"Oh, no, I'm good, thanks."

"Well come with me anyway."

"Oh, sure, ok!" Keisha dropped her iPhone in her handbag and followed Ivan through the maze of cubicles to the corner break room. No one else was there. Ivan took his union coffee cup from the cabinet and washed it.

"So what kind of cases have you been working on so far?"

"Lots of different ones. Self-employed people, overstated deductions, some dependent exemption cases where I get to play King Solomon, ha ha, earned income credit, Schedule A itemized deductions, oh, and I have a hobby loss case."

"Any innocent spouse cases?"

"Yeah, one. Wife claims she didn't know her husband took money out of his IRA and didn't report it on the return.

"You believe her?"

"Um, well, no I don't. Here she goes claiming she didn't know about the money but then they go build a new deck. Money had to come from some-where."

"So you're denying her claim?"

"Yep."

"Sounds right to me."

"Isn't that what you do mostly? Innocent spouse?"

"Lately, yes. The way it works, as you'll soon find out, you work an issue well and you're suddenly deemed the expert and every case that comes through the door with that issue is yours. Except for this one."

"That's cool. Do you like doing innocent spouse cases?"

It was a simple question but Ivan wasn't sure how he wanted to answer it. Ever since he lost Nancy, the type of work he did made little difference. What did make a difference to him? What really mattered, he asked himself as he carefully poured his coffee and milk and stirred until the he felt Keisha noticing his prolonged stirring. It was this: Liz, Alice, comfortable shoes, decent air conditioning, Turner Classic Movies, and a good cup of coffee. Not work. But he wasn't going to reveal all that to Keisha, young, fresh, and eager. Not going to spill his soul to someone who looked at Facebook more than at someone's face.

"I like them a lot. Especially when I grant them the innocent relief. Which I almost never do. What I like more, though, are the actual assessment cases leading up to them. Finding the source of the deficiency. Especially if it's criminal. Like the one I recently had."

"Oh, you recently had a criminal case? What happened?"

"He went to jail."

"You put him in jail?" Keisha said almost gleefully.

"I didn't. Tax evasion was only a fraction of his crime. His wife is claiming innocent spouse."

Keisha laughed out loud, "Ha. Yeah I bet!"

"Sometimes these audits require some keen forensic accounting skills. Which I think is what's going to be needed with our case."

"Oh, wow. Is that taught in any of the training class we're gonna get?"

"That's more on-the-job training. Which is what you will get working with me."

"I gotta say, it's hard for me to think that a big city newspaper like the *Times* is not gonna report their taxes correctly. I mean, knowingly."

Ivan took a sip coffee. "Did Sabrina tell you anything else about the case? Why it was selected for audit?"

"Nope. Just that it's gonna take a lot of work and whether I'd like to work with you on it."

"And you said?"

"I said yeah, sounds intriguing."

"Working with me sounds intriguing?" He smiled a little.

"Oh! Yeah, no, I mean yeah." Keisha laughed, a bit taken aback.

"I'm kidding."

"I know that."

"So tell me, Keisha. What article were you reading on your iPhone?

"Oh, about a mosque in south Philly."

He paused a moment and chose his next words carefully. "If I remember correctly, and I hope you don't mind me asking, I don't think you were wearing a hijab in the revenue agent training class I taught about a year ago."

"Yeah, that's right. I wasn't Muslim then. I wasn't anything. But I have a friend, and we've been friends since we were kids – same friend who told me about the article, by the way - who became a Muslim and invited me to go with her to her mosque. At first I said no, what for, why should I do that? I was never much of a church goer. So she says to me, what do you believe in? And I said I don't know. And she said something that made me think. She said, 'if you don't know where you're going, then any road will take there. And you don't know what's waiting for you at the end of that road'. And then she says, come with me, I'll take you down the right road and I'll stay with you all the way so you don't get lost. So I went with her to her mosque. And I liked it. I liked the people there. They were very friendly. They made me feel welcome and at home."

"Which mosque is that?"

"In Overbrook but they're building a bigger over in North Philly. It's gonna be huge. It's a Ahmediyya mosque."

He frowned. "I don't think I ever heard...."

Sabrina's secretary Tina knocked on the opened break room door.

"Ivan? Sorry, don't mean to interrupt, but your conference is here."

Instinctively Ivan checked his watch. "Wait a minute, I don't have any conferences today."

"Well, the guy's here and said he's here to see you."

"Who is he?"

"Well, jeez, I don't know. Thought you would know if you had an appointment with him."

"Well, I don't. Can you get his name and let me know?"

"No prob." Tina left.

"Sounds like you're on an interesting journey. I'd like to hear more about it if you don't mind."

"Absolutely, don't mind a bit."

"But getting back to our case, the file is thick."

"Yeah, I noticed that."

"Unusually thick. We have a lot of digging in there to do before we meet with the people at the *Times*."

"That's fine with me. Just give me a shovel. Ha ha!"

Tina returned. "Says his name is Leslie Glassman. And you're right. No appointment but he got your letter and wants to see you."

"What's his hurry?"

"Yeah, that's what I was just thinking. In a hurry to be audited or what?" Told him you'd be out to see him in a jiff. That's ok, right?"

Ivan sighed. "That's fine. I'll see if I can find his case file swimming somewhere in my in box gasping for air. Let's go, Keisha."

"I'm following you!"

"While I meet with Mrs. Glassman, I want you to start going through the file and let me know what expense items you'd like to tackle."

"I certainly will. And thank you, Ivan." Her smile lit up the room.

*　*　*

Ivan found Glassman's skinny case file in the middle of a pile of other folders sitting on his visitor's chair. While he worked the Eddie Malano case, other files had sat for months. Now that Ivan has been handed another big case, they'd sit a lot longer. But Glassman's sudden and unexpected appearance moved his meager folder to the top of the waiting list. Ivan flipped through it: another innocent spouse case with the usual claim of being totally unaware of the spouse's unreported income, except for one thing. It was the husband pleading innocent.

The IRS waiting room was much like a dentist's where you sat anticipating pain. People, Glamour, Photography, and Architectural Digests lay untouched on a small table in the center. No mere glossy magazine possesses the magic to alleviate the pain, nor could most people who made their way out of the office afford the items advertised in them—not after leaving, at least.

Ivan observed Leslie Glassman sitting stiffly in one of the hard chairs clutching a brown IRS envelope, perhaps thinking that by assuming the spirit of the room, he might get into the IRS's good graces. Above him, the faces of the President and the commissioner of the moment looked down on him. Ivan walked towards him and practically stood on top of him before Glassman looked up.

"Mr. Glassman, I'm Ivan Samuels. What can I do for you today?"

Glassman got up, pushed his wire rim glasses further up his nose, and nervously gave Ivan's hand the most unrythmic handshake Ivan had ever experienced. He was tall and skinny like a sickly tree, much like his case file. He was in his mid-forties and what was left of his thin blond hair was short. The top of his head was essentially bald.

"Oh, Mr. Samuels" he said in high-pitched, jittery voice," thank you so much for seeing me. I know I should have made an appointment, you're probably so busy with much more important cases than mine."

Sobbing from the get-go. "Not at all," Ivan reassured him. "Tell me what I can do for you today."

"Well, I got your letter here so no doubt you read my innocent spouse claim. What I'm here to ask you, to tell you that is, is that I really need to keep everything discrete. I'm sure you can appreciate that, right? You must go through this all the time."

"Well, to tell you the truth, Mr. Glassman, those letters get spit out and mailed long before your file gets personally hand-carried to my in-box by the very conscientious secretary we have, of which we have one, so if there is a lag time between the arrival of my letter and my reviewing your file the fault rests entirely with me, and I apologize for that."

"I see. Well, can we go somewhere to talk? You can call me Leslie, by the way."

"Ok, Leslie, we can talk right here."

"Here? Are you sure?"

Ivan scanned the small and empty waiting room and nodded his head. "I'm sure."

Leslie reached into the IRS envelope, pulled out a yellow folded paper and handed it to Ivan. "Here."

Ivan unfolded it. "A post office box and a telephone number."

"I want to ask you, Mr. Samuels, I mean, I'd really like to ask you to send all future correspondence to that post office box please and that's my cell number."

"Sure, no problem. That's it?"

"If you read my file you'd know why."

"I'm sure I would. But since I didn't, would you care to tell me?"

Leslie took a seat as if his legs suddenly went boneless, and Ivan, though he hadn't planned to, felt he needed to do the same. Now both sat under the commissioner's watchful eye.

Leslie leaned forward, his voice hushed. "If my wife finds out I filed that innocent spouse claim, I'm as good as dead."

Ivan grimaced. What to do with that information? Does that mean if a letter inadvertently got sent to the home address and his wife killed him, the government is culpable? Does he report this to Inspection? Did coming out to speak with Leslie without an appointment make him a schmuck?

"I hope you're not serious," Ivan said, trying to make the situation disappear.

"I'm dead serious. Can I show you something?" Leslie lifted up his right pant leg. On his white hairless shin was a black and blue bruise.

"She did that to me last night. And for what? Because I forgot to tell her she got a phone message. I shouldn't have picked up the phone, that's what I should have done. Should have just let it ring. Let the answering machine get it. See what I mean? And that's just last night. It's awkward for me to be telling you this, I mean, you're the IRS for crying out loud, but you need to know this because it goes to the heart of my innocent spouse claim. I had no idea the taxes weren't paid or filed late or even what my wife makes. She's a nurse and she has a cosmetic business on the side. Believe it or not, I've had to get medical treatment because of her."

Ivan nodded sympathetically. All this additional information actually put his mind at ease, as he would not be totally responsible if something did go awfully wrong at the Glassman household.

"It's none of my business of course, Mr. Glassman, but have you ever thought about getting a divorce? It might save your life. I'm not kidding. Believe it or not, you're not the first guy I've seen in this situation. I'm not even talking about the tax part of it, and I don't know if the spousal abuse is enough of a reason to grant your innocent spouse claim. I'm not saying it is or isn't, I'm just saying I need to know more, but not now. I'm just talking about your well-being right now."

Leslie nodded. "I appreciate that Mr. Samuels, really I do but that's completely out of the question and I don't want to get into that right now, thank you."

"Ok."

"I see, well, when do you think you'll get around to my case?"

"I'm going to put it on top of the pile so I would say soon."

"Ok, well, I don't want to take up any more of your time right now, so thanks for seeing me." Leslie got up and offered his hand. Ivan took it and felt like he was holding onto an out-of-control electric drill. "Would it help if I send you the hospital records?"

"You can do that."

"And please don't forget, only mail me at the post office box and call me on my personal cell. This is the first time I've ever done something behind her back and I'm very nervous."

"I see that. But you should know at some point she's going to have to be contacted."

"What? Why? Why?"

"To get her side of the story. That's all part of the process, the investigation."

Leslie stared at him as if he was just told he had cancer. Then he looked down at the worn carpet. "Mr. Samuels, I don't know what to do now. We owe thousands of dollars and it's all because of her and I'm getting stuck paying for it. And now you're telling me if I file this innocent spouse thing she's going to find out? That can only make my life worse. What do you think I should do?"

"Tell you what, I'll review your file and then call you. On your cell, of course. We can figure out what to do then."

"I don't know," Leslie said as if his world had completed disintegrated below him.

Ivan put his hand on Leslie shoulder. "I promise I won't do anything until you and I have a discussion. Ok?"

"Yeah." Leslie stared down at the pea green carpet, rubbing with his foot like a horse.

Ivan put his hands on both of Leslie's shoulders. "Get a grip Leslie. We don't have to decide anything today."

"Right, ok," Leslie answered like an obedient child.

"It's good that you came in today."

"Yeah, ok. You'll call me?"

"I will." Ivan led him out the door.

"You'll call me, right?"

"I will, Leslie I will."

Chapter Four

𝔓𝔥𝔦𝔩𝔞𝔡𝔢𝔩𝔭𝔥𝔦𝔞 ℭ𝔥𝔯𝔬𝔫𝔦𝔠𝔩𝔢

Be Wary of Thy Neighbor

by Sandra Wolf

Philadelphia, May 15 - On February 23 earlier this year, Elwood Almond, dressed in Muslim garb, approached Philadelphia police officer Jay Harman sitting in his patrol car and fired several shots at point blank range, critically injuring Officer Harman. At his arraignment, Almond readily confessed to his crime, claiming he had committed the crime at the behest of ISIS, with whom he had been communicating via the internet. Currently he is serving a life sentence at the federal penitentiary in Beaumont, Texas.

A few weeks later, Philadelphia resident Jalaal Arian was arrested in Philadelphia for providing ISIS a 'kill list" via the internet containing the names and addresses of U.S. service men and women throughout the country. ISIS planned to disseminate the list to their most ardent supporters.

One month ago, Catharine Reese, nicknamed 'Jihad Joan' by the FBI, conspired to murder cartoonist Howard Blake, who had drawn and published what she deemed to be an offensive picture of Mohammad. She had planned to subsequently flee to Syria to join ISIS, leaving her children behind. She was arrested before getting anywhere near Blake.

In addition to their professed allegiance to ISIS, Elwood Almond, Jalaal Arian and Catharine Reese were all members of the Masjid Center of Philadelphia.

The Masjid Center of Philadelphia is located in the south Philadelphia neighborhood largely owned by former Philadelphia 76ers basketball star James Warren. Warren, a convert to Islam, now goes by the name of Jamil Abdullah Hakim. Through his

Hoops Housing Foundation, Hakim has rid his old south Philly neighborhood of its drug problem and rehabilitated blighted buildings into attractive, affordable homes for the largely African-American community. Hakim has also improved education through the charter schools program and helped establish achievement-oriented youth centers. Almost singlehandedly, he's revitalized his old neighborhood and improved the economic lives of the local residents.

At the center of Hakim's neighborhood is the Masjid Center of Philadelphia.

This house of worship has played host to a number of events and speakers sponsored by the Muslim Alliance in North America (MANA). MANA is an affiliate of the much larger Muslim Brotherhood of America whose stated purpose includes "unifying its efforts to present Islam as a civilization alternative."

Almond, Arian and Reese were Hakim's personal guests at several MANA meetings held at the Masjid Center.

Along with being a board member of MANA, Hakim is a member of the National Ummah Movement (NUM) which seeks to "establish sovereign Islamic enclaves ruled by shariah (Islamic) law within major cities across the United States." Last year's regional conference of the National Ummah Movement was hosted at the Masjid Center. Almond, Arian and Reese were Hakim's guests at this conference.

In a report on the NUM conference posted on MANA's website, Hakim says, "Hoops Housing Foundation is here for the people, and the people are here for Islam. By the Blessing and Mercy of Allah, the efforts of HHF serve as a national model for what can be done with commitment, compassion, focus and careful planning and execution. Just another proof positive of the words of the Qu'ran."

The Hoops Housing Foundation recently received $1.6 billion funded largely by grants from the State of Pennsylvania and the city of Philadelphia; grants funded by taxpayer dollars. How much of that money funds the Masjid Center remains unclear. However, the tie between HHF and the Masjid Center is undeniable.

Last March a Muslim man was admitted to Pennsylvania Hospital with deep lacerations on his right wrist. The man informed police the imam at the Masjid Center of Philadelphia accused him of stealing cash from the Masjid and attempted to cut off his right hand as a form of Qu'ranic punishment. The man denied stealing the money. Police later searched the mosque but could not locate the imam. They did find a machete. According to the police report, Hakim denied any knowledge of the incident and had no information on the whereabouts of the accused imam.

Ten years ago, James Warren was an NBA basketball player who got his way on the basketball court. Now Jamil Abdullah Hakim is a supporter of the Muslim Brotherhood. His Masjid Center of Philadelphia is a meeting place for ISIS adherents and terrorists. Is this how Philadelphia should be putting its tax dollars to work?

* * *

Alex Anderson walked into publisher Conrad Bensons' office fully prepared. He'd been troubleshooting fallout from outraged police chiefs, embarrassed councilmen, exposed clergy, and damaged CEOs all his professional life. But now he found himself in the position of explaining how a *Times* reporter found its way to his competitor's front page; how a woman from the Midwest half his age outsmarted him.

Benson sat at his expansive glass-covered oak desk. The bay window behind him overlooked the Pennsylvania Convention Center.

"Talk to me, Alex." Benson ordered.

Alex leaned back with his hands clasp behind his neck. Appearance was everything.

"What would you like to know?" Alex asked.

"I have a Barnes Museum board of directors meeting at the Union League, then an executive committee meeting at the Kimmel Center, and then a meeting with the trustees of Penn. And later this afternoon with our own CFO about this absurd IRS audit coming out of nowhere. Should I be concerned?"

"I'm not the accountant."

"No, you're not. You're the executive editor with a renegade reporter publishing an article in our competitor's newspaper. How did that happen? But more importantly, what are you going to do about it?"

"I spoke to Jack in legal. He said she absolutely breached her contract. We could sue her."

"Sure, we could do that." Benson took a sip from his water bottle. "Is that the best approach? Would that be your approach? Have you spoken to her?"

"Not yet."

"Why not?"

"She's not picking up."

"What was your last discussion with her?"

Alex shrugged. "It was about the article. I told her were doing some fact-checking. When we were satisfied about all the facts, we'd schedule it."

"You suppose the *Chronicle* did any fact-checking?"

"How could they? The article came out early this morning."

"And you think she first sent it over to the *Chronicle* last night?"

Alex considered this.

"We need to do damage control here. What's your plan?"

Alex cleared his throat. "The article is mostly conjecture. The only readers who will believe there's a dangerous Islamic enclave in Philadelphia are those who think that already. She's writing for the choir, so to speak."

"Don't let being pissed off because you got outsmarted get in the way of objectivity. I can see lots of people of good-will believing her and getting scared. Rumors will start to fly that we have a "no go" zone here in Philadelphia. We can't allow that. Of course, the *Chronicle* doesn't give a crap about that. They're just after a story. So what's your plan?"

"To run a series of articles on the diversity of our neighborhoods. About why our differences are our strengths. As Philadelphians we're proud of our inclusiveness and it's something we should celebrate."

"I like it. That'll make the *Chronicle* look a bunch of Islamophobes."

"Exactly. I thought we'd interview some of the folks in Muslim neighborhoods while they're doing their shopping, and kids doing their homework, playing on the basketball court, playing a musical instrument, dads riding bikes with their kids. Take some pictures. Show how they're just ordinary folks like the folks in Fishtown, with families, with the same concerns and struggles like the rest of us. Some worship in churches, some worship in synagogues, some worship in mosques. We all worship. We're simply a city that practices the freedom to worship in our own way, which is what America is all about. Our freedoms."

"Clever. It may very well work. It could strip her story clean. Offset it completely. Show there's no basis to it at all, just hyperbole. That's good. Needless fear. That's the theme. Portray her as a fearmonger. Play up the point that it's our diversity that binds us, that we all get along fine, Muslims, Catholics, Jews, regardless of our differences or color or sexual orientation. Don't forget the gays. Play that part up too. That'll make us look even better. We all live together, but she's trying to tear us apart. And that's why she's no longer with the *Times*. We don't sue her, Alex, we fire her because she no longer ascribes to the morals of the *Philadelphia Times*. Suing her will make us look bad. The giant *Times* suing a young lady. That won't make us look good at all. But letting her go because she's an irresponsible journalist, that's the way to go. Who's writing the articles?"

"I'm thinking Doug. He did a great job on that pedophile priest."

"Ok, Doug, I like Doug. Inform Miss Wolf that she's fired effective immediately. By certified mail, regular mail and email."

"I'll do that."

"Great idea, Alex. I just hope it works."

"Why shouldn't it?"

"I hope it doesn't backfire."

"We'll do an article a week for four consecutive weeks. We'll overwhelm her so that her one article will look ridiculous and full of hate."

"I hope so."

"I know so. The *Times* reputation is at stake here. You know me, Conrad, I've been doing this a long time."

"I hope you're right. Her article could start a riot. It's actually a security issue, when you think about. The *Chronicle* should have realized that. But they're too stupid and don't give a crap. Anyway, I gotta go. I need you later for a talk with our controller about the tax audit.

"I'll be here."

Conrad grabbed his brown sport jacket hanging on a wooden hanger on the coat tree and walked out. Alex was in no hurry to get up from the comfortable chair. He stared out the window past the convention center, in the direction of Sandra's house. She'd been a good lover, while it lasted.

Chapter Five

Ivan picked up his phone to call the *Philadelphia Times.*

After listening through the tedious menu of recordings—which, of course 'has changed'—a live woman's voice came on; "*Philadelphia Times*, can I help you?"

"Ivan Samuels of the Internal Revenue Service. I believe the person I need to speak with is Brad Middleton."

"Glad you don't want to speak to me."

"Why not?" Ivan replied pleasantly. "Doesn't have to be about taxes."

"Ok, so like maybe you can solve my problem with my ex? Could you put him in jail for me? Cops tried that already. I bet he does owe taxes. Do you go to jail if you owe taxes?"

"That depends," Ivan said.

"Can I give you his name?"

"I would need more than that."

"Like what?"

"Are you really ready to go down that swarthy path?"

She sighed. He could hear the self-mockery in her voice. "I guess I don't. He's still the father of my kids. Why am I telling you this? Hold on, please."

"This is Brad." The voice was chipper.

"Ivan Samuels, from internal revenue. I'm sure I'm the last person you want to hear from today."

"Actually, no, we were expecting your call. Not necessarily today, but soon. We got your letter. In fact, we're having a meeting this afternoon. Any heads up you can give me?"

"You have something to tell me?"

"Like what?"

"Whatever you want to disclose upfront. Make everyone's life easier."

"We have nothing to hide, Mr. Samuels. Don't you guys give us a list of things you want to see so we can have it ready for you?"

"We do. And then we give you another, and another."

"I know that."

"I'll send that first list soon, but I can tell you now, it will include compensation, gifts, office expenses, loans, travel and entertainment expenses, and income, subscriptions and advertising income."

"Advertising income? You want to check if we're reporting all of our advertising income?"

"Especially from June through September, and from November to January. For all three years."

"We know this is a three-year audit. What we don't know is why."

"Why three years or why the *Times*?"

"Both whys."

"You probably know any entity can be audited to assure it's in compliance with the federal tax laws. And while I don't know specifically why the *Times* got selected – I don't do the selections – but I do see that the *Times* hasn't been audited for quite a long time. Maybe the selection committee folks decided your time is up, no pun intended. Maybe overdue."

"You're wasting your time."

"Why would that be?"

"We have carryforward losses as long as my grandfather's necktie. Whatever adjustments you want to make—and you won't find anything material, I can promise you that—will have no significant impact. That's why I'm saying you're wasting your time. And our time. And our money and the taxpayer's money."

"I only work here."

"You want to see all the advertising income for those months you just mentioned?"

"Everything over $5,000."

"Our outside accounting firm is going to be handling the actual audit, Warner and Baker."

"Is Fredrick Stacy still with them?"

"Yes. He's the tax manager. He'll be handling it. Personally."

"Should I be calling him then?"

"Sure. Meanwhile I'll start work on the list you just gave me."

"I assume you gave him power of attorney?"

"He does, in fact I can fax you over a copy. His phone number is on it so you can call him."

The fax arrived and sure enough, the power of attorney was Fredrick Stacy—the same accountant who represented the Levittown Luncheonette where Ivan had discovered the underground casinos owned and operated by Eddie Malano.

Chapter Six

As she turned into the parking lot of Temple University, Liz's iPhone sprung out the Beatles' 'The Long and Winding Road' ringtone. It was lying face up on the passenger seat. Liz tapped it and Gregg's voice rose from the cushion.

"Hey, just wanna remind you, six thirty tonight."

"Tell me again?" She was looking for a spot close to the building.

"You're kidding me, right?"

"No, no, I remember. The concert. Who are we seeing again?"

"Tell me you're kidding."

"Ok, I'm kidding."

"We talked about it just the other day. I got the tickets a week ago."

"I remember. Fleetwood Mac." She could tell from his voice he needed reassurance. "I can't wait, really."

"You just renewed my faith in you."

"I'm just a little preoccupied."

"Test coming up?"

"What do you know about tests? When was the last time you even took a test?"

"That would have to be ten years ago in high school. I aced it but hating taking it. Hated studying for it. Hated everything about it. What was the point if I was going to be an electrician like my uncle?"

"Well, you made it work," she said, turning a corner.

"That's right. Now I have my own business and pay my own rent for my Mt. Airy apartment. Which I would be happy to share with you. If you only would."

"Ah finally, I found one."

"What?"

"A parking space close to the building."

"Did you even hear what I said?

"Of course I did." Carefully she pulled in between two vans. "You want me to live with you. I know. Right now, I'm trying to get in touch with my journalism instructor. She didn't show up for class today."

"I see. Yeah, you told me about her. The *Times* reporter."

"And she's not answering her phone or returning my emails."

"Well, she's probably busy working on a story."

"The thing is, this morning an article of hers came out in the *Philadelphia Chronicle* even though she works for the *Times*."

Liz felt Gregg thinking.

"That could explain it. She's probably taking a lot of shit for that. Wait till the dust settles."

"It's so unlike her."

"What is? Not picking up her phone or publishing an article in a paper she doesn't work for?"

"Well, both."

"Is she a real friend of yours though? I mean, you're her student."

"Now you're starting to sound like my dad."

"How should I take that?"

Liz laughed. "You met him. You tell me. Anyway, I gotta go. The Wells Fargo Center, right?"

"That's it. Concert starts at seven. We'll meet at six-thirty and get a beer at Chickie Pete's?"

"Now who's not remembering?"

"Beer for me, Merlot for you. Got it."

"Deal. Listen, I'd like you to do me a favor."

"Anything for you."

"Read the article. It's online. Tell me what you think."

She knew the request was a challenge and his silence told her he was thinking how to answer.

"What's it about?"

"The Muslim neighborhood in South Philly."

She also knew Gregg didn't like controversial discussions. It was an effort getting him to share his opinions about the world or politics; she wasn't even sure if he had any. Maybe he found life safer that way. But now she was extending him an invitation to her academic, journalist, political world where, up until this moment, he had only been a spectator.

"I've actually done some work in that neighborhood."

"Really! Did you notice anything?"

"Like what?"

"I mean like, whatever. Like anything out of the ordinary."

"You mean like home-made bombs, no, didn't see any of that. I guess I remember seeing Muslim do-dads around; books, Koran I guess, those hats they wear, pictures of mosques on the wall and maybe pictures of their guru or whatever they would call him. Nobody tried to convert me or anything. Nobody offered me seventy-two virgins. And even if they did, I wouldn't take them. I have you. I was just the cable guy."

"You're into sports, right?"

"Hah, you know I am."

"Heard of James Warren?"

"Who hasn't? One of the all-time great Seventy Sixers basketball stars."

"Well, the article is about him. He's a Muslim now."

"No shit."

"Sparked your interest?"

"Oh, yeah." She knew he was just saying that to please her.

"Ok, so read the article. It's called 'Be Wary of Thy Neighbor." And I'll see you tonight and you can tell me what you think. At Chickie and Pete's."

Liz tapped the "end" button, and a picture of Liz and Gregg in front of the LOVE sign at the corner of 15th and Market appeared on the screen.

* * *

Gregg had met Liz at a party two years earlier. That afternoon her hair was layered in light shades of oranges and blues. She wore a sleeveless knee-length dress with what looked like slapdash paintbrush strokes of yellow, pink, light green, light blue and a bit of purple against a canvas of black and white horizontal stripes from neckline to hemline. Gregg noticed her at the punch bowl and walked over.

"You know, watching you from over there, I couldn't help noticing that your hair not only matched the orange punch but the sky. Can I pour you?"

Not waiting for an answer Gregg took a glasslike plastic cup, ladled out the punch without scooping any ice cubes, and handed it to Liz.

"Here you go." Liz smiled at him and took the cup. Then he poured one for himself.

"So are you on the side of the bride or the groom?" he asked, doing his best to bring forth her voice. It was his family friends' thirtieth wedding anniversary party at the Seaport Museum at Penns Landing.

"The daughter's. I'm a friend of Lana. Thanks." Liz took a sip, looking at him.

"Lana's terrific. Our family's been friends with the Nolans going way back. Me and Lana knew each other as kids."

"We met a couple of years ago in high school," said Liz. "She's been really helpful."

"That's her. Always helpful. She's helped me figuring things out, business-wise and stuff. How did she help you? If I may ask?"

"Oh, I don't know. Stuff. Like finally getting me to come out to this party. Don't want to get all that into it while I'm enjoying this delicious punch you poured me." She took a sip. "Have you been to the Seaport Museum before? I haven't."

"Yes but no. Meaning I've been here hundreds of times but always for some event, like today. Come to think of it, I've never actually seen the museum. Would you like to?"

"Sure." She held out her glass. "But first I'll take a little more punch."

As they explored the museum, he told her all about himself and what he did: from climbing on telephone poles and city streetlights to burrowing beneath pavement to install wire; who he knew and worked for, from real estate mogul Blake Brockstein to jazz bassist Wade Orkman; where he hung out, the Laurel Bar and Restaurant in south Philly and the Gun Range off Spring Garden for target practice. Gregg could tell she enjoyed listening to everything he said. He was convincing her, without knowing it, that it was time for her enjoy her own life. The day after the Nolan party, he took her to the Mustard Greens, a Chinese restaurant on 2nd Street and South. He continued asking her out, and to his mild surprise she continued saying yes. They went to Philly games, the zoo, the Franklin Institute, the Barnes Museum, Longwood Gardens. On their third date, she told him about her mom dying of cancer, and that knowledge made him feel more protective of her. Telling him was part of the healing process, and Gregg was glad she had chosen him to be part of the process.

But after that conversation about the concert, Gregg wondered where their relationship was going. He was starting to wonder if he would need his own healing process.

Chapter Seven

After Alex told Doug he had a special assignment for him the young writer smirked with pride. "So we're at war. I love it!"

Alex had hired Doug fresh out of the University of Pennsylvania, impressed with his cynical stories he wrote for the Daily Pennsylvanian: the hypocritical school administration, the bloated varsity sports budget, the silliness of Greek fraternity. Alex saw a lot of himself in Doug. Not quite the rascal that would cause disturbance and get arrested, Doug was what Alex would call radical-lite. He was tall and lanky with tight black curly hair just a bit too long to look serious. He walked with a confident swagger favoring the left every time he got up to go to the bathroom, and he sported a thin highlighter tucked behind his ear.

"That's how I want you to approach it, Doug. Every word a bullet, every sentence a gun, every article a bomb. But to our readers it needs to read like human interest and pride in our city. There's the dichotomy, there's the challenge, there's where you come in. The way you took on the Catholic clergy exposing them as pedophiles. That was your war on child abuse, your war, Doug, defending the innocent. When we uncovered police corruption, we were doing battle for the hard-working taxpayer who slaved away at their factory jobs to put basic food on their families' tables. Think of yourself as a warrior, a knight, and your pen is your sword. I know you enjoy the battle, Doug. That's why I'm sending you to the front for this crucial task."

"So Sandra doesn't work here anymore?"

By now everyone had read her article in the *Chronicle* and noticed her absence. They also noticed how she changed, listened to her changing. Listened to her talk about how the 9/11 attack changed her view on the world. It was displayed in her nuanced slants in features and editorials, her siding with American involvement in Iraq and Afghanistan—a slant Alex shunned. Alex strove for the perception of neutrality sprinkled with seeds of doubt. Alex prided himself on his journalistic subtleties and expected the same from his journalists. But Sandra's stories supported young policemen risking their lives while their young wives put their children to bed; chastised how NPR scorned religion but gushed over gay rights; exposed college professors' hidden anti-American agenda. Alex could not abide points of view other than his own getting equal space.

Sandra was Alex's find. He could let her slide occasionally but only to a point. That point had come. He had decided she had to go, but at his choosing, not hers! Instead, it was he who was tricked by her sudden asylum to the *Chronicle*. It troubled him. And it worried him that Doug and the other reporters knew it.

"She was fired. Effective this morning. As I think you know, she was no longer a good fit for our paper."

"You're absolutely right." Doug echoed.

"She wasn't one of us. She was from Ohio. An outsider. Not like you. We have a great staff here, and we have to keep it great."

"Absolutely, and I thank you for this opportunity. But you must admit her article was intriguing."

"You believed it?" Alex looked at him sternly.

"I…I didn't say that. Just that it was intriguing. I was only intrigued by it. Not that I believed it."

Alex asked himself if Sandra's article place doubt in everyone's mind.

"That article, Doug, I'll have you know, makes every Muslim in his city look like a terrorist." Imaginary fumes bellowed from Alex's angry eyes.

"That piece was nothing but a pile of profiling. Unadulterated Islamophobia. That's why we didn't print it. That's why the *Chronicle* did. That's why she's gone."

Doug nodded his head. "I totally agree."

"Are you sure you're up for this job, Doug? Because if not..."

"Of course, of course I am! I was just…"

"You were just?"

"Just sayin'."

"This paper has a reputation to uphold. Don't you think? We don't destroy people on a hunch. If we destroy someone, it's because the facts do the destroying, not us. We just tell it. Tell the facts. Tell it the way it is. Not the way we think it is. Or the way we'd like it to be. You're right Doug. What she wrote was intriguing because it was all fantasy. Fantasy is intriguing. And I'm glad you see it that way. What about everybody else?"

"I think, I'm sure, everyone sees it the same way you do. I'm sure."

"Ok, good. Now get out there and make the world a better place."

Chapter Eight

Liz handed the parking attendant twenty dollars, then followed the arrows to the first open space. As she searched for a spot, she recalled Sandra's article about this area in South Philly where the neon lights of Wells Fargo, Citizens Bank and Lincoln Financial could give the impression 36th and Market was the financial district of Philadelphia. It was not. It was the heart of Philadelphia's sports and entertainment center.

Sandra's article explained that these glowing names were nothing more than high-priced ads. There was a time when the names of these facilities had true meaning. Like Veterans Stadium, to honor the veterans of all American wars. Before that it was Shibe Park, after Ben Shibe, president of the Philadelphia Athletics. Sandra interviewed former Phillies star and broadcaster Richie Ashburn who said of Shibe Park: "It looked like a ballpark. It smelled like a ballpark. It had a feeling and a heartbeat, a personality that was all baseball."

As Liz approached the Wells Fargo Center entrance, she remembered Sandra wrote that this multi-shaped, multi-tiered structure had undergone multiple name changes, not because ownership changed but because banks merged; from Corestates to First Union to Wachovia and the Wells Fargo. Sandra explained that it had been named the Spectrum by its president Lou Scheinfeld because of the broad range of events held there; 'SP' for 'sports', 'E' for 'entertainment,' 'C' for 'circuses,' 'T' for 'theatricals,' 'R' for 'recreation,' and 'UM' as 'um, what a nice building!" Before the Spectrum it was John F Kennedy Stadium, a name, Sandra opined, that never should have changed.

After handing her ticket to an elderly attendant, Liz made her way through the crowd to the souvenir stand. She noticed fans her father's age sporting pony-tails, women dressed as Stevie Nicks wannabees in sinuous, sparkling oversized dresses and flowing golden hair. In some way, Liz found herself connecting with them all. Gregg knew what music to like.

She picked up a rectangular shot glass and handed her credit card to a sales-girl with a lip ring and red hair that was half shaved. Her appearance reminded her of the hairstyles she explored after her mother died. For a moment she wondered if the salesgirl was going through her own transformation, but dismissed that thought when she gave Liz a big smile along with the bubbled wrapped shot glass and told her to enjoy the show.

On the escalator, she looked over the crowd below and saw eager faces. Unlike at a Flyers game, tonight there would be no losers.

Gregg was already waiting at the counter of Chickie's and Pete's. To his left, in front of the seat saved for Liz, was her Merlot in a wineglass. In his hand was a bottle of Yard's beer. If she had to profile - an exercise Sandra taught her - Liz would say the guy sitting at the counter was reliable, generous, eager to please. She planted a kiss on his lips that she hoped expressed gratitude. Gregg was taken aback.

"Wow, that's a first."

"What is?" Her face stayed close to his, a leg sliding between his two. "Oh, you mean me arriving early?"

"Ah, I mean… that fragrance. It's new."

"Yeah, I knew you'd pick up on it. And here's another." She handed him the small package.

"Whoa. Full of surprises today. I'm overwhelmed. And you haven't even sat down yet. Here."

He handed her the wine. "They had had all sorts of different vintages, so I picked the one I thought you'd pick."

"Mmm," she sipped. "Just what I needed now."

"And I have something for you to match the fragrance." He reached down for a bag beneath his seat. "Something to remember tonight," he said, handing her a plastic bag that read 'Wells Fargo'.

She pulled out a baseball cap that read Fleetwood Mac. She immediately put it on and smiled.

"You look really cute in it."

"Yeah? Now open yours."

Gregg carefully undid the bubble protection. "Oh, what a cool shot glass. Another token to remember this night" He placed it on the counter. "And I'm gonna launch it with a shot of Yards."

Liz watched as Gregg filled the shot glass to the top and took it all in one gulp.

"Yards never tasted so good."

"Neither have you." She grinned when he blushed and looked confused. "Where are our seats?"

"They're high but close to the stage. Should be able to see their faces with these." He pulled out binoculars.

"You think of everything."

"I thought of something else too, but I'll save that for later."

"So what did you think?" Liz continued, shifting the mood.

"About what? Oh, you mean the article. I didn't forget. I read it. Scary if it's true. And I'm not saying I don't believe what she wrote in the article. I just don't know if her conclusions are right."

"And what would that be?"

"That Muslim anarchists live here in Philadelphia and James Warren is its ringleader. That's a stretch. I mean she gives a lot of information to make it worth considering. But I don't know. How do we know it's all true? "

A thought occurred to Liz. Gregg was an electrician. When he installed a line of wire, there was no doubt. But with journalists, their lines were not always so clear. Many times they were nuanced.

"That's fair," she said. We don't know. But we should find out before the shit hits the fan, don't you think?"

Liz finished off her Merlot and put the wine glass down on the counter.

"We?" Gregg asked.

"I think Sandra is on to something. Why do you think it was published in the *Chronicle* and not the *Times*?"

"Maybe the *Times* had their doubts too."

"If that's true, what it tells me is that she felt so strongly about this story that she defied the *Times* and got it published in the *Chronicle*."

"So I take it you still haven't been able to reach her."

"I've been trying all day. Emailing, texting, calling. Nothing." Lights in the lobby went off and on.

"Ok. Let's find our seats, shall we?" Gregg slipped off the stool, took her hand and led her to the closest entrance of the ellipse shaped arena. She followed him through the narrow walkway towards the stage, which was at the end of the basin below, as wide as a full a basketball court. They had a clear view directly over the stage. A few seconds later the steady beat of Mick Fleetwood's drum was heard over the din of the audience settling in. Something stirred on stage and suddenly lights glared on John, Lindsey, Christy, Mick, and Stevie as they brought forth "Listen to the wind blow, watch the sun rise…"

Before today Liz had only a mild interest in Fleetwood Mac. It was Gregg, a regular guy from Philly, who was expanding her music horizons. Liz listened to the words of "Landslide" and fell into a spell of reflection. The words talked to her and carried her mind to think of her life, her mom, her dad. Indeed, this song was Liz's dad's favorite. When Stevie came to the line "Can I handle the seasons of my life?" Liz felt a jolt of loneliness and the painful question for which there will never be an answer, the question she pushed away. But every time she did, it managed to creep back into the forefront of her mind – why? Why was her mom taken from her so soon?

Liz leaned her head on Gregg's shoulder as she heard Stevie croon "…but time makes you bolder even children get older and I'm getting older too…."

"Not you, Stevie!" Someone in the audience shouted and there was an applause. Liz wasn't sure if the applause was for Stevie or the fan who shouted.

* * *

Outside, Liz instinctively checked her iPhone.

"You're not going to believe this."

"Don't tell me, bad news?" Gregg asked.

"She published another article."

"Well, that's good news. In the *Times* or *Chronicle*?"

"The *Chronicle*. I'm calling her."

Liz speed dialed Sandra's number, but it went right to voicemail. The mailbox was full.

"Gregg, I'd like you to come with me somewhere."

"I got just the place. I've been spying over it for weeks now, waiting for the right moment. It overlooks the river."

"No, that's not what I mean. I mean, we will, we will. But right now I want you to follow me to Sandra's house. I want to knock on her door. I need to find out what's going on with her. I need to go now. And I need you to come with me."

Liz tried to make out the expression on Gregg's face. Confused, doubtful, disappointed, paralysis.

"Where does she live?"

"Society Hill area. On Pine Street."

He shrugged. "Ok, sure, let's do it."

"Thanks so much, Gregg. You're a sweetheart for doing this. I know it's not what you expect, and neither did I. But I just feel I have to go and make sure she's all right. Where are you parked?"

"Near you."

Liz did a double take. "That's kind of amazing since I got here after you."

"I don't mean here in the lot. I mean your house. I parked my truck there and took the train to here."

"Oh. I see. Pretty clever." She took his arm. "This way then."

Liz clicked the car doors open, started the car and sighed. Weaving out of the parking lot after an event was like pouring cement into a narrow funnel. Even though Liz's car was angled straight towards the exit, other cars slipped in sideways and got ahead of her.

"You want me to drive us out of here?" Gregg offered.

"Yes, please. Let's get out and switch seats." She put the car in park. "That'll give me time to read Sandra's article."

Chapter Nine

The Philadelphia Chronicle

Behind Closed Doors

By Sandra Wolf

Philadelphia, May 16 - Last month three Muslim men dressed in full body Muslim woman burqas robbed a bank in west Philadelphia. These outfits which only allowed eyes to show seemed perfectly normal to the bank's guard, its managers, and the patrons. Numerous Muslim women dressed in this style go in and out of that bank daily. But on that day, one "woman" pulled out a Chinese SKS military style rifle and told everyone to lie on the floor, threatening to kill everyone if anyone moved. As they ran out with $40,000, they shot a police officer.

All three were caught. In separate interviews, each said he met and befriended the others at the Masjid Center of Philadelphia headed by ex-76s basketball star James Warren, today known as Jamil Abdullah Hakim.

Since this is not the first time Muslims arrested for terroristic crimes had ties to the Masjic Center of Philadelphia, it is worth taking a closer look at who else attends and who else visits.

Kadeen Mussta is the president of the United Islamic Movement and an officer of the Jawala Scouts. Kadeen does not wear a whistle around his neck or take his troops on nature walks through Fairmount Park. But he does take seven-year-old to seventeen-year-old boys to the Poconos where they dress in military fatigues, learn combat techniques and shoot each other with paint balls. The older boys practice shooting targets with real guns. There is no visiting day for parents, and security is tight. It's like a military fortress amid timeshare vacation land. Resort personnel are apprehensive about crossing the scout master's path out of fear of retaliation. They can't even get federal law enforcement agencies to investigate this imposing boot camp because everything they do is within the letter of the law.

The Philadelphia address for the Jawala Scouts is the same as the The Masjid Center of Philadelphia which, according to their website, is "dedicated to the full implementation of the Qur'an and the Sunnah of our beloved Prophet Muhammad."

The Masjid Center of Philadelphia has invited members of the Interfaith Center of Philadelphia and of the Interfaith Committee of Canada. This sounds positive until you realize what these groups stand for. Hussein Ibrahim of Philadelphia's interfaith group laments, "America is the most wicked government on the face of the Earth. If only Muslims were clever politically they would take over the United States and replace its democratic government with a caliphate."

A caliphate is an Islamic state led by a supreme religious leader known as a caliph. Caliph means successor, a successor to Islamic prophet Muhammad. His Canadian counterpart, Mahfuz Daaoodi exclaimed that "stoning is good for the soul." He doesn't comment on what it could do to your brain if a stone hits you in the head.

There is Baasim Faaz. Veiled by his membership in the Interfaith Center's Religious Leaders Council of Philadelphia, he holds a leadership position on the board of the Muslim Alliance in North America (MANA) along with Warren and Sabat Mohammad a co-conspirator in the 1993 bombing of the World Trade Center.

At this point there seems to be enough reason for a full-scale investigation of the Masjid Center of Philadelphia. So why hasn't there been? No official of any law enforcement agency has been able to supply an answer. The question is, how much more terroristic activity tied to this mosque must take place before they do so?

* * *

"Can you speed it up a bit, Gregg?"

"Not really."

Liz looked up and saw the slow-moving traffic.

"Well, whatever you can do. I'm worried."

"She's obviously fine. She just published another article."

"I know. It's what she's saying, who she's attacking in these articles that bothers me. And then not being able to communicate with her."

"Did you try texting her?"

"Of course. I told you."

"Emailing?"

"Duh! And nada."

"We should be there in about 15 minutes. That will put us there about midnight. Think she'll be ok with us showing up at midnight?"

"I don't think she is okay. That's why we're going."

Liz was glad to see Pine Street well lit, a testament to the community's concern about crime. Muggers were less likely to attack someone on a well-lit street, and more likely to be spotted by a neighbor looking out the window.

They parked across the street. Liz quickly got out and Gregg followed her up the few steps to Sandra's townhouse front door. She could see light from a lamp through tiny crystallized door window, and the floating bubbles of a screen saver on a monitor. She knocked. A moment later, she knocked again, harder. No response.

"Does she own a car?" Gregg asked.

"She does."

"All these townhouses have a one-car garage in the back. Let's walk around to the back and see if it's there."

"Good idea."

They walked to the end of the block, turned right, and right again into the common easement shared by the neighbors on Pine and Spruce. Blue recycling and trash bins stood at the tip of each home's footprint, neatly arranged for easy trash pickup.

"This is not a good sign," Gregg said when they got to the back of Sandra's house.

"What isn't?" Liz asked.

"Tomorrow is trash day. Everyone has their containers out and ready. Except Sandra."

Liz pulled at the handles of the sliding garage door. "Locked."

"Try the back door."

The back door was three feet from the garage door. "Locked."

"What do you want to do?"

"I don't know, Gregg. But I think we should do something. Maybe we should call 911?"

"And say what?"

"Say she's missing?"

"But she's not missing. She just published an article in the *Chronicle*. Maybe she's sleeping."

"But the trash bins. You said that's not a good sign. I think you're right."

Gregg nodded his head. "I could probably pick the lock."

"You can? How?"

From his inside jacket pocket Gregg took out a pocket tool case and pulled out a tension wrench and a small packet of picks.

"Oh wow. Why do you have that?" Liz asked.

"I use it for work. Comes in handy when I need to get inside somewhere and the door's locked. Doesn't happened too often but when it does it's a time saver. I happened to need it today."

"Won't we get in trouble for breaking and entering? It could be alarmed."

Liz watched him test the door himself, then the garage door.

"I'll try the garage door. If the car is not there, she's away."

"Can we then re-lock the garage door?

"Sure. We just click it back shut."

"Ok, let's do it."

"You sure you want me to?"

"Yes. We're doing it. We're doing it together."

"You're sure? I mean I want to, but it feels like we're Bonnie and Clyde."

"Go ahead. Whatever, we'll know more if we can open the garage. That's what you said, and I think you're right."

"Yeah, okay."

Liz watched him squat down and slide his wrench into the bottom of the lock socket. Then, with the wrench inside he began inserting the pick, feeling for the pins. Liz stood close, watching his face, thinking: this is what he must look like when he works; focused, steady, patient. He worked the two tools together, slowly penetrating the inner chambers of a small, hidden, intricate mechanical world. Gregg worked with precision. After a few minutes, Liz thought it was not going to happen. She felt surprisingly relieved. Maybe this was not the right thing to do, tampering with private property, trespassing. Maybe getting herself all riled up over her unanswered cell calls to Sandra was neurotic. There was a perfectly good reason why the calls were not being answered. Why was it any of her business anyway, Liz thought? So what, if she saw the laptop with the screen saver on and the desk light on? Sandra must have left it that way and went to bed. She was about to tell Gregg to stop.

"Bingo." The lock clicked. Gregg looked up at Liz. "Do you want to open it or should I?"

Liz took a breath. "You."

Gregg stood up, grabbed the garage door handle, and pulled. The door sprang open. There, in the dark, in the eerie silence, snuggled quietly in this small compartment, innocently rested Sandra's Subaru. For Liz, seeing the Subaru was like finding Sandra.

"Ok, we just broke into her garage." Gregg touched the car. "It's cold, so she hasn't driven anywhere. The car being here and the lights on means she's probably home."

"Maybe we should call the police now," Liz said.

"And tell them what?"

"We have reason to be concerned. Her car is here, the garbage cans are not out, and her things have been left on in the living room. And she's not answering her phone. Or her texts."

"And maybe she just fell asleep and left the computer on and forgot to put out the garbage."

From both ends of the driveway easement red and blue flashing revolving lights of two police cars headed towards Gregg and Liz.

"They must've read our minds," Gregg said calmly.

"Shit, quickly, put your tools in my bag." Gregg discretely dropped the lock-pick tools into Liz's open purse. "I think we're in trouble."

"Good thing I left my Glock in the truck."

Both police cars stopped about ten feet away from Gregg and Liz, sandwiching them in. Four doors opened and four big Philadelphia police officers emerged. The closest one was a tall, muscular woman, her blonde hair tied in a bun and tucked under her police officer cap. Her partner was shorter, stocky, with a very somber expression on his square face. Liz felt he was acknowl-edging to himself he just prevented a disaster from happening.

"What do we have here, children?" said the woman officer. She was in her late thirties. "You two live here?"

Neither Gregg or Liz answered. Then Liz perked up. "Not exactly."

"Then what are you doing here at midnight?"

"My friend," Liz said. "Maybe you know her? Sandra Wolf? She writes for the *Philadelphia Times*. She lives here."

"So where is she?"

"That's what we're trying to find out. She's not answering her door. And we tried calling."

"Why is that garage door open?" asked the male officer.

"We don't know," Liz answered.

"What do you mean you don't know?" the male officer asked. "Was it opened like that when you got here?"

"Not exactly," Gregg said.

"Not exactly meaning what—exactly?" says the woman officer.

"We just pulled it up and it opened," Liz said.

Gregg looked at Liz and said, "That's correct."

"Well, that's funny," said the policewoman. "Because we got a call saying someone was tampering with the lock."

"Whoever called you was mistaken," Liz said. "We were just worried because she wasn't answering her door or her phone. In fact, we're still worried."

"What you should be worried about is being arrested for trespassing," said the policewoman.

"We think something happened to her," Liz said.

"Looks to me like you're stalking her. Does it look like that to you, Carlos?"

"Looks exactly like that that to me. What are your names?"

"Liz. Liz Samuels and I'm a student at Temple and Sandra is my journalism instructor. And we are not stalking her. We're worried about her. Is there any way you can find out if she's okay?"

The two male officers from the other car shined their flashlights over the outside of the house, scanning the windows, back door, roof. One walked over and tried the back door. The other went into the garage to look over the Subaru.

"All locked," one of the other officers said. "No sign of entry."

"Nate, you and Orlando check around the front door," said the police-woman, then turned back to Gregg and Liz. "Let me see your IDs."

Gregg reached for his wallet in his back pocket. Liz opened her small purse and pulled out her driver's license from a side zippered compartment, careful to keep Gregg's tools out of sight.

"And what is your name, officer?" Liz asked as politely as she could.

"Officer Barbara Duncan. my partner over here is Officer Carlos Sanchez. What do you do for a living, Gregg?" She said looking over his license. "Besides being an organ donor."

"Me, I'm an electrician. Lived here in Philadelphia all my life. Work all over the city."

"Ah. Liz, when was the last time you spoke to Sandra?"

"That would be Monday." Liz answered.

"In person? By phone?"

"In class."

"You said she works for the *Times*," said Officer Duncan. "Did you call the *Times*?"

"Actually, she may not be working for the *Times* anymore," Gregg offered.

"Really? What do you make of this Carlos? First she works for the *Times* and two minutes later she doesn't."

"Sounds like bullshit to me. Sounds to me like you was both trying to break in and rob this house."

"Ok, no, we're not robbers," Liz began sob. "I mean, really, do we look like robbers to you? Geez. What Gregg meant was that she just had an article come out in the *Chronicle*. Forget that. That's not important right now. We just came to see if she's okay, that's all. We just came from the Fleetwood Mac concert at the Wells Fargo. Want to see my ticket?" She wiped away a tear.

"Hey no shit, my sister was at that concert," said Officer Sanchez.

Officer Duncan looked at Gregg and Liz, making Liz feel she and Gregg were dressed in clown outfits.

"Front door is locked," said Officer Orlando. "No sign of entry."

"Did you look through the window in the door and see the light from her computer?" Liz asked, wiping away another tear.

"She fell asleep and left the light on," said Officer Orlando. "So what?"

"I leave my computer on all the time," said Officer Sanchez.

"You better not be," Officer Duncan said to Officer Sanchez.

"At home, I mean."

"What about the trash cans?" Gregg said. "Hers is the only one not out."

Officer Duncan gave them back their IDs. "I really should arrest both of you for breaking and entering and for trespassing. And probably for lying. But I'm going to let you go with a warning. If I find you here again, you'll both be arrested. Now get lost. Go home."

"But something is not right," Liz said. "I'm telling you. "Something is not right." She stifled a sob.

"What's not right is the two of you being here in the middle of the night breaking into a garage. We can arrest you right now for attempted robbery, trespassing and loitering. Or you can leave now."

Liz and Gregg saw themselves surrounded by four big, strong Philadelphia police officers, all looking at them with perplexed amusement. Liz wanted to say more, wanted to convince them that her premonition was correct, but looking at their eyes, she saw they were tired of her.

"You're absolutely right, officers," said Gregg. "We're going. Thank you for not arresting us."

"Now do your friend Sandra one favor before you go, Gregg." said Carlos. "Close that garage door."

The sound of the garage door closing sent a tremor down Liz's spine underscoring the fact that Sandra's whereabouts remained unresolved. Shaking her head, Liz allowed Gregg to lead her out of the alley to her car.

They drove West on I-76 Schuylkill Drive, passed the houses on boathouse row outlined in yellow lights that glisten on the river. The moon was full and bright against a dark, cloudless sky. There were few cars on the road and no cops in sight. Liz was speeding. She gave Gregg a quick look and saw disappointment. What began as an evening of music and promise, was ending in frustration.

"Look, I'm not saying the police were right and you're wrong. I mean we were wrong. But I can see where the cops were coming from."

"You think I'm neurotic," Liz said, eyes looking straight ahead, hands firmly on the wheel.

"No. Of course not. I do think it's odd she doesn't call you back or email you back and that her garbage cans are not out."

"Do me a favor. Take out my phone from my purse. Oh, and you might as well take your tools back."

"Oh, right. Ok, got your phone."

"Now look up George and Candice Wolf in Blue Ash, Ohio. Go to AnyWho."

"Who are they?"

"Her parents."

"Yeah. And what, you wanna call them?"

"Maybe."

Gregg began to tap.

"There are several Wolfs."

"Find George and Candice."

"Ok, George and Candice Wolf. I think I found them."

"Ok. Now call the number."

"I think this is a mistake."

Gregg called and waited for the ring.

"Ringing now."

"Touch the speaker."

Gregg did so and both listened to George and Candice's phone ringing.

"We're so glad you called and we're so sorry we're not here to pick up. We want to hear what you have to say so please leave us a message and your phone number even if you think we have it. We will call you back as soon as we can. God bless."

Liz took the phone from Gregg's hand and put it to her ear. "Hi, Mrs. Wolf. My name is Liz Samuels. I'm a Temple student of your daughter Sandra here in Philadelphia. Could you just give me a quick call back on my cell when you get a chance? Thank you so much."

Liz handed the phone over to Gregg who put it back into her purse.

"You think I should not have made that call, right?"

"I think it could have waited."

"For what?"

"For a day or two. There's more we could do. Call the *Times*, call the *Chronicle*. Call Temple University.

"Well, here we are." Liz parked her car in front of her house, turned off the ignition and stared. She alternated between looking at the moon and the oily spot on the sun visor. Then she looked into the window of her house.

"Uh oh, you're in trouble. I see my dad waiting up for me." Gregg looked towards the house. They watched Ivan open the refrigerator, take out what appeared to be a beer, then walk back to the living room where a flat screen TV showed a black and white movie.

"You know what, Gregg?"

"What, Liz?"

"I am worried about Sandra, yes, but I want you to know I'm glad we did what we did. And I couldn't have done it without you."

"Oh, well, really?"

"Incredible you were able to pick the garage door lock. And that whole scene with the police, I never did anything so daring in my life." She leaned over, put her arms around him.

"And this cap you bought me means more to me now than just the concert."

Chapter Ten

The Philadelphia Chronicle

Abused Muslim Wife Heads Women's Shelter

By Sandra Wolf

Philadelphia, May 18 - Abisha Sallez was a 28-year-old Muslim mother of three who fled to a women's shelter three years ago. Now she is a supervisor at the Women's Shelter of North Philadelphia, the shelter that rescued her.

Abisha's journey to this point in her life was an arduous one. The abuse she suffered began one month into her marriage. At first it was verbal, then emotional and mental, and finally became physical.

The physical abuse began after the birth of her second daughter. Her husband wanted a boy. He began accusing her of doing everything wrong: cooking, cleaning, and not having a son. The Koran, he told her, tells a husband to beat his wife if she does wrong. Her parents agreed. They also told her that if she returned to their house and went astray while living in their house, it would be better to stay with her husband and endure the abuse. So she stayed. Even after she gave birth to a son, the abuse continued.

Abisha had nowhere to turn. Her local mosque had already sided with her husband. She couldn't go to the police because that would bring shame and even more abuse. So she remained, believing and praying it would stop, telling herself her children needed a father, trying to convince herself that one day this sacrifice would be rewarded. One day it was rewarded with an assault on her pretty face leaving a broken nose. That's when she finally left.

Abisha found solace outside the Muslim community at a women's shelter in North Philadelphia. At first, she was afraid of how the other women would respond to her Muslim clothes, diet and rituals. "I was a curiosity," she admitted. "Most of the women were surprised to learn abuse took place in religious homes." But soon she was accepted as a fellow resident, as a woman with the same troubles and needs as their own, toting three children. With the approval of her mosque, her parents brought her children to her.

Abisha went from resident, to mentor, to employee caring for the newcomers and reaching out to other Muslim women who found themselves in similar situations.

"I am grateful that I found a place of peace and want other Muslim women to know that there is no reason to remain with an abusive husband," Abisha explained. "If I could finally break away, all such women can break away. It is difficult. You will be told it is against Allah's will. But you have to believe this is not so and find peace."

Chapter Eleven

The next day, as Ivan paged through the *Philadelphia Times'* tax returns, he couldn't help but think about his father on a cruise ship and thought about the similarities between a heart attack and an audit. While the possibilities of both are always present, measures to mitigate both are available. Medication and exercise for the heart, receipts and documentation for the audit.

A tax return that disclosed its tax liability was like a well-toned body, looking honest from the outside, possible corrosion on the inside. Ivan recalled marathon runner Jim Fixx, who died from a heart attack jogging at age of fifty-two. An autopsy—like an audit—revealed Fixx's three severely atherosclerotic blocked arteries. His problem was genetic, unresponsive to statin and Gatorade—completely natural and likely unavoidable. But with a corporate tax return, the disease was always man-made, always deliberate. You pray to God for good health, but you roll the dice you won't get audited.

The *Times'* tax returns had every reason to escape scrutiny. For the last eighty years, its tax history was impeccable. But eighty years ago, it wasn't. Its owner at the time, Max Biscuit, was thrown in jail for tax evasion. Biscuit's incarceration stemmed from his deep involvement in organized crime. He was sensible enough to keep his personal exploits far away from financial intermingling.

Ivan's scrutiny of the *Times'* returns confirmed what he already knew. Anyone who followed the plight of the paper for the past several years knew about its financial struggles to stay afloat. It has been peddled from owner to owner more times than a mediocre baseball player prior to the free-agent era. It bounced from holding company to hedge fund. It battled revenue losses, decreasing advertisements, circulation slowdowns, and competition from online news sources.

Desperate to survive and teetering on bankruptcy, the paper laid off journalists, stringers and clerks. Exactly what, Ivan asked himself as he sat in his cubicle flipping page after page of negative numbers, did the FBI think was going on at one of the nations' most venerable newspapers, with so much on its plate that dogs awaited the overflow? Funneling funds to an offshore tax haven? Skimming? Illegal expenses? Unreported income? Always under the public spotlight, exactly what could this paper think they could get away with? What did the FBI know and but not saying? That was Ivan's job, to find out.

"Hey, hi, oh, I don't mean to interrupt. Were you about to make a phone call?" Keisha was standing outside his cubicle with a cup of coffee.

Ivan took his hand off the phone. "I thought you didn't drink coffee."

"Oh no, this is for you. I know you take a coffee in the afternoon so here you go." She placed it on his desk.

Ivan eyed it with surprise. "Well, no one has ever done that before. That's very kind of you, Keisha."

"Oh, that's okay. I just wanted to tell you that I've been going through the *Times'* tax returns and I was thinking…."

Ivan took a sip of coffee then looked up at her. "Thinking is good, Keisha. Are you going to tell me what you were thinking about?"

"Ha ha. Yeah, I just wanted to see your reaction. I mean they have all these carryover losses going back years. So I wanted to ask you, is this typical? I mean are we really going to disallow enough expenses to overcome these losses?"

He took another sip of coffee. "Good questions. In fact, those were my questions when I audited a greasy spoon diner in Levittown. It looked like a small mom and pop outfit, so how much more taxes could they possibly owe? But what did I find? A front for illegal gambling. I'm not saying the *Times* is using their printing press to make counterfeit money. But they were selected for audit for a reason. So we just do our job."

"Ok, I hear you. Hey, I see you have today's *Chronicle* sticking out of your backpack. Did you read it?"

"Just the sports section on my way to work. I read the rest on my way home. By that time, it's old news and it doesn't bother me as much."

"Oh, because I thought maybe you read the article about the shelter for abused Muslim women. It's written by the same journalist who wrote the other article we were talking about."

"That one in fact I did read. My daughter pointed it out to me this morning. What did you think of it?"

Keisha nodded her head up and down. "I totally understand what she was going through because I'm actually helping some Muslim women at my mosque in the same predicament. I don't doubt anything what the article says. But the thing is, it makes all Muslims look bad and it's not that way. I just wanted you to know that."

"Ok, what way is it?"

"What I'm finding out is, learning about Islam and dealing with these women, because I'm kinda new at this, is there's a lot of misinterpretation going around, especially by Muslim men who treat their wives like second class citizens, who think they are following Allah's commandments and believe they are like Allah in their household and punish their wives if they don't follow his rules. But this is a total misunderstanding of the Koran. In fact, Islam teaches kindness. I just wanted you to know that."

"If it teaches kindness," Ivan focused on her, "why is there all this unkindness?"

"That's where the misinterpretation comes in. So for example there's a verse that says "men are the protectors of women because Allah gave more to one than the other and because they support women from their means." That verse teaches that men are supposed to protect women. But a lot of Muslims believe this means men have power over women and allows them to do whatever they want to do if their wives don't obey them. This misinterpretation gets so carried away, sometimes by a whole Muslim community, that it's impossible to reverse it. So these abused women, like the one in the article, have no choice but to flee from their communities. Some come to our mosque, where we give them a warm welcome and find them a place to stay. That's part of what I do.

I just wanted you to know that since I saw you had the newspaper and would be probably reading that article."

"That sounds like quite a responsibility, Keisha. Must be emotionally draining for you."

"Hey you know what? I actually find it uplifting. Spiritually uplifting."

"I can understand. Well, I'm about to do something mundane. In fact, the only uplifting part is lifting up the phone to call the *Times'* accountant. Who, by the way, was the accountant for the Levittown diner I was telling you about. Want to sit in on it?"

"Oh, ok sure. Where should I put these files?"

"On the floor is fine."

Ivan dialed. "Looks like we're matched up again," Ivan said to Frederick Stacy on the phone.

"If I didn't know better, I'd say you were on a fishing expedition in my private lake." Stacy put his cell phone on speaker as he was driving, if Ivan was interpreting the sounds right. Ivan put his phone on speaker so Keisha could hear.

"We go where the fish bite."

"You're not targeting me, are you, Ivan?"

"You know better than that."

"This is not like the diner in Levittown."

"What is it like?"

"You know I was just surprised as you were about the gambling going on there, right? We're square on that right? And they still owe me my fee, by the way."

"You cooperated. I didn't forget."

"And it will be the same here. Brad told me what records you want and we're gathering that up now. But I really don't get it. Everybody knows it's a losing operation. The publisher's CEO is speaking to the mayor and Congressman Dix to get the whole damn audit scraped. They're very well connected. We may not even meet."

"I wish him good luck with that."

"The paper supported both the mayor and the congressman in the last election. Benson feels they owe him."

"Maybe they do. We don't."

"I get that. That's one of the things that got Nixon in trouble. We could probably be ready next week."

"Do you want to schedule something now?"

"Text me some dates that are good for you and I'll get back to you on which ones are good for me."

"This is the government. We don't text."

"Email me then."

"I need to interview the publisher Conrad Benson and the editor, Alexander Anderson directly."

Ivan heard a moment of silence. "Expect pushback there. But listen, I'm on your side. I'll do my best to arrange it. But Ivan?"

"Yeah?"

"You're wasting your time."

"That's what you said about the Levittown diner." Ivan hung up.

"Got a job for you Keisha. I want you to prepare the interview questions for the editor, Alexander Anderson. Ask about his travel expenses. I want you to make him squirm."

"Oh, yeah?" She grinned brilliantly at him. "Oh, ok. I'm on it!"

Chapter Twelve

Ivan carefully carried three cups of Starbucks coffee to Liz and Alice and placed them on the center table which was surrounded by three oversized soft chairs. He sat in the empty one. The two women were already heavy into conversation.

"She's published three articles in four days and she's not taking my calls," Liz said. "What do you make of that?"

"She's probably banging out another one and doesn't want to be disturbed," Alice reassured. "I'm that way when I'm writing a brief. Don't take it personally."

"I'm sorry. I'm just not buying that."

"So what do you think?"

"That something is wrong. Like I was telling Gregg."

They sat near a fake fireplace in a corner, away from the many clusters of students hovering over laptops. The building was primarily the University of Penn bookstore, but like seemingly every other place people gathered these days, it also had its own Starbucks. Alice wanted to come here, she told Ivan, because it made her feel nostalgic.

"I've noticed," said Ivan squeezing the thick armrest, "up until today there's nothing small about Starbucks; the chairs are outsized, the fireplace imposing, and the one toilet they have in the men's room is the kind for the handicapped. But now they finally have small."

"Small toilets?" Alice asked.

"Cup size. I got that for Liz because she never finishes even tall."

Liz picked up her small cup and looked it over. "Too small."

"We can switch," Alice offered.

Ivan took note how careful Alice was not to act like a replacement for Liz's mother. Alice's life was rich with close friends with whom she'd shared insights on all matters of life: love, family, friendships, legal and financial. She came off as a cobra in the court room, but to the people who knew her best she was a warm and serious friend. She would be that person for Liz—not as a mother—that was not her turf. That space was strictly in the realm of memory. She would be Liz's friend.

"Not answering emails, not answering texts," Liz recounted more for her father than for Alice.

Ivan glanced at his watch. "What time is our reservation?"

"Six thirty," Alice answered. "Not that we really need one at Chima Brazilian All-You-Can-Eat Steakhouse. Is that the time you told Gregg?"

"I told him to call me to find out. He'll probably call."

A cell phone rang. Liz reached for hers, but it wasn't ringing.

"It's your phone, Dad."

"Oh," Ivan said, reaching into his pocket. "Who would call me? Everyone I know is right here." Ivan flipped up his phone. "Hello? Yes, it's Ivan. Who? Martinez?"

"Yes," answered a heavily accented voice. "Martinez. Friend of Diana. We with your father."

"What do you mean?"

"On cruise ship."

"Oh." Ivan felt his mind twisting like the infinity sign. He remembered his father telling him calls were expensive; no calls, except for emergencies.

"Where is he?"

"Well, first he fall down. They take him off the ship. To hospital. But I with him though. No worry."

"What do you mean he fell down? Fell down where?"

"On way to breakfast. Just like that."

"And now he's off the ship? Where?"

"Belize."

"What do you mean Belize?"

"We in Belize right now. I packed everything. His suitcase with him now."

"Let me speak to him."

"He a bit groggy. Maybe nurse. I give her to you."

Ivan covered the mouth of the phone and said to Liz and Alice, "My father is in a hospital in Belize."

"What!" Liz shrieked.

"Hello, Mr. Samuels?" The nurse had a slight accent which Ivan assumed was Belizian, but spoke with much more confidence in her English than Martinez. "This is Maria, the nurse here. Your dad is stable right now."

"What exactly happened to him?"

"We believe he had a heart attack. We're keeping an eye on him."

"Can I speak to him?"

"Mr. Samuels, your son is on the phone and wants to speak to you."

Ivan faintly heard his father in the background.

"Ivan? He's here?"

"He's on the phone."

"Oh. On his way?"

The nurse handed the phone to Harold.

"Ivan, where are you?"

"What happened to you? Are you in any pain?"

"No pain now. Was I in pain?"

The nurse's voice answered faintly. "You were. We gave you painkillers."

"Dad, Martinez said you fell on the way to breakfast."

"I don't remember having breakfast. Am I in a hospital? Not much of a hospital, if you ask me."

Ivan put his hand over the mouthpiece and addressed Liz and Alice. "He doesn't know where he is." He took his hand away.

"Put the nurse back on, Dad."

"He wants to talk to you."

"Yes, Mr. Samuels?"

"Maria, what's the game plan at this point?"

"Well, he's not in any condition to go back on the ship. He's too fragile to fly home by himself. He needs to stay here at least for a few days so we can monitor him."

"And then what?"

A brief pause.

"To be honest with you, Mr. Samuels, you should get him to a hospital in the states."

"You just said he can't go back on the ship or on a plane."

"I said he can't go by himself. You need to put him on an air ambulance."

Ivan got up and walked towards the bookshelves where there were fewer people. Liz and Alice followed him, leaving their coffees behind. They found themselves in the travel section. He looked at Liz's anxious face. Alice's expression was calm and steady.

"Do you know any?" Ivan asked.

"I don't, sir."

"What about the hospital administration?"

"You mean the front office. I don't think they will know. There was someone here from the cruise ship. Maybe she can help you? I can try to get her back here for you."

"Yes, please. Meantime, can you put Martinez back on?"

"Let me see if he's still here."

"What do you mean?"

"He may have left."

"He can't do that. Get him back please." Hand over mouthpiece. "Now she tells me Martinez may have left."

"Yeah, Ivan?" said Martinez.

"Martinez, the nurse said my dad may have had a heart attack. He needs to get to a hospital back home. Where's Diana?"

"She on the ship."

"Why is she on the ship? Why isn't she with him?"

"Only me. And the ship, she about to leave."

"Tell Diana she has to stay with him."

"Diana on the ship. I did everything. I pack his bag. I get the lady from the ship to talk to you. There's nothing else I can do. I need to go back on the ship."

"Wait a minute! You can't just leave him in Belize! He just had a heart attack, for Christsake!"

"I sorry. I give you back to the nurse."

"Mr. Samuels?" said Nurse Maria. "The doctor would like to talk to you."

"Mr. Samuels, this is Doctor Hadera." Ivan switched the cell to his other ear. The new voice had a heavier accent than Nurse Maria, and it was harder to pick out words. "I am the physician taking care of your father. Your father came here very weak and dizzy."

"How is he now?" Ivan asks.

"We are taking some tests, echocardiogram. It looks like he had a mild heart attack. I don't think he had a stroke. It doesn't look that way. He is talking."

"So what's the game plan?"

"I'm not saying this can happen, but sometimes if you get a heart attack another heart attack can follow soon after. I'm just letting you know."

"The nurse said I should get an air ambulance and get him back to a hospital in the states."

"That would be a good idea."

Ivan shook his head and started tapping his foot to the floor. The doctor had no faith in himself or the hospital he worked in.

"How do I do that?"

"I think the American Embassy has a list of reputable air ambulances. I'll have them call you. At this number?"

"Yes."

"Or you can google."

"Can you believe this?" Ivan started to pace. "How do you find an air ambulance on google?"

"I can try to do that." Liz offered.

"The important thing is, he's at a hospital so he's being taken care of," Alice tried to sound reassuring, but it sounded to Ivan Alice didn't believe that herself. His phone rang.

"Mr. Samuels, this is Selma at the American Embassy in Belize. Doctor Hadera at Karl Heusner Memorial Hospital gave me your number."

"Yes."

"They asked if I could help you find an air ambulance that can take your father back to the United States. Do you still need help with that?"

"I would, yes, that would be good."

"Well, I have good news. Air One Ambulance should be able to take him tonight. Did your father have travel insurance?"

Ivan blinked. "I don't know. He has Medicare."

"Medicare doesn't cover you outside the US." Selma paused a moment. "Can I give you the name and phone number so you can call the service directly?"

"Are they in the states or in Belize?"

"In the states, of course. This one is in Cape Canaveral."

"Ok, give me the number. Wait, I have nothing to write with."

Liz spoke up. "Just repeat the number dad, and I'll plug it right into my phone and call them right away."

They did so, and a moment later Liz's phone was ringing.

"Air One Ambulance. Is this Mr. Samuels?"

"Yes."

"We were expecting your call, sir. We're sorry about your father and hope we can help. So here's what we can do for you. We can send an air ambulance to Belize, equipped with a hospital bed, hospital supplies, two nurses and pilot and co-pilot. Where do you want us to bring your father?"

Ivan looked at Liz and Alice. "To Philadelphia.," he told the man.

"What hospital in Philadelphia?"

"Lankanu. Its actually in Wynnewood, a suburb of Philadelphia."

"So to review, we will be flying from Cape Canaveral to Belize, picking up your dad, flying him to Philly and putting him in an ambulance to Lankanu Hospital. Do we have that right?"

Ivan paused. "I, yes, that's right."

"Very good. I need your credit card information."

"Oh, how much is this going to be?"

"It comes to roughly twenty-six thousand dollars. Maybe a little less or more."

"That's impossible. I can't do that," Ivan said.

"You can try to call other air ambulances if you like, if you can find one that can do it for you. We all charge just about the same. It's up to you, sir."

Ivan looked at the books surrounding him, about all the placing you can go and things you can do all around the world.

"What did he say?" Alice asked.

"They want twenty-six thousand dollars. They want my credit card. I don't have that kind of credit."

Alice thought for a moment. "But your father does, I would think?"

"I would think he does."

"How fast can they get him here?"

Ivan brought the phone back to his ear.

"Are you still with me?"

"Of course, Mr. Samuels."

"How long will this all take?"

We can have him at the hospital some time tomorrow."

"Tomorrow." Ivan told Alice.

"Here's my credit card. Your father will reimburse me when he gets back. And after he recovers."

"Are you sure, Alice?" Ivan said with a mixture of relief and embarrassment.

"Let's get it done, take it." Slowly, Ivan accepted it as if it were a precious piece of ancient porcelain. Alice was making the difference between life and death for his father. Slowly, he read the number and information from the card.

"Thank you, Mr. Samuels. You father will be safe with us. He'll be with you in Philly in no time."

Ivan handed Alice back her credit card, feeling awkward, asking himself why he didn't decide to be a lawyer or a doctor or own a chain of Starbucks. As Ivan handed Alice back her card, the melody from Fleetwood Mac's 'You Can Go Your Own Way', Liz' new ringtone, chimed from her phone.

Chapter Thirteen

"Hi, Gregg?"

A woman's voice responded, and she sounded worried. "Is this Liz?"

"Oh. Yes. Sorry."

"This is Candice Wolf. I got your message. Have you spoken to Sandra?"

"No, have you?"

The voice sighed. "Not in days. We tried calling everywhere, cell, home, work. We're pulling our hair out here. We weren't sure what to do next. Call the police? Then I remembered your message, so we thought we'd call you."

"Hold a sec. Dad, it's Sandra's mom. Remember I was telling you I couldn't reach her? I know we're dealing with Grandpa, but they need help."

"Do you know where she lives?" Alice asked.

"I do, as a matter of fact."

Ivan said, "Tell her we'll drive over to Sandra's house right now. Let's go." Ivan led the way out of Starbucks.

"Candice?" Liz walked behind Alice. They were outside, but Liz still had her phone out. "We're going to go to Sandra's house now."

"Oh, really? I don't want to put you through any trouble."

"You're not. I'm really worried about her too."

Ivan beeped the wireless door opener of his Toyota Avalon. Alice sat shotgun, while Liz slid into the back.

"Tell Candice we'll call her when we get to Sandra's," said Alice. Liz did.

"Where am I going?" Ivan asked.

"Society Hill area. 759 Pine Street." Liz answered.

Ivan took a deep breath and made a U-turn in the middle of the road, heading south on Chestnut Street past the brick row house fraternities.

"Here's what I think we should do," said Alice. "We call 911 and ask the police to meet us there. We call Candice when we get there and have her talk to the police."

"Sounds good to me," said Ivan, making his way through city traffic.

Alice dialed.

"911. What's your emergency?"

"Yes, can you have the police meet us at 759 Pine Street. Our friend Sandra Wolf lives there and no one has been able to contact her in over a week including her parents who live in Ohio. We're afraid something happened to her. We're on our way to Sandra's house now."

Ivan drove under the Drexel Bridge past the 30th Street train station and the old post office.

"I can arrange for them to meet you there."

They passed the storefronts of shoe stores, thrift shops, the YWCA and what Ivan knew was a former Korean brothel raided by the police.

"Would it be possible for them to break in if necessary?" Alice asked.

"That'll be their call. Your name is?"

"Alice Dykman."

"Okay, Miss Dykman, the police will meet you there in a few minutes."

Ivan was able to hear the dispatcher on the phone. He looked over at Alice and saw her cringe at "Miss". "Thanks."

Ivan made a right on 10th Street to Pine and followed Liz's direction to Sandra Wolf's brick townhouse. There were no parking spots on her street.

"Go around to the back. We can park by her garage."

"You sure?" Ivan asked he drove to the back.

"I'm sure."

"You've been here?" Alice asked.

"Yeah, once. Here. Park here."

Ivan stopped the car in front of the garage and turned off the ignition.

The three of them walked up the lit tree-lined street. They passed first-floor windows with opened wooden shutters painted in deep colors of patriot blue, barn red and forest green. Some had Tidore rectangular flower boxes. Ivan put his fingers in Sandra's flower box and came up dry. The flowers were wilted. Not a good sign.

Liz walked up the few steps to Sandra's front door, tightly gripping the iron banister. Ivan knew the grip was not for balance but comfort. She knocked, she rang the bell. She tried the doorknob. Nothing.

"I can see a light through the window." Alice said.

"Does she own or rent?" Ivan asked. "When you speak to her mother, ask her that."

"Pretty sure she rents," said Liz."

"There was a real estate agent sign on one of the windows we passed," said Ivan. "I'll walk back to get his number and call him to see if he knows who owns this house. Liz, you should call her mother back now."

Liz pulled out her cell phone and touched Mrs. Wolf's number.

"Liz?"

"We're here, Mrs. Wolf, and Sandra is not answering her door."

"Oh, please, God. George, she's not answering her door!"

"Liz, this is George, Sandra's father. Is there any way you can break in? Break a window?"

"My dad is trying to find out who owns the building," Liz said. "The police will be here soon. Hold on I'm getting another call."

"From Sandra?" George raised his voice.

"Gregg? Sorry I can't talk now. We're at Sandra's house. No, she's not. I got a call from Sandra's mom. Remember I called her? I'll call you later."

"Sorry Mrs. Wolf."

"I say they should break in," said George. "A window or something."

Ivan came back. "I just got off the phone with the realtor. The owner lives in Palm Beach Florida. So that's not going to help us."

The police arrived. Slowly their car doors opened and two officers stepped out. Out of the corner of his eye, Ivan saw Liz's face brighten in recognition.

"What do we have here, people?" said the first officer, a tall blond woman.

Alice approached them. "I'm Alice Dykman, I made the call to 911. Candice Wolf, the mother of Sandra Wolf who lives here, is on the line." Alice offered her phone to the woman. Ivan saw her badge: Duncan. "No one has been able to contact Sandra in over a week. Her parents live in Ohio."

"You say it's her mother on the phone?" asked Officer Duncan.

"Yes, Candice Wolf is her mother." Alice said, still extending her arm to the officer, who reluctantly took the phone.

"This is Officer Duncan. Who am I talking to?"

"Candice Wolf, Sandra Wolf's mother."

"And when was the last time you spoke to your daughter, Mrs. Wolf?"

"About a week ago. It's not like her not to call me. I'm at my wits end trying not to panic. Can you get in there somehow?"

"Do you know anybody who might have a key, Mrs. Wolf?"

"I don't."

"This is George, Sandra's father. Can't you just break in?"

"It's not that simple, Mr. Wolf."

"It's just that simple. Just do it. You must!" George shouted.

Liz said, "Do you remember me? From several days ago? We were in the back, me and my boyfriend. We told you she wasn't answering her phone then, remember?"

"I remember I didn't arrest you," Officer Duncan said, raising her eyebrows. Ivan and Alice looked questioningly at Liz.

"You saw the computer on," Liz continued. "It's still on, and still no one has heard from her. We need to get into this house."

"If there's ever a situation where there's an exigent circumstance, it's here." Alice added.

Officer Duncan looked at Alice and squinted. "Are you a lawyer?"

"Why, yes I am."

Office Duncan handed the phone to Alice and the two police officers sauntered up the few steps in a way that told Ivan they were doing everyone a favor. They knocked, tried the doorknob, rang the bell. Officer Duncan took out her phone. "I'm calling my supervisor. If he gives the okay, we can try doing this the easy way first, with plastic, and if that doesn't work, we can do it the hard way with a crowbar."

While Officer Duncan called her supervisor, Liz put her arms around Ivan. "What do you think, dad, what do you think?"

He thought about what they may find inside; he thought about his father in a medical center in Belize hoping he would hang in there until he was airlifted to Lankanau.

"Be prepared," he told Liz.

After getting the okay from their supervisor, Officer Sanchez sliced and diced and shimmered his credit card near the door latch to no avail. Officer Duncan handed him the crowbar. Sanchez placed the thin end of the iron crowbar between the door and the jamb right above the lock. He pushed several times with both arms, then even more times with his whole body. Nothing. Officer Duncan, in sync with Sanchez, added her body to the push. After several pushes, the lock broke and the door opened.

A warm, oily putrid whiff swished out, taking everyone by surprise. It hung there, mingling with the outside air. Officers Duncan and Sanchez, guns drawn and aimed at the floor looked at each other grimly.

"You all wait out here," Officer Duncan said.

As they stood near the steps, Ivan looked down at Liz. Her upper lip was lapped over the lower, the way it had taken shape after her mother's passing. He put his arm around her, looked at her eyes and saw the coming of further suffering.

"Tell me this is not real," Liz whispered. "Tell me this is a dream." She buried her face in her father's chest. Ivan felt the warmth of his little girl's tears soaking through his shirt. Her cries were at first muffled, like a kettle of covered boiling water. The she cried out, "No! No! No!" The echoes bounced off the row home windowpanes of Pine street. Lights turned on, front doors opened. Heads stuck out to see what it was all about.

* * *

Holding Liz' phone with Sandra's parents on the line, Alice stood ready to do whatever was necessary. She read the pain on Liz's face and felt it from the Wolfs in the palm of her hand. They had heard Liz cry out, and she could hear them shouting to each other.

From inside the house they heard the two-way radio static and the voice of Officer Duncan: "We have a '5292' female, Caucasian, in her thirties at 759 Pine St. We searched the house, all clear. Send the crew."

Officer Sanchez came out, trying to appear professionally detached, as he addressed Ivan, Liz, and Alice.

"I'm… I'm sorry."

Alice reached out to hand the cell phone to Officer Sanchez. "You need to tell the parents. Have you ever done that before?"

"No ma'am." Nervously, Officer Sanchez took the phone. "This is Officer Sanchez." All heard rapid voices of anxiety through the cell phone.

"Ma'am, sir. I'm…I…I'm very, I'm very sorry. We're not sure what happened here. The medical examiner is on his way."

"Are you sure it's her? Are you sure it's our daughter?" cried George.

"Are you asking for someone to positively identify her?" said Officer Sanchez.

"Yes," said George.

Officer Sanchez turned to Liz. "Ma'am, the parents are asking, would you, can you positively identify her?"

"Don't ask me to do that," Liz put both arms around her father and buried her head in his chest.

"I could identify her," said Alice. "I've seen her at city events. I know who she is."

"Ok then. Follow me, please."

"I'll call you back, Mr. Wolf." Alice said.

Alice had had her share of walking into a room filled with anxiety, where the drama between the legal combatants was so toxic even those on the peripheral needed a respirator. But nothing in her past prepared her for the suffocating reek that floated and permeated the entire first floor of Sandra Wolf's townhouse. The usually undeterred attorney followed the thick body of Officer Sanchez as he led the way through the thick stench. Alice turned around to see the larger frame of Officer Donovan behind her. Both police officers had flashlights on. When they reached the living room the first thing Alice saw was the 17-inch computer monitor and the squiggly laser-like lines of a screen saver. The second was the bloated and blue petite body of Sandra Wolf, sprawled out on the carpet, flies hovering, larvae nestled within.

Alice suppressed a gasp. Besides seeing her uncle in a casket at a viewing, Alice had never seen a dead body before, and certainly not as part of a group of first responders. The police officers shined their flashlights on the body. Sandra's face, which Alice remembered as pretty and sweet with soft eyes, lay still and cold, her eyes bugged out like a baby owl. Around her face and neck Alice observed small nodes of red rashes. She was wearing a pink sweater, stretched as a result of her sudden overblown belly, and black nylon stockings. Her black and highlighted signature hair lay without luster, like spilled paint from a can. Her leather desk chair was overturned with its four wheels hanging uselessly, like shoes about to slip off a foot. Next to the chair were a pair of high heels, expensive. Duncan, Sanchez, and Alice quietly looked the scene over, heads bent as if in mourning, trying to make sense of it all.

"Ms. Dykman, can you identify her?" Office Sanchez asked, quietly and apologetically, as if his question may be misinterpreted as a disrespectful intrusion of the moment.

"Yes. I recognize her. It's Sandra Wolf. The reporter for the *Philadelphia Times*."

"I'm no doctor," said Officer Donavon, "and maybe I shouldn't be saying this, but it's just us here now, but from my experience it looks to me she was choked."

Alice took in the scene. "You're saying that because...?"

"The red spots I see on the neck and the big eyes, and the chair being on its back. My guess she was choked from behind while sitting on the chair and pulled off the chair. It's not the first time I come across a scene like this, believe it or not."

They paused. "See the dark purple of her fingertips? Means she's been here awhile. Ok, you ID'd. We can get out."

As they made their way out, Alice asked, "So if you're correct, how did the person get into the house? It was locked when we got here."

"Maybe it wasn't locked when he got here. I say "he" because, you know. I think it's a "he." Maybe she let him in. Maybe he was with her all the time and they got into an argument."

"And locked the door on his way out?" Alice put in.

"He didn't have to lock it. It locks from the outside when you close it. I'm just surmising here. It's the crime scene investigator's and detective's jobs to sort out the possibilities."

"Could be any of those scenarios," Alice said.

"Or none of them," Officer Donavan admitted. "I've been surprised before."

When they were outside Alice dialed the Wolfs number and handed the phone to Officer Duncan. "Her parents?" Officer Donavan sighed and took the phone.

"Did you...see her?" Liz asked Alice.

Alice rolled her mouth. "I did, Liz. I did."

Liz's eyes began to well up with tears.

"Do they know how even? Or why?" Liz asked.

"It's not clear."

"I mean was it a natural cause? Aneurysm or something like that?" Liz asked.

"I don't know. The crime investigator and medical examiner are on their way. Probably won't be definitive until there's an autopsy. Oh, looks like they're here."

Chapter Fourteen

A van with the words "MEDICAL EXAMINER" and another with the words "CRIME INVESTIGATOR" arrived and double parked. Liz watched them get out of the vans and take over. The medical examiner headed straight inside the house. One crime scene investigator with a high-quality camera began taking pictures of the entrance, then disappeared inside the house. A gloved investigator dusted the metal handrail, the doorknob and window. Another drew sketches in a book. An investigator came out with plastic bags filled with shoes, a cell phone, a half full bottle of Snapple diet peach iced tea. One investigator carried out Sandra's laptop computer.

Another investigator came from around the corner and said to Officer Sanchez, "Look what I found in the trash can in the back." He held up a plastic bag containing a necktie. "A Jerry Garcia tie."

It hit Liz that the concern for Sandra that she alone carried for days and tried desperately to share, had now been taken out of her hands.

Officer Sanchez approached Liz. "Detectives will want to talk to you."

"What about her parents?" Liz asked.

"My understanding is that they're making flight arrangements."

The three were left alone, huddled together, but soon they were not alone, as they felt the presence of neighbors gathering around. Liz heard them talk.

"Do you know what happened?" said a young woman in sweats, standing on her toes.

"No idea. I thought you would know," said another woman walking her dog.

"Who lives there?" another man asked.

"Beats me," said another man walking two dogs. "I just moved here last month."

"I know," said an older woman with serious expression. "Sandra Wolf."

"Never met her."

"She's a journalist at the *Philly Times*," said the older woman.

"I'm just sayin', I never met her."

"Are you sure this is her house?" said an older man. "I think hers is further down."

"I'm sure. I've seen her. This is her house."

"Does anyone know what happened?" said the man walking the two dogs.

Liz wished they would all shut up. Another police car arrived and two people came out, a middle age, stocky white male with short, curly gray hair, and a younger, taller straight-haired black female. Officers Donovan and Sanchez approached them and led them into the house.

"Those are the detectives," said older woman.

"This can't be good," said another neighbor.

"No shit."

After what seemed to be hours to Liz but only ten minutes, Officer Donavan came out with the two detectives. Her chin pointed to where Ivan, Liz and Alice huddled together, as if creating a protective shell for Liz. The detectives approached them.

"I'm Detective Valerie Moss," she said. "From homicide. This is Detective Frank Lopez. You're Liz?"

Liz nodded.

"Can we ask you all to come over here with me away from everybody so we can talk?"

They followed the detectives to the other side of the entrance, away from the crowd. When they were away from the crowd Moss turned to them with a serious and sorrowful look.

"I can't imagine what this is like for you," Detective Moss said to Liz. "And you're Alice?"

"Alice Dykman."

"You ID'd the body, is that right?" Detective Lopez asked.

"Correct."

"And you're sure it's Sandra Wolf?"

Alice nodded at him slowly. Liz wondered if Detective Lopez would question where Philadelphia was on a map even if it was circled in red.

"We need to ask you some questions," said Detective Moss, looking at Liz.

"Yeah, okay."

"Office Duncan tells me Sandra Wolf was your teacher at Temple, is that correct?"

"That's right. And a journalist for the *Philadelphia Times.*"

"When did you see her last?"

"The last time," Liz repeated. Framing the question that way brought a chill to her lips. "That would be Monday. She didn't show up for class on Wednesday." Looking down at the brick sidewalk she added, "Never thought that would be the last time."

"I know what you mean," Detective Moss said. "Was that the main campus in North Philly?"

"No. Center City. On Market Street."

They were interrupted by the sounds of screeching brakes and sliding doors of Action News and NBC vans. In an instant cameras, lights, wires, microphones, and newscasters spewed out like a swarm of hornets.

"There goes the neighborhood," said Detective Lopez, "Pain in the ass. But that's America."

Detective Moss asked Liz, "So was there anything out of the ordinary about her that day? That class?"

"Nothing. We spoke afterward as usual. She offered to take me along to an interview, sort of as an onlooker or shadow. She wasn't just a teacher to me, you know."

"Interview with who?"

"Didn't tell me."

"Did you speak to her after that, on the phone or email?"

"As I keep saying, she wasn't answering."

"When was the first time you tried to contact her after Monday?" Detective Lopez asked.

"I guess Wednesday."

"Officer Duncan told us she and Officer Sanchez saw you and your boyfriend at the back of the house," said Detective Lopez. "Says you were tampering with the garage door. What about that?"

Liz looked at Ivan and then at Alice. "It was stupid, I know. But we looked through the window first and saw the light. And her computer screen. I just knew something was wrong. So I – we – I guess I, wanted to see if her car was there."

"Was it?"

"Yeah. Which made me wonder even more why she wasn't answering my calls or my emails. But nobody thought it was a big deal. Not Officer Sanchez. Not Officer Duncan. They were ready to arrest me."

Liz looked past the detective towards the front door of the house "Oh!" She buried her face in her father's chest as the medics carried out the body bag and pushed it onto the truck.

"So now what?" Ivan asked Detective Moss over Liz's head.

"They do an autopsy. Figure out the cause of death for sure. Forensics goes through the DNA and fingerprints. They do a death certificate which will state the cause of death. The press will be all over this. Liz, do you have any thoughts who might have talked to her or contacted her since you last spoke with her?"

Liz's mouth crunched up and tears welled out. She tried to suppress it, but she started to cry, loud and sputtering like a faucet with intermittent pressure. With a supreme effort of will, she managed to compose herself after a moment. She sniffed hard. "What's weird is that she published three stories this week for the *Philadelphia Chronicle*."

"And you said she worked for the *Times*," said Detective Moss.

"And what's weirder, if she's been gone for almost a week, they were published after she was dead."

"You read the articles?"

"I did."

"What were they about?" Detective Moss asked.

"The Muslim community in Philadelphia."

"What about it?"

Liz paused, pondering how to respond to Detective Moss' question. "A lot about it. A lot of questions about it. You need to read the articles."

"Looks like you got a lot of interviews ahead," said Ivan.

"I need to ask you, Liz. Did she ever say anything about having enemies?"

"She was an investigative journalist," Alice put in. "I would think she had plenty of enemies."

"I was asking Liz," Detective Moss said to Alice.

"I can't think of any. Anyone in particular," Liz said.

"Maybe who she wrote about became her enemies," said Ivan.

"We'll look into that. Meanwhile, I need contact info for all of you." Detective Moss took out a pen and opened her pad.

Ivan and Liz wrote down their information. Alice gave Detective Moss her card. Meanwhile police unraveled several layers of yellow tape. As she watched, another pang went through Liz's chest. But this time the pang was different; not the pang of sadness and shock but of transformation; she felt a change taking place in her mind, in her heart, her disposition; a change from sadness and anger to determination. She felt the wetness in her eyes drying as she observed the scene before her with new clarity; not the clarify of understanding of what took place or why, or even how, but of purpose.

"Detective Moss, what can I do to help?" Liz asked.

"Just be available."

"No, I mean more. I mean really help. I want to help find who killed her."

"This is a job for the police and detectives. It's not for ordinary citizens like yourself to be involved in. But I know what you can do. Sandra's parents are flying here tomorrow morning to identify and claim their daughter. Maybe you can meet them up at the airport? Bring them to the medical examiner office? Meet me there. That would be a great help. To them and us."

Liz didn't answer.

"Let me give you my card. You let me know."

Liz took the card and looked at it. "What you're asking me to do is the hardest thing anyone has ever asked me to do. But I will. I will pick up Sandra's parents from the airport and meet you at the morgue."

Chapter Fifteen

While the road off Route 30/Lancaster Avenue leading to a sprawling landscape of rich grass, exotic plants, and shrubberies could be mistaken for the entrance of a well-endowed university or resort, no one knew better than Ivan that the focus of this institution was on healing the sick. He knew the place well, the looping hallways, the coffee kiosk, the parking garage with its token-operated toll booth. It was where his mother Sarah had spent her last few months battling heart disease. It was where his father would battle his.

Ivan parked his Toyota at the emergency room parking lot. Through the open sunroof, he listened to the stillness of dawn and saw the sun rise over West Philadelphia. He was alone among a full lot of parked cars. He took comfort in this sight. The cars made him feel less alone, giving him the moral support to go on.

Ivan had received a call from the pilot that the plane had landed in Philadelphia's Northeast airport. A little later he received a call from the hospital saying his father was settling in to monitors, IVs, EKGs, echocardiogram, coronary angiogram and a cardiac catheterization.

Ivan stood at the entrance to his father's emergency room space, separated by a curtain so thin everything on the other side could be seen in silhouettes. His arm was hooked to an IV of saline. Plugs and buttons punched into his arm and chest led to monitors with green digital lines. They gave off an occasional gasp but otherwise emitted a steady stream of blips. Dad's heart rate was high, his blood pressure was up. He was unshaven, white hair disheveled, his mouth opened a crack and drooling. Near the entrance sat his pot-bellied red suitcase hastily stuffed by Martinez along with a small black carry-on. Ivan did a quick scan of the other early morning emergencies and thought, only his dad had travelled an arduous distance to reach these sacred quarters of healing, only he had left fine dining and first-rate entertainment to come here and possibly die.

Ivan sensed someone next him. "Excuse me, hi, is this your dad? We were waiting for you." A young, petite and perky nurse, too perky for so early in the morning, looked up at him.

"That's him," Ivan pointed with his chin to his father who was sleeping.

"He's stable. We got him on the bed no problem. We've taken his blood pressure, which is on the high side. We're giving him Toradol, a mild pain killer. He doesn't seem to know where he is or what happened. Do you have his insurance?"

Ivan pondered. "He's on Medicare. I don't know about his supplemental." Ivan eyed his black bag. "Anybody look in there?"

"Oh, we can't do that. That's his personal stuff. But you can."

"Has he been seen by a doctor?" Ivan asked.

"A few already."

"Did they confirm he had a heart attack?"

The nurse wiggled her shoulders and bent her head slightly towards Ivan. "I'm supposed to let the doctors tell you all that. But it'll be an hour, maybe more before they come around here again. Yes, he did. I know he was flown here. Where was he? If I may ask?"

"Not in his right mind."

"Huh?"

"What's the game plan from this point?"

"Well, once a bed becomes available, he'll be admitted. Probably in a couple of hours. We have coffee. If you need anything, my name is Carol."

"What's your name if I don't need anything?"

She gave him a questioning look, then caught on. "Oh, well, then it's Leroy! You're funny."

"Why am I funny?" Harold grumbled. His half-opened eyes looked at Ivan. Above him, the blank TV stared down on him as if in disapproval. When he tried to move around with all the attachments, Ivan thought, he looked like an oddity at the Ripley's Believe It or Not Museum he father took him too when he was a young boy.

Harold spoke again. "And where the hell am I?"

Carol approached him. "Good morning, Mr. Samuels, I'm Carol, your nurse. You're at Lankanu Hospital. We're going to take good care of you here. Can I get you anything? Are you comfortable?"

Harold lay on a narrow bed under a thin white sheet wearing a pea green hospital gown. His bed was raised enough to get a good view of the nurse station beyond which Ivan and Carol were standing. He lifted his left arm to examine the heparin lock stuck in his vein.

"I make a living." Harold quipped.

Carol broke out in hearty laugh, surprisingly vigorous, Ivan thought, for such petite woman. Then he saw her name tag said Connetti. Italian.

"Now I see where your son gets his sense of humor. You remind me of my uncle Sal. You see this button here?" Carol pulled a cord from a wall panel of assorted wires. "If you need me, you push this button, ok?"

Harold pushed the button. "Like this?"

"Exactly," Carol said turning off the red light.

"So what am I doing here?"

"You know what, I'm going let your son tell you. I'll be back."

Ivan noticed his father's expression, a mixture of annoyance and guilt, and wondered which sentiment would spring forth first.

"I know. I screwed up."

Ivan felt relief. "Yeah, well, we can talk about that. The doctor will come again soon to talk about what comes next."

"I'm not having an operation."

"Do you remember at all what happened? On the ship?"

Harold looked at his hands, shook his head. "Not really. I was walking. Next thing I knew I was in that hospital. And then on a plane with nurses. And now here." Looking up at Ivan he said, "This is Lankenau. Where Sarah was."

"Right. And your so-called friends left you in Belize so they could enjoy themselves for the rest of the cruise. Including Diana. What do you make of that?" The moment these words came out he regretted them. Now was not the time.

Harold's eyes darted back and forth as if an enemy lurked and about to pounce from any direction.

"What could she do? She's not a doctor."

"Let's forget about that for now and focus on getting you back in shape. Liz will be visiting you later."

"That'll be nice."

"Are you hungry?"

"Not really. Pissed."

Ivan sat on the edge of the bed. For the first time that morning, Harold looked directly at his son, with a mixture of sadness and gratitude.

"Maybe you should consider moving back to Philly," Ivan said.

"Don't be ridiculous. I have life in Florida. And it's cold here. Which is why I left in the first place."

"Just keep it in mind as a thought."

"That's all it'll ever be."

Ivan looked up at the TV. It reminded him of the face of the great and powerful Oz.

"When was the last time you watched the news?" Ivan asked. In his own right his father was a news junky, even if it was only CNN and the Miami Herald.

"Before I left on the cruise."

"Should I put it on?"

"What the hell."

Ivan took the remote laying to the right of Harold's head. He pressed the red button and went to Channel 6.

"But the big story on Action News is the sudden and bizarre death of *Philadelphia Times* journalist Sandra Wolf, found dead last night in her home in the Society Hill section of Philadelphia. Police are calling it a possible homicide as it appears she may have been strangled by an unknown assailant. Police can't say when the homicide took place but there's speculation that it may have taken place several days ago. A spokesperson for the *Philadelphia Times* confirmed Ms. Wolf had not been heard from for several days. But oddly, articles allegedly written by Ms. Wolf appeared in the *Philadelphia Chronicle* as recently as Saturday. When we asked the *Philadelphia Times* if she had left the *Times* to work for the *Chronicle* the spokesperson for the *Times* had no comment. When we asked *Chronicle* editor Michael Banks, here's what he had to say…"

A written quote against a white background appeared on the screen with the raspy voice of Michael Banks, as if he was chewing on sand.

"First off, everyone here at the *Chronicle* is just shocked, couldn't be more shocked, and our hearts go out to her family. Such a shame, such a talent. It's very upsetting for this to happen to a journalist, or anybody for that matter. You asked about the articles. As a matter of explanation, we received all the three articles at the same time and we published them this past week over the course of several days. Of course, we didn't know, when we put out the stories, we didn't know what happened to Sandra. But truth be told, she had approached us a few weeks ago in fact, to let us know she was writing some pieces and had her doubts then about whether the *Times* would publish them. She asked us if we would be willing to do so. She showed us the articles and we told her yeah, you let us know when."

"Action News asked *Times* editor Alex Anderson to comment on the *Chronicle*s' statement but the long-time editor, who is usually not at a loss for words, had no comment. Two of Ms. Wolf's articles that appeared in the *Chronicle* last week were about former 76ers basketball star James Warren and the South Philadelphia Muslim community. When we asked police officials if there was any connection between James Warren who now goes by the name of Jamil Abdullah Hakim and the death of Sandra Wolf, we were told the investigation is ongoing. Action News attempted to reach James Warren at home and at his mosque but could not be reached for comment. Sandra Wolf was thirty-four."

Ivan stared at the screen as if homing in on the pixels would help him connect the dots to the Sandra Wolf story. If Sandra Wolf worked for the *Times*, why did she need to send those articles to the *Chronicle*? Why didn't the *Times* publish them? Was Sandra's death somehow connected to the FBI's interest in the *Times*? Where did his audit fit into all this?

"Poor girl," Harold said. "She's worse off than me."

Chapter Sixteen

Detective Valerie Moss was accustomed to interrogating thugs for assault, armed robbery, rape, drug dealing, and now that she was promoted, murder. It took only one interrogation to grasp the incongruity of it all; moving up the ranks rewarded her by letting her get in the faces of the most ruthless. On one hand, she was proud of escaping her wrenching West Philly neighborhood of crumbling concrete and bullet-holed bricks, banged-up cars, crack use and prostitution. Turning away from her brothers wallowing in their whirlpools of despair, she left. But did she truly get away? Her job called for looking into the eyes of conscienceless killers who, if it weren't for the heavy metal shackles locked around their ankles and wrists, would leap across the wobbly interrogation table to rip out her throat — not because they faced life in airtight prisons, but because the clever investigative skills and wit of the detective who would put them there were those of a woman.

Today was different, way different. First, this was not the cagey Philadelphia Police Office of District 3 crowded with losers. This was the venerable and well-respected office of the *Philadelphia Times*. Here, the people she would be interviewing did not spend the greater part of their lives destroying other people's lives and scheming ways to weasel out of getting caught. Rather, they were people who prepared for a great career, in a legitimate profession, and spent every day and sometimes all day doing their personal best to tell the truth. At least she hoped so. And second, it was Sunday, the day after the discovery and broadcast of the inexplicable death of their colleague.

To make it easier, everyone agreed to come into the office, where Detective Moss and Detective Lopez would conduct private interviews, including with publisher Conrad Benson and editor Alexander Anderson. First, though, Benson wanted to address the whole group. Moss watched as people in various attire — business to beach casual — filtered into the conference room followed by Benson, Anderson and another suited-up gray-haired man she didn't know. At last, about twenty employees stood around a well-worn oak conference table which, had it ears and a brain, would know more secrets than the Central Intelligence Agency. No one took a seat.

Benson began. "Appreciate all of you coming in this morning. This Sunday morning. Needless to say, this is a sad day for all of us. We're all shocked by the terrible news about our fellow employee, colleague, and friend, Sandra Wolf."

Heavy pause, thick as tomato paste.

"Of course, to us she was more than an employee. She was part of our family. And this," Conrad stretched out his arms, "was her home.

"This horrifying event is something we have never experienced in the history of the *Times*, I don't think." He turned to Alex for confirmation. Alex nodded. "Sandra was Alex's shining star." He again turned to Alex, who remained stoic. The other employees stared at him with blank faces that appeared to say, 'guess I'm nobody.'

Conrad continued. "I know all of us have our own religious beliefs. Or maybe you don't have any religious beliefs. That's your private matter. But I'd like to ask if you would all indulge me with a moment of silence and say your own prayer, or just visualize positivity for Sandra. I think that would be the appropriate thing to do now." He turned and nodded to Alex, standing a bit behind him to the right. Conrad bowed his head down in prayer. Alex stared straight ahead.

Detective Moss eyeballed the crowd, took the opportunity to make a mental note of the body language in the room. Some, being good subordinates, bowed their heads; some closed their eyes, others remained motionless, eyes open, like waiting for "The Star-Spangled Banner" to end at a Phillies game. She also used the moment to mentally separate those she thought were probably innocents from persons of interest.

After a few adequate but awkward moments, Conrad continued. "Thank you all for that moment. I'm sure that would mean something to Sandra. I know it's a very strange and challenging time for all of us here at the *Times*. But we will get through it. I promise you. I've arranged for a psychiatric social worker to come to the office tomorrow if anyone feels the need to talk to someone."

A pause, a clearing of the throat.

"We don't know how or why this terrible tragedy occurred, but we need to find out. Not that that will bring Sandra back to us, but still it must be done. Detectives Valerie Moss and Frank Lopez from the Philadelphia Police Department are assigned to investigate Sandra's death." Conrad nodded in their direction; Detectives Moss and Lopez remained still. "They are here to learn more about Sandra to help them solve this mystery. They will be speaking privately with all of you. We want you to feel comfortable when speaking to the detectives. We are also mindful of your legal rights. To that end we have here today our in-house counsel, Jack Finch who has offered to sit with you for these interviews. Detective Moss, do you want to say anything to the group before you get started?"

Detective Moss took one step forward. She looked at the mostly young faces staring at her. Some looked pensive, some bored.

"As Mr. Benson noted, I'm Detective Valerie Moss of the homicide division of the Philadelphia Police Department out of District 3. This is my partner Detective Frank Lopez. I first want to say how sorry we are for the loss of Sandra Wolf. I didn't know her personally, but I knew her name and her work, so in that regard, she wasn't a stranger to me. And I also want to thank you for agreeing to come in today, as opposed to us all going down to the station house. My aim today in speaking with you to is to find out more about Sandra Wolf. What you know about her, especially the last time you saw her. Anything and everything you can share with us will help. Sometimes small things can be everything. As you probably heard, the victim – Sandra – your friend and colleague—appeared to have been strangled in her home. We don't know who, we don't know why, we're not even sure exactly when, but maybe something can come out of these conversations today. I know most of you don't have your own office, so we'll talk privately with each of you in this conference room, one at a time. Does anyone have any questions for me at this point?"

Silence. Then Doug asked. "Are we required to have the attorney sit with us?"

"Good question," Detective Moss answered. "No, you are not. That's up to you."

"Okay, thanks." Doug said.

Valerie Moss had trained her eyes to see everything without moving them, like a blind person trained his ears to hear every subtle sound. It was a skill that kept her alive. It was a skill that has helped make her a sharp detective. It was a skill she was using now, getting glimpses of reactions to the young reporter's unexpected question. The reactions were almost unnoticeable. It was the stiff ones, the motionless ones that gave off the strongest vibe. And the stiffest one, she noticed, came from Alexander Anderson. Valerie had planned to interview him first. She now decided to interview him last. She also decided not to interview the reporter with the question first, even though he was listed first on the printout the *Times* secretary handed her when she arrived.

"Detective Moss?" Standing before her was a young, tall, athletic woman, blond hair in a ponytail wearing shorts and sneakers.

"Yes?"

"I don't mean to sound like a jerk or anything, but can you take me first? I have this special sorority reunion that we planned for months and it's happening this afternoon. I mean, if you can't, I totally get it."

"Have a seat. The rest of you stay close. We'll do this as quickly as possible." What she really meant was, we will take all the time we need.

Chapter Seventeen

From Benson's office Anderson, Benson and Finch watched the employees go in and out of the conference room with the detectives, then head out the door.

"Looks like no one wants you, Jack," Benson observed, sitting at his desk. Anderson and Finch stood.

"You don't need a lawyer," Jack noted, "when you have nothing to hide."

"Nevertheless, I thought it was the prudent thing to do to have you here. So they know we're supporting them."

"Oh, I agree. No question about that. You did the right thing. But I wanted to ask you Alex, since you knew Sandra best, the police said there was no indication of forced entry. I was wondering if you knew if Sandra had a boyfriend?"

Alex looked up from his cellphone. "I don't. She was a private person in that regard."

"It's the detectives' job to find the killer," Benson said. "Ours is to run a paper. Alex, we're still going forward with those pieces Doug is working on, correct?"

"I never told him to stop," said Alex. "Which reminds me, I need to finish my own editorial for tomorrow. Excuse me."

Alex went to his office just as Doug entered the conference room to talk to the detectives. He wondered if Doug would be telling the detectives about his assignment and how that would reflect on him. He wasn't worried. He was ready for whatever questions the detectives threw at him. He turned on his computer and browsed to see how other news sites wrote about Sandra's murder. What he read astonished and amused him. One conspiracy theorist said the murder took place in a mosque and her body taken back to her home to make it look like a burglary gone bad. Alex had chosen senior staff reporter Janet Walker to write Sandra's obituary. He had 'paired' Sandra with Janet so Janet could show Sandra the city, introduced her to public officials and the like. It seemed only fitting to give Janet the assignment, and she treated it with love. The obituary discussed Sandra's insights, instincts, her integrity. She interviewed George and Candice Wolf, who told her how much Sandra loved working at the *Times*. "Best job she ever had," Candice told them. Janet was forbidden, however, to say a word about the articles published in the *Chronicle*.

Alex watched Doug's body language responses to the detectives' questions, nodding his head, shaking his head, lifting his shoulders. Alex took a sip from his Seattle coffee and tossed the cup in his trash can. Five minutes later, Detectives Moss and Lopez walked into his office, taking notice of the awards and certificates of honor hanging on the walls.

Detective Moss took a seat and said, "Tell us about your relationship with Sandra Wolf, Mr. Anderson." Detective Lopez stood.

"Sure. I met her for the first time eight years ago when she came in for an interview. She had driven all the way from Blue Ash, Ohio, jut to talk to us. That alone impressed me. Shortly into the interview, I recognized her potential. She was looking for an opportunity to grow with a big city paper and we gave her that opportunity. I hired her and she excelled. I'm sure you read Sandra's articles. She's brilliant. Was."

"So why did you fire her?" Detective Lopez asked.

"We didn't fire her."

"We just interviewed Doug. He told us you told him you fired her," Lopez countered.

"I told Doug what I wanted him to believe. You can check with personnel."

"You didn't answer my question," said Detective Moss.

"I'm sorry. I thought I did. What was your question?"

"Your relationship with Sandra Moss."

"Professional of course, one of mutual respect. We didn't always agree on everything, as you probably gathered. We have a certain standard at the *Times*. Standards that we uphold at all costs. So even when a star reporter such as Sandra, and she was a star, a superstar, if we feel a piece doesn't quite meet up to those standards, and I'm not talking about writing standards here, I'm talking more of policy standards, we don't run with it. Obviously, Sandra had a different point of view and I respect that, we're all entitled to our own point of view. This is America. The First Amendment is sacred. We just had a difference of opinion."

"What do you mean by "at all costs?" Detective Moss asked.

"I'm sorry?"

"You said you uphold your standards at all costs. What exactly does that mean?"

"Am I on trial here? It's a figure of speech. Meaning if it doesn't meet our standards, we don't publish it."

"Tell us Mr. Anderson," said Detective Lopez, "what was it about those articles that didn't meet your standards?"

"Those articles were accusatory and lacked validation. I was not going to have the *Times* go on record accusing one of the most well-respected members of our community, who has done so much development for the black community, and a famous Philadelphia sports celebrity, of being an un-American terrorist supporter. We'd be opening ourselves to a lawsuit."

"Never stopped you before," said Detective Lopez. Alex took this as a swipe for the *Times* attacks on the Philadelphia Police.

"When was the last time you saw Sandra?" Detective Moss asked.

"That would be Tuesday. Tuesday afternoon. She was on her way to interview the head of the teacher's union, Simon Kraft. You should speak to him."

"Right now we're speaking to you. What was your last conversation about?"

"About her interview with Kraft. I emphasized she should try to nail down what would Kraft want to prevent a school strike."

"Did you have a relationship with Sandra that went beyond professional? Did you have a romantic relationship with her?" asked Detective Lopez.

Alex chuckled and sat back in his leather desk chair, clasping his hands behind his neck. "That's always the question, isn't it? Was the boss having an affair with his subordinate."

"Again, you didn't answer the question," said Detective Moss.

"No."

"Tell us where you were since the time you saw Sandra leave the office Tuesday to interview Mr. Kraft," said Detective Lopez. "And don't leave anything out."

Alex sighed. "Let's see. Tuesday, Tuesday after she left I was in the office. I was on the phone. I could probably give you the names of the people I spoke with. I was working on an editorial about a possible casino on Penns Landing. Maybe you read it the paper on Wednesday? A lot of people are frantic about it. I personally think this will be a positive development for Philadelphia. You guys probably disagree because it'll mean more work for you. Anyway, then I went home and had the dinner my wife left in the refrigerator."

"Was your wife home when you got there?" Detective Moss asked.

"She was not. She was out with her friends. She does that now and then."

"Did you go out after you got home and ate?"

"Nope. Stayed home."

"What time did your wife come home?" asked Detective Lopez.

"Can't say for sure. It was late. I was already in bed when she came home. I was beat."

"So nobody saw you after you left the office on Tuesday?"

"Maybe. I don't know. I can't think of anyone."

"So from the time you left the office until your wife came home, nobody could vouch for you? Is that it?" Detective Moss asked.

"Just the leftover turkey in the fridge."

"What's that's supposed to mean?" snapped Detective Lopez.

"I mean you could ask my wife if she saw any leftover turkey when she got home. She'd probably say no because I ate it all. That's all. I'm not trying to be smart. Sometimes things I say come out that way. Sorry."

Alex noticed how Detectives Moss and Lopez looked at each other with skepticism.

"Really, I was just thinking how I can prove I was home. That's all. Didn't mean anything by it."

"Okay, now let's hear about your Wednesday," Detective Moss asked, jotting something done in her notes.

"I must admit, that was a confusing day for us at the *Times*. I was sitting with Conrad talking about how to deal with Sandra's article in the *Chronicle*. Do we fire her? Do we sue her? Is this her way of telling us she quit? All these questions came up and we were talking it through. But we didn't fire her."

"Did you try calling her?" asked Detective Moss.

"We tried calling but she didn't pick up. We thought she didn't want to talk to us. Obviously we were at a turning point. We thought maybe she just wasn't ready to talk to us."

"Did you go to her house?" asked Detective Lopez.

"Why would I do that? Just because she wasn't answering her phone?"

"Because that's where she was found dead."

Alex pulled his chair closer to his desk and eyed both detectives. "Do I need to call Jack in here?"

"You tell us," said Detective Moss. "You go to her house. You get into an argument with her over the article. Things get out of hand. I don't blame you for being angry. She was your employee. She was being insubordinate. You could have just fired her right then and there."

Alex's voice was tight. "Except I wasn't there and I didn't kill her. And I didn't fire her. And that conversation you're making up never happened."

"Right now, you're the only one with motive."

"I could give you a list of people with motive. Starting with the people she wrote about in that article."

"That article and the other two articles came out after she was dead," said Detective Lopez.

"Am I under arrest?"

Detective Moss put on rubber gloves, stuck her hand inside the trash can, and fished out Alex' Seattle coffee cup. "Not before we check your DNA."

Detective Moss leaned over Alex's computer and yanked out the mouse's cord. Dangling it in front of his face like the tail of a real mouse, she said, "I'm sure you have plenty of these mouses running around here. We're gonna check for fingerprints on this too. If things work out the way you say, I'll just feed it to the cat."

Chapter Eighteen

Unlike many modern-day airports in major cities where terminals are spread through swaths of acreage, all the Philadelphia airport terminals are reachable by one straight road off I-76. Terminal F is the last terminal, reserved for short, domestic flights on small jets.

Ivan glanced over at his daughter in the passenger seat. She stared straight ahead. Did losing a parent prepare you for bonding with parents who'd just lost a child? When Nancy died, nothing anyone could say mattered. He was sure it would be that way in a few moments when they met George and Candice Wolf.

Inside the terminal Liz spotted a slim, tall, elegantly dressed but clearly distraught woman coming down the escalator. She was wearing a tan knee-length skirt with matching jacket and a beige, buttoned blouse. The combination of class and grace was a tip-off, but her gray-streaked black hair swinging freely just above her shoulders clinched it. She had to be Sandra Wolf's mother. Liz noticed the sleepless look around Candice's piercing blue eyes, a round soft-skinned face like her daughter's. She wore pale lipstick.

The man with her was trim, slightly taller, with closely cropped salt and pepper hair, wearing a gray sport jacket, gray pants, and black shirt. He had thick eyebrows that arched over small green eyes, a slightly protruding nose, and tiny pocks on his bristled facial skin.

Both looked shellshocked, as if they had just landed unexpectedly on the planet Pluto.

Liz walked towards them, unsure of the right way to say hello. "Liz," Candice said, opening her arms to embrace her. "Oh Liz, Liz, bless you bless you." Liz could tell she was about to cry.

George stood a bit behind Candice and nodded, which Liz took as his appreciation for her being there as well. Liz whispered in Candice's ear. "I don't know what to say."

"Your being here says everything," said Candice.

George headed to the baggage carousel.

"My dad is outside by the car," Liz said when Candice released her.

"Okay, Okay. Right," Candice wiped away a tear. "I promised myself I wouldn't. But….no, okay, that's it." She looked at Liz and pushed out a smile. "Okay, George, find the luggage?"

"Got one. I see the other."

"Where did you say your father is? With the car you said? Do we need to take a shuttle? Can you believe we came here to Philadelphia only once to see Sandra. Can you believe that? These shoes are beginning to hurt. George, I told you I should have worn tennis shoes."

"No shuttle. My dad is right outside. Unless a cop chased him away, in which case he'll circle back."

"Got both now." George wheeled two small suitcases one blue, one red.

"Can I take one of those for you, Mr. Wolf?"

"George. And no."

Outside, Ivan leaned on the passenger side of his Toyota.

"That's my dad, there, Ivan Samuels." Ivan nodded at the Wolfs and popped the trunk, then went to grab the luggage from George.

"You can sit upfront with me, George," said Ivan. "Candice, you're okay sitting in the back with Liz?" Ivan put the luggage in the truck and shut the trunk door.

"I'd love to sit with Liz," she said, giving Liz a smile as she slipped in the back and straightened her skirt.

* * *

Ivan made his way through the cluster of idling and exiting cars, blending into the PA 291 Penrose Avenue traffic to the George C. Platt Memorial Bridge that led across the Schuylkill River and onto I-76.

In his rear-view mirror Ivan observed Candice looking out the window, taking in the urban industrial sites of oil tankers, billboards advertising army recruitment, slip-and-fall lawyers, Medicare supplement plans, and an isolated windowless building surrounded by parked cars with a sign "Gentlemen's Club." Candice looked at everything, probably to keep her mind off from where she was going, Ivan thought.

"What do you do, George?" Ivan asked. George was stoic, eyes blinking, as if he were in a dream and wanted desperately to wake up to at his desk in front of his computer.

"I'm a software engineer for the insurance industry. I make the software for insurance products."

"Got it," Ivan said.

"Been doing it for thirty-five years. And for what," he said turning a question into a statement.

Ivan glanced at him and saw his mouth and cheek cringing into the shape of pain.

"We've met the detectives handling the case," Ivan said. "Detective Moss will be meeting us where we're going."

"Are they any good?" George asked, eyes focused on the road.

Ivan took a moment to answer. "They seemed competent to me. They're still in a quandary about how the…the …perpetrator got into Sandra's house." Ivan stopped himself from saying murderer.

"Think they're capable of figuring it out?"

Ivan took a deep breath, sucking in the insult to Philly cops—but he'd have had the same question. "Do you know if Sandra had any boyfriends? I'm sure the detectives are going to want to know that."

"She never discussed that with me. Candice? What about you? Did she ever talk to you about any boyfriends?"

'Not unless her boyfriend was her boss," Candice said, still looking out at the urban sights.

"You mean the editor of the *Times*? Alexander Anderson?" Ivan probed just to be sure.

"If I spoke to her during the day, she'd tell me she had to get off because her boss was calling. If I called her at noon, she'd tell me she had a business lunch with her boss to talk about a story she was doing. Never anybody else. Only him. But that doesn't mean…"

"More than just a few times?" Ivan asked.

"Many times. And to be honest, it seemed to me they were dating. I mean, what do they need to talk about over lunch that they can't talk about in the office? And then there were times I called her at night and she was with him."

"Did she ever talk to you about any of the articles she was writing?" Liz asked.

"She told me," George answered. "She told me about the ones that came out when she…. when we couldn't reach her. I told her it sounded like a great story, too good in fact, and maybe she should be careful, maybe she shouldn't write it because her safety could be in jeopardy. Maybe her boss agreed with me and was taking her to lunch to talk her out of it. But…" George voice trailed off. "Maybe she wouldn't listen to him either."

"Ivan?" Candice pushed herself closer to the front seats, asks. "Do you think it could be him?"

Ivan mulled this over. "The editor of the biggest newspaper in Philly, over a disagreement over a story? I can't see it."

"Why not?" George said.

"Just too bizarre."

"Bizarre is just what happened to our daughter."

Chapter Nineteen

Over twenty-four years during the 1800s, Philadelphia's city morgue went from being the worst in the country to being the nation's prototype. The first morgue was just a greenhouse on Potter's Field on the 900 block of Lombard St, which was now a gentrified, desirable area of Center City. From there, the morgue moved to an inaccessible spot on the waterfront, tucked among storage bins and freight trains. In 1890 the City Council authorized a modernized morgue, and the result was a work of art. The façade had the feel of a high-culture theatre rather than a den for the dead. It boasted a colorful blend of bricks, stone, textured tiles and shiny marble and made the 1300 block of Wood Street proud. The interior was even more impressive, featuring decorative tiled walls from ceiling to floor, marble switchboards, incandescent lamps and a state-of-art refrigeration system - the envy of all morgue refrigeration facilities from coast to coast.

It reigned for twenty-four years as such— until the devastating Spanish flu epidemic did it in. Unable to sustain the mounting number of corpses created by this disease, a new, more functional Spanish Mission-style morgue was built, grimly appropriate for the disease that spawned it. This structure served Philadelphia faithfully until modernity crept in and rendered it once again obsolete. In 1971 a newer, blander building opened in the shadows of the University of Pennsylvania. It went by the politically correct title 'Medical Examiner Building.' Ivan was lucky enough to find a parking spot right in front, where Detective Moss, wearing slacks and a business jacket, awaited them.

Ivan and Liz got out right away. Detective Moss reached for the back door handle next to the Wolfs but stopped. Candice was leaning forward, her forehead on the back of the front passenger seat and her hand on her husband's right shoulder. George, seeming to stare at the parking meter in front of him, put his hand on top of his wife's, and there they remained as if these touching hands had become wires infusing energy into each other's bodies, into their minds, in order to move their souls forward to their next chapter of their lives, which was about to begin with the opening of the car door.

Inside the building, the pathologist greeted them. He was in his forties, balding, short, a bit pudgy and Asian. He wore a long white lab uniform with his name, Ozzie Moto, stitched on the pocket. Ivan got a whiff of formaldehyde and golden Givenchy aftershave.

Placing her hand gently on Candice's shoulder, Detective Moss said, "Ozzie, these are Candice and George Wolf and their friends Ivan and Liz."

"Very sorry Mr. Wolf, Mrs. Wolf," Ozzie said moving his entire body to face each of them as he said their names. Ivan got the feeling Ozzie had said he was sorry so many times, for him it was like stretching.

"If you are ready, you can please follow me?"

Ivan was hesitant, as was Liz.

"There's a little cafeteria down the hall," Detective Moss said to Ivan and Liz, "if you want to wait there."

Candice looked to George. He took his wife's arm, pulled it closer to him and followed Ozzie to the elevator. It occurred to Ivan that Ozzie, this stranger who never knew Sandra before yesterday, probably knew her more intimately than anyone else in the room.

Candice stopped. "Can they at least come down the elevator with us?"

"If it's okay with them, it's okay with me," answered Ozzie.

In the basement, Ozzie led to them to a door with the sign Medical Examiner Laboratory. There were two interior windows on either side of the door. Through the windows they saw a table with a white sheet covering what everyone assumed to be Sandra Wolf. Ozzie puts his hand on the door handle and faced the Wolfs. "OK?"

Everyone remained frozen as if in suspended animation, waiting for someone to answer. George stared at the door, unable to move. But Candice collapsed. Ivan caught her before she hit the floor. "She's fainted." Ivan said.

"Oh, my. I'll get a chair," said Ozzie.

"And some water, Ozzie," Detective Moss said.

"Of course," Ozzie agreed.

George helped Ivan ease her down to the floor.

"Candice? Candice?" George burst into tears. "Sandra, Sandra!" Ozzie returned with bottled water and a folding chair. Ivan opened the bottle and handed it to George, who put it to her mouth.

"George?" Candice mumbled. "George?"

"Take some water," George said.

Ivan suddenly felt the vibration of his cellphone. He ignored it.

"I can't," Candice said, "I can't go in there."

"It's fine, Candice," said Detective Moss. "Liz and Ivan will stay here with you."

Ozzie opened the door. Detective Moss and George followed him in.

Ozzie led George and Detective Moss to the other side of the table so they faced the window to the hallway. He put himself opposite them, his back to the window.

"Please stand here, Mr. Wolf. I'll stand here so Mrs. Wolf won't see anything when I pull the sheet. Just you two will see. Will that be all right?"

"What?"

"You just need to nod and I'll know this is your daughter."

"Nod, right."

Ivan watched Ozzie pulled back the sheet like a master artist revealing his work. The thing was, in a way Ozzie was an artist who applied his talents to bring this tragedy to life, to envision what took place, to give meaning to every bruise, every scratch, every concave, every damaged internal organ and how all of it put together could lead to catching the killer. But unlike an artist, there was never, ever any applause for Ozzie.

George looked down at his daughter's ashen face and bruised neck. The sheet was pulled back to reveal just the top of where her torso had been cut for the autopsy. Ivan swallowed, imagining Liz on that table. Gone was any beauty Sandra had owned, any sweetness, her smile that surely said without words "I love you, Daddy." He looked up quickly, unable to take more. George was holding back tears, until he couldn't. The nod was not necessary.

The three came out of the Laboratory. "Ozzie, can you bring more chairs so they can all sit while we go to your office and talk?" said Detective Moss.

"Of course," Ozzie said.

* * *

Ozzie's office was busy with record books of the deceased, transcripts of his numerous findings scattered on his desk, a pile of labeled cassette tapes. On a table in the corner were photographs of body parts, both external and internal. He showed Detective Moss photos he had taken of Sandra's autopsy.

"We are still waiting for fingerprints and DNA tests," Ozzie began, "but one thing we know, the strangulation came from behind, without her suspecting. We can tell this from the shape and angle of the bruise on her neck and thyroid cartilage.

Moss nodded. Ozzie continued. "When people are asphyxiated, a classic petechial hemorrhage develops in the eyes. This is a tiny red mark which is a sign of asphyxia caused by an external means of obstructing the airways. It was a close struggle. A crime committed in anger. Forensic did toxicological testing and found indication of some drug use."

"What kind of drug use?"

"Perhaps marijuana. Maybe her parents know something about that?"

"We can ask. Anything else?"

"There's a very involved fingerprints test that forensics use on fabric that was developed at the University of Alertay in Scotland. It's a technique called vacuum metal deposition or VMD. Forensics is using this on the tie we found. The technique uses gold and zinc to recover the fingerprint marks. We once were able to identify a rapist by pulling his fingerprint from a victim's underwear. But here I did not find any evidence of sexual assault or a recent sexual encounter."

"That's a relief."

Ozzie continued. "We did find particles of skin and a hair under her fingernails. That would indicate a struggle. She tried to scratch him. We need to look at the DNA there. Plus the fingerprints on the bottle of Snapple."

"And our techies are rummaging through her computer," added Detective Moss. "Looking at her emails, the websites she last visited to see what possible leads we could get from that. And who knows, maybe a neighbor will come forward to tell us they saw someone at the house that night. Okay, let's ask if the Wolfs or Liz know anything about any drug use."

* * *

Candice was in the middle of telling Liz and Ivan how Sandra learned how to swim at summer camp when Ozzie and Ross returned. "That's another thing she and Liz have in common," Ivan said.

"We have a delicate question to ask," Moss began.

Ivan looked over at George and Candice. He knew from his own experience as an IRS agent whatever question was about to be asked would not come out delicate.

"How delicate?" George asked.

"Do you know if Sandra took any drugs?"

George and Candice looked at each other, perplexed.

"You mean illegal drugs? Of course not," George answered. "Why do you ask that question?"

"It's only preliminary right now, but maybe marijuana?" Ozzie asked hesitantly.

George shrugged. "Maybe in college. Your forensics are so good you can go back that far?"

"We're not that good, no. No, this would be recent."

"I wouldn't know anything about that," said George.

"I would," Candice confessed.

"You would?" George stared stunned at his wife. "How?"

"We talk. She tells me things. I just listen. No judgments."

"Did she ever tell you who she might be ingesting marijuana with?" Detective Moss asked.

"Her boss."

"What! My God! Detective Moss, is this enough to arrest him?"

"Sir, we can't assume anything. The case is ongoing, and we're looking into everything. Right now, all we have is speculation."

"How long will this 'looking into everything' take?"

"Hard to say. Maybe a few days," answered Moss.

"Mr. and Mrs. Wolf," said Ozzie. "I know from experience it is a process. But I can assure you, your daughter's case is in good hands with Detective Moss. With that being said, if you like you can make arrangements for your daughter now."

Ivan watched Candice slowly folded her torso and stared at her shoes, slightly rocking in her chair without taking her eyes off her shoes; George sat straight in his chair, looking beyond Ozzie, beyond the wall behind Ozzie, starring somewhere far off, into an eternity without any care to return. Like an anchor, Ivan took George by the arm.

"George?"

"I know, Ivan."

"Do you need help making arrangements?" Ivan asked. "Anything at all?"

"We spoke to the funeral director before we left. I spoke to the priest. We'll be taking her back to Blue Ash."

"Okay. Today?" Ozzie asked.

"Too much for today. We'll go tomorrow." He swallowed. "How do you arrange to fly a – a body back to Ohio? How do we get her there?"

"That's okay," Ozzie said. "I'll give you the information you need for the funeral home."

Ivan felt again the pumping of an irregular heartbeat coming from his pocket, his cellphone, reminding him of what's coming up next.

"Can you take us to our hotel?" Candice asked Ivan.

"Sure. Anything you need," Ivan answered. "Which hotel?"

"The Doubletree," George answered, "On Broad Street."

"Good choice," said Ozzie.

Chapter Twenty

Ivan and Liz watched George and Candice pull their suitcases behind them, their forlorn backs disappearing into the Doubletree Hotel as if time and destination were no longer relevant. Ivan put the gear back in drive and made a right on Locust Street.

"Before we see Grandpa at the hospital," Liz said, "I'd liked to make a little detour."

"Detour where?" Ivan passed the narrow Juniper Street to make the next right on twelfth.

"Not far. Just keep going straight."

"Where do you want to go, Liz?"

"Here." Liz showed him the map on her cellphone with a red bubble staked in the address.

Ivan gave it a quick glance. "You expect me to see that? Tell me where exactly you want me to go."

"The Masjid Center of Philadelphia, Catharine and Ninth Streets."

"Isn't that the mosque Sandra wrote about in her articles?" said Ivan, unperturbed.

"Exactly. I want to see it for myself."

"You're becoming a real investigative reporter."

The homes in this area of south Philly were porchless three-story brick row houses with the sidewalk three steps away from their front doors. The Masjid Center of Philadelphia occupied the last two houses on the block. Between the two front doors was a window completely covered with the mosque's logo, an artsy collage of the letters MCP. Next to the window was a Plexiglass-covered bulletin board mounted directly onto the brick wall. Nothing else distinguished the mosque from the other residential homes on the block. Small window air conditioners poked out from a window on each floor.

Ivan parked his car in front of the mosque. Liz got out to read the bulletin board listing the times of prayer. Around the corner against the cement wall was a little wooden shed. Ivan peeked inside.

"Not at all what I expected," Ivan commented.

"Which was what?"

"A building like a church or synagogue."

"What's in there?" Liz asked, standing behind him.

"I see snow shovels, ice salt, cans of paint, scattered tools on the floor, planks of wood, tubs of cement and a ladder."

Turning away from the shed Ivan came face to face with a husky, red-bearded black man wearing a long white Muslim dishdasha and a black skull cap that fit tightly on his bald head.

"Assalamu Alaykum," he said in a voice softer than his frame would suggest.

"Good afternoon," Ivan replied. "Are you the imam here?"

The man cocked his head. "No, I ain't. That be Brother Ahmed. You here to pray duhr?"

"Excuse me?"

"Afternoon prayer."

"We'd thought we'd visit the mosque, if that's okay." Ivan said.

The man stared at Ivan, then looked over to Liz, who was reading notices on the bulletin board.

"This ain't a museum, sir. It's the house of prayer. It's the house of Allah."

"It says here 'all are welcome'," said Liz.

The big man squinted his small eyes at them. "Not saying you're not welcome." He pulled open the door. "We pray in fifteen minutes."

"Thank you," Ivan said. "What's your name, if I may ask?"

"Nazzir."

The interior was one long rectangular space, its brown laminate floor covered with numerous rugs lining half the length of the room. At the front end of the mosque between the front door and the window was a three-foot-high stage with two wooden banisters at each end. On the stage was a microphone stand. On the wall behind the stage was a white board with black smudges left over from half-hearted erasing. Next to the board was a sign in Arabic with its English translation beneath; "Allah loves the righteous" Qu'ran 9.7. In the opposite corner was a 6-foot-high metal fan and next to it a standalone heater. Neither was plugged in. The four walls were painted white and mostly bare except for one large framed Islamic painting. Several men in skull caps were sitting on the floor reading; a few others stood talking. The older folks took Ivan and Liz's presence in stride, but the younger ones stiffened up as if the winds of blasphemy were just ushered in.

At the farthest end of the hall was an office with a glass window. Inside was a young, slim black man in white dishdasha but without head apparel, exposing his shiny bald head. He sat behind his desk talking to another black man in jeans and a black T-shirt. The man's brown leather jacket was draped around the back of the wooden chair he was sitting on. This man was a bit older and clearly distraught. The conversation appeared to Ivan to be heated, perhaps pivotal, as if the rest of this man's life depended on the outcome of this conversation. As the man spoke, he pressed his forefinger on the table to emphasize the importance of what he was saying. His passionate speech was interrupted when the imam turned to face the strangers who had just entered his mosque.

Nazzir said, "You see Iman Ahmed is back there busy with a brother."

"I see him,' said Ivan, getting a whiff of feet and old pages.

Liz went to get a closer look at the painting. It was a design of several wide circular shapes interlocking with one another, each in shades of bronze, lavender, leafy green, rust, violet, blush, turquoise. Within each circle was an Arabic message. The center, the size and shape of a peach, was filled with pastel colors: yellow, pink, and sky blue. It also featured a message in Arabic. The north, south, east and west edges of the outer circle was ebbed out, each containing its own curvy lined design. It was rich in color, detail and meaning, and quite beautiful.

"Is this an original?" Liz asked Nazzir. "Do you know?"

"Say what?"

"Is one of your congregants an artist?"

He bobbled his head side to side. "I think yeah."

Ivan saw Imam Ahmed get up and leave his office. The man he was talking to threw up his arms in irritation.

"Look like he on his way over here right now," Nazzir said. The imam smiled widely as he approached.

"Assalamu Alaykum," he said, offering his hand to Ivan, "Welcome to The Masjid Center of Philadelphia. I am Imam Ahmed. And you are?"

"Ivan," He shook the imam's hand. "And this is my daughter Liz."

"You're very welcome. We always like to have guests. I see you are admiring this painting?" The imam was a few inches shorter than Ivan but taller than Liz. Ivan also noted the imam was the only Muslim in the room without a beard.

"Yeah, I think it's really great," said Liz. "I love the design and the choice of color. Like it's wrapped in itself but talking to you at the same time. Who's the artist?"

"Ishmael. It's an interesting thing how some people express their spirituality. We pray of course, but sometimes Allah blesses you with a creative gift, and if you use that gift to sanctify Allah, such as Ishmael does, your reward will be great. Maybe you'd like him to make something special and spiritual for you?"

"Oh, I don't know about that. I probably can't afford him. Does he only do Islam art?"

"Yes. Mostly designs like this, or maybe trees or fruit or mountains. Never people."

"You mean no portraits?"

"Correct. Nazzir, please ask Ishmael if he could break away from his canvas for a moment. These people want to meet him."

Without a word Nazzir left to get Ishmael.

"Traditionally the image of the human form is idolatry," Imam Ahmed continued. "Frankly I don't think here in Philadelphia anyone would worship a human figure, but this is a mosque and we go by that strict code. If you are interested in learning about Islam, we have classes here."

Here it comes, Ivan thought.

"Can't say we are right now," Ivan responded. "But with all that's going on in the world and here in Philadelphia we thought we'd stop in and see for ourselves."

Imam Ahmed continued to smile but both Ivan and Liz could tell the smile no longer came from the heart.

"See what?"

"The mosque, meet you, instead of just reading about it in the newspaper."

He relaxed slightly. "That's wise. You can't know Islam from what you read in the papers. Or the internet, especially. Most of it, unfortunately, are lies." The Imam's smile widened.

"I agree," Ivan said with a quick look to Liz. "You can't trust the media. Not since Walter Cronkite. So who can you trust? Who do you trust?"

"Ah, great question. For us Muslims the answer is easy. We trust in Allah. And Muhammad is His prophet. We trust the Qu'ran. We trust our community because we are building it together. Now I ask you that question. Who do you trust? Do you believe in God?"

The people in the room stopped talking and awaited Ivan's answer. Ivan felt like he was walking towards the edge of a diving board with nothing else to do but jump.

"I've been grappling with that question since my wife died," Ivan said finally.

"Oh, I am very sorry," Turning to Liz he said," Your mother?"

"She was."

"It must be very hard. Not all answers are evident. I am sure your wife was a righteous person and is resting joyfully in the afterlife. As Muslims we do not see death as the termination of life, but rather the continuation of it in another form. I don't know if that helps you, but I hope it gives you both some comfort."

Ivan nodded. "I appreciate the sentiment. But I don't think I'm there."

"Understood. I have learned never to judge someone in whose shoes you've never been. Thanks be to Allah I have both my parents, a wife, two healthy children. But I'm going to tell you something. I was not always a Muslim. I am a convert to Islam. My parents were Baptist but not church-going Baptists. Maybe that's why I got into a little trouble. But I knew, I always believed, in a creator, in an Almighty, but didn't know how. I didn't know at the time I believed in Allah, but truly, I was a Muslim and I didn't know it until Imam Walid, my mentor explained it all to me, showed me the truth. Told me to read the Qu'ran. In English of course at that time. Now I read it in Arabic. And to him I am eternally grateful."

"And you?" he said suddenly, turning to Liz. "Do you believe in the afterlife?"

Liz looked up to the ceiling and was surprised to see a Muslim design painted right above her head. She wondered if it was done by the same artist who did the painting hanging on the wall.

"All I can say is I hope you're right," she answered.

"On a lighter topic," Ivan said, "how long have you been the imam here? You look kinda young."

Iman Ahmed chuckled. "Thank you. It's my second year here. Before this I was in Florida for five years and one year in Saudi Arabia. I am grateful to Brother Jamil Abdullah Hakim for inviting me to lead this masjid."

"You mean James Warren of the Seventy-Sixers?" Ivan said.

"Amazing brother. He is an example of Allah's plan. Thanks to Him," he pointed upward with an index finger, "and Brother Hakim, we are able to serve four hundred families belonging to this masjid and its affiliate masjid not far from here. I am told the first day this masjid opened there were over three hundred people praying. A tent needed to be put up. It's a great blessing."

Ivan looked down the room and imagined three hundred people dressed like Nassir kneeling in prayer. And at that moment, Nassir returned with Ishmael behind him. He was a slim black man in his late twenties with a full black beard. He was a bit taller than everyone else there and wore all light brown, from his shoes, pants, and shirt to the knitted hijaz on what everyone could see was his bald head. There were some scattered paint marks on his shirt: yellow, green, red. His eyes too were brown but pensive, piercing and distrusting. When he reached the group awaiting him, he smirked at Ivan and Liz, clearly showing signs that he was pulled down here against his will.

"Ishmael, these people were talking about your painting," said Imam Ahmed. "They want to know more about your art. How you create this. You should talk to them."

Ishmael looked over Ivan and Liz. "What about it?"

"Oh, we were just admiring it," said Liz. "I was just saying it shows a lot of passion and seriousness. I can tell you're a very serious and accomplished artist. Congratulations."

"Are you a Muslim?" Ishmael asked.

"Oh, no."

"Are you converting to Islam?"

"Oh, not that either."

"I give my paintings for free to people converting to Islam. Otherwise it's five hundred dollars. It used to be three hundred, but I was told I was charging too little for my art."

"Ishmael, they just want to talk to you. They admire your paintings. Be nice to them."

Ishmael looked at the floor as if instructions on how to be nice were written there.

"If they are not converting to Muslim and not buying my art, we have nothing to talk about." Ishmael gave one harsh look to Liz. To the imam he said, "You brought me down for this?" Ishmael turned and left.

"I'm sorry," says Imam Ahmed. "I thought I would get him to talk to you. He is so quiet, so reclusive. I apologize for his behavior."

"No apology necessary," said Ivan as he watched Ishmael walk away until he disappeared upstairs.

"But I do have another question. I hope you don't mind me asking. It might seem a little rude."

The imam smiled gently, his polite mask firmly in place. "Sure, why not?"

Ivan looked around the room. Almost everyone was back to their private conversations. Some continued to stare at him.

"We read about it, we watch it all the time on TV, it's happening all over the world. And I know there are many Muslims in Philadelphia, but you're the first Muslim I've had an opportunity to meet and speak with. First Muslim leader, at least. So as a leader of the Muslim community, can you to tell me why, and

I mean this sincerely, because I really can't figure it out, why there is so much terrorism in the name of Islam?"

Liz did a double take. But Ivan knew, as soon as he walked in and spotted the Imam in his office, he would not leave without asking this question.

Imam Ahmed smiled. He smiled wider than he did when he greeted Ivan and Liz moments ago. A smile that told Ivan the imam was not surprised and always ready for questions like this.

"Let me put your mind at ease, sir," he said. "As any true Muslim will tell you, Islam is a religion of peace and those who cause these heinous attacks are not following the ways of Muhammad."

In the silent moment that followed Ivan felt invisible darts shooting back and forth between himself and the imam's white teeth.

"Does that include the terrorists who caused 9/11 and the Muslims who applauded the attack?" Liz piped up.

"They do not speak for Islam," Iman Ahmend said, his smile still hanging in place.

"They shout allahu akbar as they commit terrorism," Ivan continued. "Doesn't that bother you?"

"Of course it does. Don't you think we suffer the backlash from that behavior? Whenever there is one of these attacks, the Muslim community braces for retaliation from racists. It is something we must endure. We have no choice. We must persevere. But we hope education can change hearts. People like yourself who visit our mosque can see the peaceful nature and humanity of our community. We have faith that Allah will inspire you to spread the word that Islam is a religion of peace."

"The backlash you talk about. Is there the same backlash in response to Muslim-on-Muslim terrorism in Iraq?" Ivan persisted.

The door opened and three men in their twenties entered, all wearing regular clothing but with Muslim beards. They wished the imam Assalamu Alaykum and continued with their conversation, but eyed Ivan and Liz with suspicion.

The door opened again and a Muslim man and his son in white dishdasha garb entered. The father stared sternly at Ivan and Liz. His silent message was clear; he was telling them they had invaded a private space.

"Now you are asking questions that require more than a brief discussion just before our afternoon prayer. You are invited to stay and pray with us.

"We can't," Ivan said.

"Then please come back so we can talk more. Or attend our classes. Again, I am very sorry about your wife, but she is closer to Allah and that is a great gift." He offered his hand to Ivan, which Ivan shook. The imam turned to Liz and offered her his smile.

"There's another woman who's now closer to Allah," Liz said to him. "Her name was Sandra Wolf. She was a journalist for the *Philadelphia Times*. Maybe you heard about her?"

"Is that the reason you are here?" said Imam Ahmed, no longer smiling.

"She was my friend."

"I see. I read her stories. That's all they were, I'm sorry to say, and don't mean to speak ill of those who are no longer with us. But stories. It's stories like those that make the Muslim community feel unsafe, marginalized, vulnerable, hated. It makes people Islamophobic. But we must persevere and pray that Allah looks out for us."

"They haven't found the killer yet," Liz continued. "I'm sure you'd let the police know if you heard something that might help them, yes?"

Before them, Imam Ahmed's face transformed into an expression of rage, and Ivan believed they were getting a glimpse of Ahmed's former self, the person he was before his life took a turn to faith. Had he not been the spiritual leader of this mosque, Ivan was sure the imam's next move would be to strike at his daughter. Just in case, Ivan took a slight step closer to his Liz. But just as quickly, the fierceness in his Ahmed's face subsided, allowing his inner peace to once again gain control of his being.

"Of course," the imam said. "We always cooperate with the police."

"Don't mean to intrude any more on your prayer time, Imam Ahmed," said Ivan.

"You are welcome anytime. Peace be with you."

When they got to the car Liz said to her father, "Did you see how reacted when I asked about Sandra?"

"Do you think they know something he's not telling?"

"He said he read the articles and that they were lies. Is that motive?"

"Maybe. Not evidence. Remember, the article came out after she died. Ready to see Grandpa now?"

"Looking forward to it. And thank you, dad."

As they drove away from the curb, Ivan looked to his side-view mirror and recognized, coming out of the mosque, wearing a red skullcap and brown disdasha, the exceptionally tall frame and angry face of Jamil Abdullah Hakim.

Chapter Twenty-One

Nobody paid attention to Ivan and Liz searching for Harold's room on the fifth floor at Lankanau Hospital. They walked past the nursing station where the focus was on sorting medications and filling flimsy paper cups with water. They passed a room filled with a family looking dire. They guardedly slipped past slow-walking patients pulling bags of liquid on IV trees on wheels as if they were prisoners dragging a ball and chain.

Finally, they found Harold. He was out of bed sitting in a stiff wooden armchair facing the window, his back to the entrance of his private room. From that angle, the window was too high to see anything except a gray sky, perhaps an occasional bird. This told Ivan his father was not relishing the outdoors but tuning out the indoors. Ivan checked the chart hanging on a string on the bedpost to see if Harold had his dinner and evening medication. He did. He was free for the night.

"Ready for action, Dad?" Ivan said to the back of his father's head.

"Always ready for action," his father responded to his son's voice without taking his eyes off the blank sky. "What kind of action?"

"A walk down the hall. I'm here with Liz."

Harold turned to face them. His white hair still disheveled as when he first arrived, and he still needed a shave.

"Oh, Liz, I wish you weren't seeing me like this. But come here anyway," Harold lifted his arms slowly for a small hug. Liz hustled over and hugged him in kind.

"I am soooo glad to see you, Grandpa! No matter what and where and how!"

"I should be taking you out to dinner in Bar Harbor. I should be taking you to the beach off Collins Avenue. And to my cabana."

"Sounds great! When?"

"Ivan, do you know when?"

"Here's what I know." Ivan sat down at the foot of the mechanical bed which perched at an incline. "Tomorrow at noon you go in for bypass surgery. No reason to think it won't go well. Dr. Sommers is one of the best in the country. You know that, right?"

"I got no choice, is that it?"

"That's your best choice. Doing nothing is also a choice but the worst choice."

"My doctor in Florida was against surgery. She put me on a regimented exercise plan; running track; walking through the mall; fruit and vegetable diet; fish, no meat, no pizza, no eggs. Put me on Crestor to be on the safe side. And it was working."

"Is that why you now occupy these luxurious accommodations here at Chez Lankenau?" Ivan said.

"My point is, it kept me alive."

Ivan sighed and shook his head, painfully amused by his father blotting out the ordeal involved in getting him out of Belize. He could have died had he remained there.

"I know, I know," Harold said. "After the surgery there's what, there's rehab, right?"

"That right. We'll need to find you a rehab facility."

"There's one in Boca that my friend Myron Kornstein went to after his open-heart surgery. He thought they treated him right. Call Myron to find out where. Then make a reservation there."

"Travel is out for a while. I already have a list of rehab centers close to us."

"What's "a while" mean?"

"That depends on you."

"If it depends on me, then after the surgery. Make the reservation."

"Meaning how well you do in rehab. You can't travel. Not until after you've done some healing, maybe even until the rehab is complete."

Harold looked down at his hands, then up at the window.

"I feel like I'm in Alcatraz."

Liz piped up. "Oh grandpa, come on. With good behavior you'll be out of here in no time!"

Liz and Ivan saw the crinkling of the corners of Harold's eyes expressing a smile. Then, "How did I get myself into this mess?"

"Not your fault, grandpa. Could have happened anywhere."

"But it didn't happen anywhere. It happened while I was on a cruise with Diana. And her friends."

"Has she called you?" Ivan asked.

"No. Not yet."

"Are they back from the cruise?"

"This morning," Harold softly answered.

Ivan changed the subject. "When was the last time you took a walk?"

"Here? I haven't."

"Well, let's do that."

"But I'm all hooked up."

"It's just saline. Come on. I'll be on your right side, Liz will be on your left. We'll take your new friend along and tour the floor. Meet your neighbors while they're still here."

"Liz, take my cell phone from that table over there, will you? Put it in my pocket. If this robe even has a damn pocket." Harold moved his hands around the loosely belted thin hospital gown for a pocket. "I don't feel one."

"No worries. I'll stick it in my pocket for you," said Liz. "We'll get you a robe with pockets later."

In the hallway Ivan felt a sense of composure coming from the quiet and focused medical staff, all working with a depth of certainty in themselves that the lives of all the people with beds under them were on the path to full recovery. It was a good place.

Holding his father's spongy biceps, they walked slowly through the corridor. At the end were the elevators and some comfortable couches. Ivan and Liz walked on either side of Harold with the IV tree between them, its wheels shifting sideways every few feet, frustrating them with every step. Ivan thought the IV tree needed more help than his dad. But he was grateful for their time together. Ivan and Liz had taken no trips since Nancy's death, and Diana's plethora of domestic plans had kept Harold occupied.

Sitting on the plush microfiber couch near the elevators, Harold looked up at the bags of clear liquid dripping into tubes that led into his arm like an umbilical cord. He then looked down at the open-back hospital slippers, a size too small for his feet.

"Where do I go from here?" Harold asked, practically in a whisper and gazing at the carpet as if asking a nonexistent swarm of ants.

Ivan wasn't quite sure whether he meant the walk, or life. He chose the simple path.

"We could be daring and take the elevator to check out the excitement on floor six."

"No, I mean after all this."

"Have you thought of my suggestion? Staying in Philly?"

Harold looked up with consternation, clearly irritated that just because his son rescued him from a small Central American country below the equator with mediocre medical care, he thought he could run his life.

"Of course I'm going back to Florida. My life is there."

"Maybe this talk can wait."

"Not wait. It's not going to start. You don't know what you're talking about. Everything I have is there."

"Not us, Grandpa," chimed Liz. "We miss you."

He frowned. "Well, you miss me, come to Florida then."

"Yeah, you know, school and all that. But I might just surprise you."

"You don't scare me," Harold said surveying the needle in his forearm.

And then, like a contact from another planet, they all heard Liz's pocket ring. Instinctively, she answered the cellphone like it was her own. "Hi."

"Harold? Who's this? Where's Harold?" a woman's voice responded.

They could all hear the cranky angst in the woman's voice. "Is he there? Is he alright?"

"Just hold on," Liz held out the phone to Harold, shaking it up and down like a rectal thermometer. "It's Diana."

* * *

Harold stared at the crazy lines and bubble abstract painting on the wall across from him and felt like part of the painting. He had been waiting for Diana to call, wondering why she didn't call immediately after disembarking from the ship. He calculated she had driven home, showered, unpacked, mixed herself a vodka punch in her blender, and was now ready to explain why she had not stayed with him, but instead continued on the cruise he'd paid for. Liz placed the phone in the palm of his hand. Harold stared at it as if it were a live crab. He knew everyone could hear Diana's shrill voice. "Harold? Harold?"

"Talk to her or hang up," Ivan said breaking the awkward stillness.

Harold slowly brought the phone to his ear.

"I'm still in this world," Harold said to her.

"I've been going crazy. I did nothing but think about you. Nothing. All I could think about is you all the rest of cruise. What could be happening? Are you still alive? Are you in a coma? I didn't, I couldn't enjoy anything. Nothing from the time they took you off the ship. Nothing. Tell me everything. What happened to you?"

"Do you know where I am?" Harold asked.

"No. I don't even know where you are. All I know is you're not home. Are you in the hospital? Is your son with you?"

"He's with me and I am in the hospital. But not in a Miami hospital. I'm in a hospital in Philadelphia and I'm going in for heart surgery tomorrow."

"Oh, my God. Harold. So you did have a heart attack? They told me on the cruise ship that they really didn't know what was up with you. I thought maybe you just got dehydrated and they didn't allow you back on the ship."

"Maybe I was dehydrated. I don't really remember all that much what happened on the ship. I was out of it. Maybe you could tell me?"

"Oh, my God. Everybody was all around you. You were on the floor. Don't you remember? You fell. You collapsed. The doctors, the nurses on the ship, they all came. I was so frightened. I didn't know what to do."

"You were there with me?"

"Not right away. Not when it happened. I was in the jewelry store, remember? Remember I told you I was stopping in the jewelry store? Then when I saw all the commotion I came out and saw it was you."

"And then what happened?"

"Then they took you away. They took you to the ship hospital they have there."

"You came with me?"

"I went down to wait in the hospital waiting room. Then they told me they had to take you off the ship to the hospital. Martinez packed your suitcase, did you know that? And he brought your luggage off the ship and went with you. He did a very good job. You should thank him when you get the chance."

"Did you come with me too? To the hospital?"

"What could I do? There was nothing for me to do. I wish I could help. I didn't know what to do. But now I'm hearing that you're in good hands. You're with your son. You're in a good hospital. Everything is going to be okay now. You'll have the surgery and your heart will be as good as new. Lots of people have heart surgery and their lives are much better. That will happen to you too."

"Do you know how I got here? To Philadelphia?"

"No, how?"

"Never mind. Diana?"

"Yes Harold?"

"I want to ask you something."

"Sure Harold. Anything."

"I'd like you to come up here to be with me. To be with me for the surgery. I'll send you the money for plane fare."

"Oh, I wish I could. Believe me I wish I could. I want to. I really want to. But I have no more time left at work. The cruise ate up all my vacation time. If I take any more time off the bank will fire me. The other tellers are taking their vacation now. Oh, Harold, I wish I could go. Nobody knew this was going to happen. But your son is there. I'm sure everything will be alright. I'm praying that everything goes all right and you'll be back here in no time. And when you get back everything will be back to normal. I'll make you your favorite dinner like I always do. But I just can't take off more time from work."

"I understand," Harold said thinking: the surgery will have to go through my bowels because now that's where my heart lies.

"Harold, you know I love you, right?"

"Of course."

"And I would take the first flight up to Philadelphia right now if I could, you know that, right?"

"Of course."

"Heart surgery is very common. It's surgery, yes. It's a big deal, yes, don't get me wrong. But you will be fine after. I'm sure. And everything will go back to normal, like I said, and I will be waiting for you, love. When is the surgery?"

"Tomorrow."

"What time?"

"Afternoon I think."

"I will call you tomorrow morning before the surgery and talk to you as soon as possible after the surgery. Just imagine that I'm there with you. Holding my hand. You will be fine, Harold. You will."

"I know. I'll be back before you know it."

"Exactly. Okay, I have to go now. My son needs something. I will call you later, my love."

"Okay." Harold turned off the phone.

* * *

Ivan and Liz heard both sides of the conversation, and each felt their belly twist in knots. Ivan looked down at his dad, his romance shredded like confetti, part of his heart bursting with emotion, the other part to be cut open by surgeons tomorrow. Ivan was about to try some words of comfort but stopped, realizing it would be the words he would say to his daughter.

"Take me back to the room," Harold broke the silence.

"Sure thing," Ivan said as he and Liz helped him stand.

When they got to the room, Ivan said, "I have an idea."

"What's that?"

"Suppose I come back after visiting hours and sneak in a flask of Glenlevit single-malt scotch?"

"Sounds like a great idea. Bring three shot glasses. One for me, one for you, one for the nurse."

"Hey, what about me?" Liz pouted.

"You? You're my granddaughter."

Chapter Twenty-Two

The next morning, Ivan found Keisha Lamont sitting patiently in his thin-cushioned guest chair tucked into a corner of his cubicle between his busy desk and his overflowing credenza, reading from her cellphone.

"Waiting long?" Ivan said, pulling the straps of his soft leather case off his shoulders.

"Oh, hey, hi, no, not long, no. I was just reading about the journalist who was found murdered, the one who wrote those articles we were talking about the other day."

"Shocking, isn't it?"

"I mean that's crazy. I don't know what to make of it. I mean who would do that? I mean there's a lot of crazy people out there, believe me, I know. Do you think it had something to do with the articles she wrote?"

"I don't know. The articles were published after she was killed. So it's hard to say."

"The police say they still don't know anything. Do you think that's true? That maybe the police are just not telling what they know? I think they know more than what they're telling. What about you?"

"You might be right."

"Are we gonna go ahead with our audit? After what just happened there? Are they gonna want to deal with us now, with their journalist getting killed? Do you think?"

"Maybe that's what Sabrina wants to talk to us about." Ivan looked into Sabrina's office. "Her door is closed now."

"Oh, she told me to tell you that as soon as you get here we're to go right on in to see her."

Ivan knocked on her door and opened it.

"Come in both of you and have a seat. One of you close the door, please."

Keisha closed it.

"The *Times* controller just left me a message asking us to postpone the audit in light of the death of their journalist Sandra Wolf."

"What did you tell him?" Ivan asked.

"Nothing yet. I wanted to talk to you first. On the one hand they're dealing with this sad crisis, the murder of their colleague, and on the other hand we have our job to do. But it's really up to us to decide which way to go - whether to postpone or not. Keisha, did Ivan tell you about the FBI involvement in this case?"

"FBI, no he didn't."

"You told me not to tell anyone," Ivan said.

"Yeah, well, Keisha is working the case so she might as well know that. But that's really all we know. We don't know what their case is about. All we know is that they think a detailed audit might uncover something."

"Something criminal? Fraudulent?" Keisha asked.

"That's what you and Ivan are going to find out," Sabrina said.

"Okay." Keisha answered hesitantly.

"That's why I put Ivan on the case, and I thought you were just the right person to work with him. How have things been going so far?"

"Oh, it's great! I'm already learning a lot."

Sabrina turned to him. "So, Ivan, what do you think? About the postponement, I mean."

If there ever was a time to tell Sabrina about his own personal involvement in the Sandra Wolf murder case, his daughter's involvement, that he knew the detectives and knew they were looking at editor Alexander Anderson as a possible suspect, now would be the time. By all rights he should recuse himself from this audit.

"No postponement," Ivan declared.

"Oh, why? I mean I'm just asking," Keisha said.

"There's no telling how long this murder investigation will take, or how long it will take to make an arrest. Could be weeks, could be months. I noticed the murder of their colleague hasn't kept them from publishing their newspaper every day. Work continues for them, why not for us?"

"I thought you would say that and I'm okay with that," Sabrina said. "So go call them and schedule the first meeting asap."

Back in Ivan's cubicle Ivan picked up the handset and handed it to Keisha. "You make the call."

"Me? Seriously?"

"Why not?"

"I don't know. I mean, they don't know me."

"Ask for Brad. Tell him we're sorry but we can't postpone the audit and would like to schedule a time this week to start. I'm dialing him now."

"You sure?" Keisha asked again as she put the phone to her ear covered by her colorful hijab.

"*Philadelphia Times.*" Keisha heard the receptionist say.

"Yes, this is Keisha Lamont from the IRS. Like to speak with Brad please."

"A moment."

In a moment Brad picked up. "Who is this?"

"Hi Brad. This Keisha Lamont from the IRS calling about the audit?"

"About the audit?"

"We would like to schedule something this week."

"I thought it was being postponed."

"Oh, no. I'm sorry. Why did you think that?"

"Well, we spoke to Sabrina Hughes this morning about it. She said she's honoring our request to postponement because of the unexpected death of one of our journalists. Who is this again?"

"Keisha Lamont. Did Sabrina definitely tell you it's being postponed? Because she's my boss and she just told me to call you."

"Why are you calling me? I thought Ivan Samuels was handling the audit?"

"Oh, he'll be there, don't you worry. I'm assisting him. So when this week is good for you?"

"I'd like to speak to Ivan please."

Ivan shook his head.

"He's not available right now. That's why I'm calling you."

"I see."

"I'm sorry."

"We're dealing with the death of one of our journalist And you're still pushing this audit on us? Unbelievable."

"I know. We are so sorry. Me and Ivan. Us both. I felt terrible about it when I read about it in the papers. In fact, I read about it in your paper. But I thought I saw an article she wrote in the *Chronicle*. Did she recently switch jobs?"

"She worked for us. Believe me, she's on our payroll. I should know."

"Oh, okay."

Keisha looked at Ivan, who was waiting for a reply from Brad. At last, Keisha heard Brad sigh, "Okay, how's Wednesday?"

"Wednesday is good. Wednesday about nine thirty?"

"Yeah, fine."

"Great. Thank you. I look forward to meeting you, Brad."

Keisha hung up.

Ivan smiled. "Perfect. I couldn't have done it better myself. Now for the easy part. Planning the audit. Ready for that?"

"That's why I'm here."

Ivan picked up the file. "What do you notice about this file?" Then dropped it on his desk with a thud.

"It's heavy," Keisha observed.

"Right. And why is it heavy? I mean, it's a new case. Usually all we get is the tax return, so that's a pretty thin file. Here we already have reams of bank statements, cancelled checks."

"Yeah, so what's with that?"

"Pre- provided, courtesy of the FBI. I think we keep all these records in the office and compare them with the statements and checks the *Times* gives us and see if they match."

"Clever."

"How much experience do you have reconciling income?"

"Like none. I thought we learn how to do that in phase two of training?"

"This is your phase two training. Here's what you're going to do before our meeting Wednesday. You're going to tally up all the bank deposits year by year. When we get in there on Wednesday, you're going to review the income ledgers, compare them with the vouchers; then compare them with the deposit analysis you did and see if they all reconcile to the income reported on the tax return. And then see what you get."

"I already got it. A headache. No, I'm only kidding, ha ha."

"You see, you're already half through phase two."

"What are you going to do? Can I know that?"

"I'll be interviewing Alexander Anderson."

Chapter Twenty-Three

Gregg waited for Liz in front of the Land Title Building, where the *Philadelphia Chronicle* occupied a third-floor office. He knew the structure well, a two-building edifice connected by a corridor on the first-floor lobby. It had undergone numerous refurbishings since the turn of the century, with Gregg recently playing a role in maintaining its electric standards, air conditioning and heating systems. That was when he worked for the electricians' union. Now on his own, Gregg scheduled his own time, barring any emergencies. He'd agreed to meet Liz to give her moral support for her meeting with Michael Banks, the editor of the *Chronicle*.

Pushing himself away from the corner column of the building's bay window, Gregg spotted Liz among the crowd across the street in front of City Hall, the largest municipal building in the country. She looked distracted, maybe pensive. He waved both arms to get her attention. She responded with a quick gesture that seemed almost dismissive. Turning her head right to make sure no cars were speeding around the circle, she crossed the street. Gregg came to the curb, smiled, and gave her a kiss.

"Oh, I can't believe I'm doing this," Liz said taking a slight step back.

"It's an acquired taste. But if you do it often you'll get used to it. Here, let's do it again." He moved closer but Liz stepped back.

"I mean my meeting with Michael Banks."

His smile disappeared. "Oh. Why?"

"I mean, who am I anyway?"

"Sandra's protégé. He wouldn't have agreed to meet with you if he didn't want to."

"Maybe. I guess."

"Absolutely. He has something he wants to tell you. I can feel it. Why are we debating it? Let's get up there. We certainly don't want to be late." Gregg took her hand but Liz didn't move.

"What's the matter?"

"I'm sorry."

"Are you kidding? You're not going to the interview?"

"I am. But you can't. I don't know what I was thinking, asking you to come with me. I guess I was nervous. If I'm going to do this, I have to go it alone. I'm sorry if messed up your day."

"Ah, don't even worry about it. You go up there. You interview him. You'll be fine. Then you'll tell me all about it."

"Okay, I'm going. I'm so sorry, Gregg." Liz planted a kiss on his cheek. "I'll call you when I'm done."

"I'll hang around. Plenty of things to do in the city."

Gregg watched her disappear into the building.

* * *

The interview was Ivan's idea. It pained him to watch his daughter reading and re-reading Sandra's articles, fretting over the facts and frustrated about the mystery surrounding her friend's death. He told her he heard Banks say on Action News that Sandra sent him all three articles at once, as if she suspected all along Anderson wouldn't publish them.

Liz had admired Alexander Anderson. He was the beacon of journalism and had won all kinds of awards. Sandra had only positive things to say about him. But after Sandra's murder, Liz went back to read Anderson's editorials about 9/11 and noted his conciliatory approach to Islamists' grievances and claims of victimization. It was hard for her to reconcile that viewpoint after reading how the passengers on Flight 93 took control away from the terrorists, forcing the plane to crash in a field in Shanksville, Pennsylvania. Gregg promised he would drive her out there someday.

She did a google search for Islam, terrorism and homegrown radicalization in the United States. She found plenty of articles on the topics, but not a single one written in the *Philadelphia Times*. Ivan suggested she find out why.

"How do I do that? Call Alexander Anderson and ask him why the *Times* never comes up when I Google radical Islam? Yeah, that'll go over well."

"Try Banks."

"What do you mean?"

"Interview Banks. You were Sandra's student, and she was your mentor. You're a journalist for Temple News. That gives you bonafides. Call him. See if he says he's too busy to see you."

Liz called. Banks said he was very busy, but for her, he would make time.

* * *

Liz got off on the third floor and followed the signs around two corners to the *Chronicle*'s office. She sensed the office faced a back street. This told her two things. The *Philadelphia Chronicle* could not afford top floor space with a view but wanted the prestige of being in a landmark building. Her hunch was confirmed when she opened the door and found herself in a claustrophobic office crammed with desks facing one another, pillars of paper, piles of CDs, tape recorders tipping over tops of cabinets, and green tin trash cans filled with junk food wrappers and Styrofoam take-out containers. Beyond the cluster of worker bees, cornered off in a larger, glass-enclosed office, sat a bulky bald man in his forties with dark framed glasses, thin lips, and a thin, dark mustache. He reminded Liz of her childhood Mr. Potato Head. In her mind, she replaced his squashed nose, blinking eyes and thin mustache with a pointed nose, calmer eyes, thicker mustache and a full beard from her long-lost box of replacement pieces.

"Can I help you?" a young woman asked without getting up or even looking up from the document she was reading. She had a heavy face and limp brown hair pulled away from her face with dollar-store hair clips. She was trying not to let Liz' sudden appearance distract her, but clearly had no choice as her desk was closest to the door.

"I have an appointment with Mr. Banks?" Liz answered.

"Mike!" the woman shouted. "Yo, Mike!" Mike looked in her direction but continued talking fast into his cell phone, pointing several times in the direction of the floor to make a point. Seeing Liz, Michael Banks transformed his pointing to a beckoning one and held the door open until Liz came in. He gestured her to sit while still talking but made hand motions indicating he would be off soon. Liz nodded, smiled and took the opportunity to look over the hangings on the wall; Denzel Washington from the film "Philadelphia", Bruce Willis in "12 Monkeys," Gregory Peck as Atticus Finch in "To Kill A Mockingbird", former Mayor Frank Rizzo, an American Flag, a Philadelphia Eagles emblem, and a picture of James Warren dunking a basketball.

"Okay, sorry about that," Banks said shutting off his phone and sitting down. "It never ends. You'll see. Anyway, forget that, I'm all yours. Liz Samuels, right?" He reached across the desk to shake her hand.

"Yes, and thank you for meeting with me. I know you're busy."

"Everybody is busy. That's the job, getting busy people to agree to be interviewed. So, let's do it."

Liz took out her tape recorder. "Mind?"

"Record away."

Liz pressed the record button and took out a note pad and pen as well. She began.

"On Action News the other day, you mentioned that Sandra sent you the articles you published long before they saw print. Can you tell me more about that?"

Bank opened his palm out to her. "Sure. About a month ago, maybe more, I lose track, she contacted us saying she wrote these articles on the Muslim community in south Philly and she wasn't sure if they, meaning the *Times*, or to be more precise, Alex Anderson would publish them."

"Did she say why?"

"She didn't need to say why. I knew why."

Liz looked up from her notepad, surprised. "Can you tell me why?"

Banks leaned forward. "Let me explain something to you, if you haven't figured it out already. Anderson would never publish anything negative about Muslims or Islam."

Liz made a note. "Why do you say that?"

He leaned back. "Let me tell you a story. Anderson writes an editorial about some rumor going around that Israel knew about 9/11 and that's why many Jews didn't show up for work that day. Total bullshit. We write an article about Arabs dancing on rooftops after 9/11 and we back it up with pictures. Now get this; I send these pictures to Anderson and suggest that he cover the story too. I mean why not, right? Truth is I was testing him.

"Guess what? He didn't run them. Didn't even acknowledge receiving the package, which I knew he did. We covered over twenty stories about terrorist bombings in Iraq, car bombings, mosque bombings, all perpetrated by Islamic terrorists against other Muslims. The *Times*? One brief mention on page 29 in the middle of a column they call International Briefs. That was it."

"Why do you think they hardly covered it?"

"You have to know what makes Anderson tick, and I think I figured it out. Did you know he was arrested for disorderly conduct when he was a student at Columbia University back in the 1960s? He was one of the leaders of the SDS."

Liz gave Banks a blank stare. "I'm sorry. I feel really embarrassed. What's SDS?"

"Don't be. Not your fault. Students for a Democratic Society. Did you know if you Google SDS you get 4 pages of Safety Data Sheets before you get to anything about the Students for a Democratic Society? They were a group of radical students who wanted to take over everything. And I mean everything. They wanted to control the universities. They rallied against the Vietnam war, rallied for black power. At one point they took over five buildings at Columbia including the president's office. They even held the dean hostage, do you believe that? You're shocked, I can tell by the expression on your face. At that time Columbia University was supporting the Pentagon's military research which, in the mind of the SDS, was akin to killing innocent Vietnamese children. About seven hundred people were arrested. Anderson was one of them."

Liz shook her head "I didn't know anything about that."

"Not surprised." He leaned back with an enigmatic grin.

"Did they accomplish anything? The SDS?"

Banks stood up and put his knuckles on his desk. "I'll tell you what they accomplished. They accomplished destroying property and harming people, if you call that accomplishment. Garnered a lot of negative attention back then." He pointed his finger at Liz to make a point. "Anderson was in the forefront of that. So I was thinking about who Anderson is, what makes him tick. Why he ignores and refuses to cover radical Islam. And then it dawns on me. He sees radical Muslims as the modern day SDS. As kindred spirits. The SDS hated America for what it was. Well, so do radical Islamists. They want to take over the world with Sharia law; the SDS wanted to take over the world with leftist ideology. Radical Islamists don't care who they hurt. Well neither did Anderson and his ilk. In his heart and in his soul he's still a radical. But now he's a respected member of the civilized world. He can't outwardly do the things he did when he was a radical SDS student at Columbia, so the next best thing he can do is lend support to the current trend of radicalization, and that trend is radical Islam. Make sense to you?"

Liz looked up at Banks, who still stook with his fists on his desk. "I … well… I don't know. I never thought of all that. You make it sound like it could make sense."

Banks sat back down. "Let's break it down. Let's talk about intolerance. Would you agree that radical Islam is intolerant of others who don't believe like they do?"

"Okay, yeah."

"Look at the countries where Islam rules. Saudi Arabia, Iran. Can you be a Christian in Saudi Arabia? Or a Jew? Can a woman walk around without a hijab? You know the answer to all those questions is no. What about leftists? Are they tolerant of different points of view? Are they open to the views of conservatives? See what I'm getting at? Kindred spirits; leftists and radical Islamists."

"But let me ask you something," Liz said. "Wouldn't you say leftists are mostly non-religious? How can you say they're kindred spirits with Islam when Islam is a religion?"

Banks shook his head. "I'm talking about radical Islamists. Not the Islamic faith and not all Muslims. Most Muslims do not think that way. In fact, they're like the silent majority. I'm talking about the ones who do. Those are the ones who make all the noise. Remember the Doors song "When the Music's Over?" You probably don't. Jim Morrison shouts out "we want the world and we want it now!" Well, radical Islam wants the world, but they are more patient. They are more calculating. That's what Jamil Abdullah Hakims's neighborhood is all about. It's about encroachment. They encroach, without their encroaching being noticed. City officials are letting it happen, hell, the government is paying them to do it so long as the neighborhood is getting cleaned up. And the media, like the *Times*, are mostly their cheerleaders. But Sandra, bless her soul, she took notice. She figured it out and wrote about it and found herself up against her intolerant leftist boss. You're either a leftist or you're a bad person. You either believe in Islam they way they do or you're an infidel. No wiggle room for either. That's why Anderson would never publish Sandra's pieces and that's why she came to us. Did you say you're doing a story for the Temple News?"

"Yes, that's right".

"Good luck in getting them to let you print anything I'm telling you." He looked at his watch.

"I notice you have a picture of Jamil Abdullah Hakim on your wall there."

Banks looked at the picture and shook his head. "No, that's James Warren. There's a difference. I'm a Sixers fan. Not a Hoops Housing Foundation fan."

"I want to ask you, Mr. Banks...."

"Mike, call me Mike. You say Mr. Banks and I think you're talking to my grandfather."

"I have one last question." She turned off the recorder. "This is off the record. The police still don't know who killed Sandra. They have no one in custody. Do you have any thoughts as to who might have killed her?" She paused a moment. "Do you think it could be Anderson?"

Banks leaned back in his chair and chuckled. "Anderson? He'd have to be zonked out of his gizzard to do something that stupid. I mean, yeah, he was a radical and rioter and an anarchist. But a murderer? Over an article he didn't want published? Can't see it. Did you speak to Abisha?"

"Who?"

"The Muslim woman Sandra befriended and wrote about in the third article."

"I haven't."

"Speak to her. Her husband might be wacko enough to do it. But what do I know. I'm just a journalist."

Chapter Twenty-Four

The night Sandra Wolf was discovered murdered, the 700 block of Pine Street was bustling with revolving police car lights, media and medical examiner vans opening and slamming shut, and curious know-it-all neighbors dressed in their housebound attire.

Now one bored police officer sat in his silent patrol car guarding the quartered-off 'no-go zone' message of yellow crime scene tape. Detective Lopez walked up to him with two cups of covered Wawa coffee and tapped on his window. The police officer rolled it down and Lopez handed him a coffee.

"Thanks," said the police officer.

"Anything new here I should know about, Ray?" asked Detective Lopez.

"You mean besides the usual crap questions like 'find the killer yet?' 'Any suspects?' 'Why aren't you out there looking for him instead of sitting here doing nothing?' Shit like that? No. What about your end?"

"Expecting to hear soon from forensics."

"Keep me in the loop will ya? It's lonely here."

Detective Moss stood in front of the house, surveying it from roof to steps, as if the identity of the murderer laid hidden somewhere in the bricks, the mortar, the doorknob, the wilted flowers.

"So what are you doing here today?" Officer Ray asked.

"Trying to figure out what happened," Detective Moss answered. "Trying to make sense of it." She pulled out a pair of rubber gloves from her back pocket.

"Does it ever?" Officer Ray took a swallow of coffee.

"Never," Lopez said. "Even when the murders are solved."

Inside the house, Moss tried not to let the rancid remnant odor of decomposition get to her. She felt the floor sinking from the weight of tears. The imprint of Sandra's decomposed body was beginning to fade, and Moss got an eerie feeling, that so too would be her memory, leaving it up to her and Lopez to keep Sandra's name alive.

The swivel chair was still overturned and seeing it gave Moss a jolt.

"It looks to me," Lopez began, "she was sitting in that chair, pounding away at her computer; someone comes up from behind, strangles her with the tie, like in the Hitchcock movie "Frenzy". He's strangling her, pulling her up from the chair; she struggles, the chair overturns; she's kicking, arms go wild and crazy, and then she collapses right there." Lopez pointed to the imprint.

Moss looked at the chair, then at where Sandra's body had been found.

"Does she know her attacker?" Moss asked. "Does she see his reflection on her computer screen?"

"Maybe she did. Then how I just described it could be what happened."

Moss nodded her head. "Okay, now let's assume she doesn't know the attacker, doesn't know he's in the room. And doesn't see him through the computer screen because she's busy typing away."

"The question then is, how does he get in?"

"Maybe he was already in."

"No sign of forced entry," Moss noted.

"Maybe he had a key?"

"Why would he? Did she have a boyfriend who let himself in? Did they have a lovers' quarrel?"

"Except she didn't have any lovers. Except maybe Anderson," said Moss.

"Yeah, I know we grilled him hard on that and he denied it. Doesn't make sense to like him for it."

"He has a history of having a bad temper going back years," Moss said.

"I know bad tempers. My dad had a bad temper. With a bad temper you hit someone impulsively, like my dad did to me and my mom and then it's over. We have forethought here. Definitely more than just a bad temper."

"Okay, let's talk about the tie. A Jerry Garcia tie. Isn't that the kind of tie Alexander Anderson would wear?"

"My brother wears Jerry Garcia ties. Not that he knows squat about Jerry Garcia. He just likes the design."

Moss said, "Let's assume she doesn't know the attacker. He picks the lock, lets himself in. She doesn't know he's there, he sneaks up."

"And dumps the tie in the trash can behind the house thinking the trash truck will pick it up, except that it don't because the can wasn't put out for them to take. He didn't figure that."

"And he doesn't steal anything," Moss added as her phone rang.

"Can you get fingerprints off ties?" Lopez asked but Moss was talking on her phone.

"Oh? Great, we'll be there." Hanging up, she turned to Lopez. "That was Gupta in forensics. They got results."

"Ah, just when I was about to crack the case."

* * *

Forty years ago, children living near north eighth street and Poplar in Philadelphia would have attended school in a three-story brick building with long narrow windows in sets of three. After being abandoned for decades, it became the place where hair, blood, spit, semen, and man-made items of every sort, from paper to plastic to cloth, were parsed and dissected for DNA, finger-prints, and traces of drugs. There was also a digital lab that got into the more antiseptic guts of desktops and laptops. It was here at the forensics department that Detectives Moss and Lopez met with Suhar Gupta, the senior forensic science analyst in charge of coordinating the efforts of the many technicians dedicated to the task of connecting the dots, dashes, lines, fragments, pixels, and plasma that, with any luck, would lead the detectives to the murderer.

Suhar Gupta had one of those faces that was always happy even when there was nothing to be happy about. He was most happy at work in his white cotton lab robe, pecking particles he hoped would lead to the perpetrator. He came from India twenty years ago on a student visa to study biochemistry at John Hopkins University, but he supplemented his studies with binge watching NCIS, CSI, and Law and Order. The binge-watching led him to fall in love with forensics. The thought of solving a mystery from the confines of a laboratory fascinated him. Now a naturalized United States citizen, he spent most of his waking hours in the old school building fleshing out evidence to help solve over three hundred homicides a year in Philadelphia. The murder of Sandra Wolf was his highest profile homicide so far, and he was eager to reveal his findings to the detectives. He brought over two chairs so Moss and Lopez could sit with him in front of his computer screen.

"First let's talk about Sandra," Gupta said as he clicked an icon folder labeled 'Wolf'. "We got her DNA from the mouth of the Snapple bottle. We took her fingerprints and matched them with the Snapple bottle too, as well as the keyboard of her laptop. There were no other fingerprints on the Snapple bottle or the keyboard. We also fingerprinted the upturned chair and found only Sandra's prints. We did this for a baseline."

Moss sensed Lopez's impatience and injected before Lopez got verbal. "Got it. So far so good."

"Right. Now let's go to Alexander Anderson. His fingerprints are in the system, and they matched his mouse and coffee cup. We also picked up his DNA from the lip of his cup."

"For a baseline, got it," Lopez said.

"That's correct. Now it starts to get more interesting. We tested the fabrics."

"By fabrics you mean the Jerry Garcia tie?" asked Detective Moss.

"That but not only the tie. We tested the lingerie she was wearing, her underwear and bra. It looked new, newly purchased I mean, with a Victoria's Secret label. I'll get to that in a minute, which you will find most interesting, I assure you. Getting back to the fingerprint test. It is a difficult thing to get ridge details and impressions from fabrics. I think my colleague Ozzie told you about it?"

"He told me," said Moss. "Frank wasn't with me at the morgue."

"So I will explain for Mr. Lopez. We use a technique known as vacuum metal deposition. It creates something like a photographic negative, where colors show up as their opposites. Fabrics with a high thread count like silk, nylon and polyester are best for revealing fingerprints. Like we have here. "

"Cutting to the chase, what do we have here?" Lopez asked.

"What we have here is Anderson's fingerprints on the lingerie and on the tie."

"You're shitting me!" Lopez exclaimed.

"I kid you not."

"You're saying that Alexander Anderson, the editor of the *Philadelphia Times* murdered Sandra Wolf?"

"Detective Lopez, have you heard of Linus Pauling, the two-time Nobel prize winner in Chemistry and Peace who also paved the way for the discovery of DNA?"

"Can't say I'm acquainted with the guy, no. What's he got to do with this?"

"Professor Pauling always told his students to ask themselves, "What does the evidence require us to believe? Not what do our minds and hearts want the evidence to confirm, but exactly what is the evidence telling us, even though we may wish it would tell us something different. This is the standard we go by here at the Philadelphia Office of Forensic Science. We pride ourselves on being unbiased professionals; we collect, process, analyze and interpret to assist you in finding the answer to who, what, where, when, but not always why but many times how during an investigation. That's what we do."

"Hey, I got it. I didn't mean no disrespect."

"None taken. But now I want to show you what we found on Ms. Wolf's computer. We see emails to Michael Banks, the editor at the *Philadelphia Chronicle* starting at ten p.m. Tuesday. They are talking about the articles she wrote and they decide they will be published starting Wednesday, then Thursday and Saturday. There is also an email to Abisha Sallaz letting her know the article about her will be published in the next few days."

"Who?" asks Lopez.

"Abisha. She is the subject of the third article that was published on Saturday," Suhar answered him.

Moss looked at Lopez. "Anderson lied to us." Then to Gupta she said. "You mentioned something about Victoria's Secret?"

"Yes, I didn't forget. We contacted Victoria's in downtown Philadelphia to track down any recent purchases of these specific items together. In fact, they found a sale of these two items purchased together last Tuesday. It was charged to the credit card belonging to Alexander Anderson."

"The hits keep coming," said Lopez.

"You can be the judge of that after I tell you this. It was delivered to the Doubletree Hotel the same day."

"Why there?" Moss asked.

"Anderson booked a room there for that night." Suhar answered.

"So let me piece this together," said Lopez. "Wolf and Anderson are together in the hotel room. She puts on the Victorias and goes home with them on. But that doesn't put Anderson at her home."

"You're forgetting the tie," Suhar said. "We found his prints on the tie."

"Why is his tie at her house with his fingerprints?" Lopez said outloud.

"Maybe he went home with her," offered Moss.

"But he booked the room for the night. Why go to her house?" Lopez asked.

"Maybe they had an argument about the articles and she left?" said Moss.

"So what's he doing at her house?" asked Lopez. "Make-up sex?"

"Maybe that was the idea and things got out of hand," said Moss.

"So let me see if I understand this," said Lopez. "Anderson goes to her house. She lets him in. Things get out of hand and he strangles her with his tie. Then dumps it in the trash behind the house. Is that what you're saying here? 'Cause if you are it still don't make sense to me that he would do that."

"So what's your theory?" Moss asked Lopez.

"I ain't got one yet."

"I think we should stop by the Doubletree," Moss said. "See what we can find there."

"I agree," said Suhar.

"Is there anything else, Suhar?" Moss asks.

"Not now. We are still looking at possible skin fragments we found under the deceased nails. As soon as we get something conclusive I will contact you."

"That'll nail 'im," said Lopez. "Pun intended."

Moss shook her head in disapproval. "You did great, Suhar. Thank you for all your hard work."

"Oh, no, thank you."

Chapter Twenty-Five

With both hands on the wheel while driving to Center City, Lopez asked, "So what do you think?"

"He lied to us. He told us he went straight home from work. I'm liking him as the perpetrator."

Lopez said nothing. Moss looked over at him.

"You don't?" she asked.

"Murdered her over a disagreement about articles. Does that sound like much of a motivation to you?"

"He got angry. He's a hothead. Emotions got the better of him. I'm open to other ideas."

"I don't got none yet."

Moss and Lopez approached the front desk of the Doubletree Hotel where two clerks ignored them as they were deeply engaged in a conversation about Game of Thrones.

Moss put her badge in their faces and looked at their name tags. "Dwayne, Kate, we're Detectives Moss and Lopez. We need to confirm you booked a room last Tuesday to an Alexander Anderson."

"Oh, wow," said a befuddled Dwayne, "the police. Cool."

Kate moved closer to get a better look at the badges. "Okay, yeah, I see."

"Alexander Anderson, Tuesday," Moss repeated. "Please check."

"Okay. No problem," said Kate. "Detective Moss and Lopez, let me take a look here on the computer. Hold on one minute please." Kate plugged away at the computer.

"Were either of you working here last Tuesday evening?" Moss asked.

"That would be me," Kate answered "I've been working my ass off here lately with my husband out of work."

Moss showed her a picture of Sandra. "Happen to see this woman?"

Kate stopped what she was doing to look at the picture. "Oh, yeah. I do remember her. That's the reporter. The murder! Shit! Yeah."

"You did?" said Dwayne.

"Do you remember what time?" Lopez asked.

"Time? No, not exactly. Evening sometime."

"You saw her entering or leaving?" Lopez asked.

"Leaving. Definitely. I saw her leaving. And she was in a hurry, I remember."

"Here, let me continue looking this up," said Dwayne as he moved closer to the computer. "Let me do something here while you talk to them."

"Do you remember what she was wearing?" Moss continued.

"Wearing? Hmm. Gee, I don't know," said Kate. "Nothing struck me. Regular clothes."

"Regular meaning work attire, or regular meaning, hangout clothes?" Moss pursued.

"Oh, business clothes," Kate said. "I do remember now, she was putting on her shoes."

"What do you mean?" Moss asked.

"I mean, I saw her standing while putting her shoes on and then she hurried out."

"Notice anything else? Did you see her coming out of the elevator?"

"I didn't. But you know what, now that I think of it. I saw the emergency exit door closing right behind her. That one." Kate pointed to the emergency door. Moss and Lopez looked where she was pointing, behind them and to the left.

"So maybe she was coming from there? I don't know. Maybe I'm wrong."

"That's good, Kate. Was there a man leaving with her?" Moss asked.

"Oh, no. Just her. By herself definitely."

"Do you know if she took a cab or drove her own car?" Lopez asked.

"I can't see outside from here. Maybe the bellhops would know?"

"Got it," Dwayne announced. "Alexander Anderson booked the penthouse suite."

"Oh, that's on the twenty-third floor," Kate explained. "Then I guess I'm wrong on her taking the stairs."

"We'd like to see the penthouse suite." Lopez said.

Dwayne said, "Let me check if anyone's in there now."

"Take your time."

"Just takes a second. Nope, its vacant."

"Has anyone had it since Tuesday?' Moss asked.

"As a matter of fact, no. I'll have one of the bellmen go up with you and let you in."

"We appreciate it," said Moss.

"Do you know who killed her?" Kate asked. "Do you think it might be this Alexander Anderson guy?"

"It's an open investigation."

"Oh my God. I just realized," Kate put her hand over her mouth. Then took it off. "Could I be the last person to see her alive?"

"Oh wow," says Dwayne. "Yeah, you might. One of the last, at least."

The bellman took Moss and Lopez up to the 23rd floor. He inserted his special key pass allowing the elevator to bring them up to the penthouse. He inserted a different key pass to open the door where Anderson and Wolf began their Tuesday night. Moss and Lopez put on their gloves and instinctively turned on their flashlights.

"I can get the lights f'y'all," the middle age bellman said and began turning on all the lights.

Lopez went to search the bathroom while Moss opened the wardrobe and looked inside. She peeked behind the TV. She lifted the coffee maker that still emitted a lingering aroma of coffee.

There was a square Doubletree ashtray on the night table. The rim was a bit raised and covered the inside circumference. She looked inside and noticed a tiny butt tucked in the corner. She turned the ashtray upside down and shook it a few times. A butt fell out on the night table. Moss bent over to exam it. It was a quarter of an inch long and pressed thin to the width of a blade of grass. To Moss the butt appeared handmade.

"Come here, Frank, and tell me what you make of this," she called out.

Frank came out of the bathroom, flashlight in hand. "Whatcha got there?" He shined his flashlight where Moss pointed. He snorted and shook his head in disbelief. "What you got there is definitely a roach."

"Roaches?" the bellman bellowed. "I'll get housekeeping on that right away."

"The butt of cannabis," said Lopez. "Weed. Marijuana."

"We need to get this over to Suhar," said Moss.

"Absolutely."

Moss's cell rang.

"Moss here," she answered, annoyed at the interruption. Listening to the person on the other end, she looked at Lopez. "You're kidding! You're not kidding. You keep him there, do you hear me? We're heading back now."

"What's going on?" Lopez said.

"You're not going to believe this," she said staring at him.

"Test me."

"A guy just came into the precinct who said he saw a man in front of Sandra's home Tuesday night and said he could identify him if he saw him again."

"No shit. This is our lucky day," said Lopez.

"You can take us down now, sir," Moss said to the bellman.

"Sure, no problem. And don't you worry about the roaches. I'll get house-keeping on it right pronto."

Chapter Twenty-Six

At the precinct, Moss and Lopez found a large young man seated in a corner. He wore a black Spiderman T-shirt, arms covered with design tattoos, a tuft of blond hair on top of his head and shaved over both ears. He was impatiently pumping one leg.

"Mr. McGinnis, I'm Detective Moss and this is Detective Lopez. Thank you for coming in. Sorry we kept you waiting for so long. We understand you may have some information about the Sandra Wolf case?"

"You sure took your sweet damn time," he said, rubbing his fingers through his hair. "I didn't have to come here. I'm doing you a favor. You know that, right?"

"Mr. McGinnis, we're very grateful that you did," said Moss. "It's an open investigation and my partner and I are working nonstop. Please forgive us. Why don't we go into the conference room."

"Yeah whatever." McGinnis got up. He was a foot taller than either Moss or Lopez.

"Would you like some coffee or soda?" Moss asked, looking up at him.

"Naa. You can cut the bullshit."

They led him into the conference room, where metal tables and chairs loudly scraped the floor when moved or pulled out.

"So what can you tell us, Mr. McGinnis?" asked Lopez.

"Like I told them out there, I was riding my bike that night, and after watching the news it clicks that I rode my bike right by that house, that same house and then I remembered some asshole opens his car door and almost knocks me over when I'm riding by."

"And you're sure it was in front of Sandra Wolf's house."

"Yeah, sure as shit. The house on TV. That was the house where I rode past, like I said. It was when he got out of the car."

"Then what?" Lopez asked.

"Then what? I'll tell you then what. I call him an asshole for almost hitting me when he opened his fucking door."

"Did you get a good look at him?" Moss asked.

"Good enough to recognize the asshole if I saw him again."

"Did you see him go to the house?"

"Why do you think I'm here? I'm not making this shit up."

"Did you see him go into the house?" asked Moss.

"Like I said, I was riding my bike. I didn't stick around. His car door opens like out of nowhere. He ain't even looking where he's going or what he's doing like he's the only dude on the street. I called him an asshole, or maybe a dick-face, I don't remember which I used for him, either one would fit. And I looked back to see what he would answer me but he don't. He don't say shit. He just walks away towards that house."

"So if I understand you correctly, Mr. McGinnis. Tommy is your first name?"

"Yeah Tommy, or Angel. My friends call me Angel."

"Why do they call you that?" Lopez asked.

"Cause I have this look, like an angel. My friends say my hair is like a halo. That's what they say, so that's cool with me."

"We'll stick with Tommy if that's okay."

"Yeah, whatever."

Moss continued. "If we understand you correctly, you saw the man get out of his car and walk to the front door of Sandra's house."

"Right. He was going to that house for sure."

"What you're telling us is very important," Moss reassured him. "It's very helpful to us. Do you think you can describe him to a composite artist?"

"You mean describe him and an artist draws him? Sure, no sweat. I can do that. Absolutely cool with that."

"You really have to think hard about what he looked like," Moss continued. "The artist will show you pictures of eyes and noses and mouths. You pick the one that matches the closest."

"You got pictures of goatees?"

"What?"

"A goatee. He had a goatee."

Moss froze and looked at Lopez.

"Yeah, we got pictures of goatees," Lopez said.

"Let's do it then."

"Thank you, Tommy. We'll be right back with the artist."

Outside the conference room Moss said, "Bring that roach over to Suhar right now and tell him to drop everything."

"You got it. So maybe you're right."

"If the composite looks like Anderson, that, and with all the other evidence, we'll bring him in for a line up. See if Tommy can ID him."

"If he can do that, then Tommy is right. Anderson is an asshole."

"I'll stay here with the artist, see what happens with that."

"Later." Lopez left.

Chapter Twenty-Seven

When Ivan got to the Philadelphia Times building, Keisha was already waiting outside, her laptop strapped over her blue business suit jacket, her purple hijab framing her smile.

"I know, I'm early. I didn't want to be late."

"How early were you?" Ivan wore a gray sport jacket, blue Dockers pants, black Rockport shoes, light blue shirt with a striped blue and gray tie. His ponytail peeked from under his Indian Jones hat, his sunglasses too pale to make a difference.

"Oh, about twenty minutes. No big deal. I'm ready."

"I'm not worried. I told Brad I want to begin with interviewing Anderson and then Conrad Benson."

"Oh, okay. Who's Conrad Benson?"

"The publisher. We want to hear them tell us how the company runs, who does what, ask him to describe a routine week; who approves the travel expenses and how they are approved. We want to hear all this from them."

"And you're going to ask all the questions, right?"

"No, I changed my mind. You are. I prepared a list." Ivan reached into his sport jacket pocket and pulled out a folded piece of paper. "Questions for Anderson about his travels, questions for Benson about internal controls."

Keisha took the paper and looked it over like it was a key to a treasure map. "Okay. You sure?"

"Frederick Stacy, their outside accountant, promised to have all the documents we asked for. Between that and the interview, we'll be busy all day."

"Especially since we don't exactly know what we're supposed to be looking for."

"We're looking for pornography."

Keisha cringed. "What did you say?"

"What I mean is, we'll know what we're looking for when we see it." Ivan smiled. "You ready?"

"I thought I was a minute ago."

"You are. Let's go."

They took the elevator to the eighth floor and passed through glass doors under the sign "Philadelphia Times."

"Ivan Samuels and Keisha Lamont here to see Brad Middleton and Frederick Stacy," Ivan said to the woman at the front desk whose hair was Viagra blue and Big Bird yellow.

"Oh yeah. You're the IRS. I'm Prim. I spoke to you on the phone. I was getting ready to rat on my ex to you."

Ivan noticed the spider web tattoo on the back of her hand between her thumb and forefinger. "And you're ready now?"

"Yeah, I dunno. Gotta think more about it. Don't want my kid to hate me. I'll let them know you're here." Prim picked up the phone and hit one button. "IRS is here."

"Bring them in," Ivan heard Brad's voice.

"Come on with me," Prim got up from her chair. She was slim and shorter than Keisha. "Careful not to trip on the leads."

Keisha looked down, expecting to see wires but saw only the laminated wooden floor. "Where?" she asked.

"Heh, heh, it's my newspaper joke."

"That's actually pretty funny," Ivan said with a smile. Keisha smirked.

They followed Prim through the hallway, passing cubicles and pictures on the wall of the Liberty Bell, Ben Franklin, Betsy Ross, Phillies former stars Mike Schmidt and Pete Rose, Rocky Balboa—and then Ivan did a double-take. Keisha, walking behind him, almost bumped into him when he stopped walking. Prim sensed she was no longer being followed.

"This way," she ordered.

Ivan stared at a painting that resembled the one Liz had asked about at the Masjid Center of Philadelphia.

"Where did you get this painting?" Ivan asked.

"Oh, yeah," Prim said. "Not your typical Philly scene, is it?"

"Do you know why it's here?"

"I have no idea. You'll have to ask them."

"They bought it?"

"Hey, I only work here. That's a Brad question. Let me get you to where you'll be and Brad will be right down and you can ask him all your tax questions and art questions."

Prim opened the door to a conference room. There was a long rectangular table with extension cords and internet cables sprouting from a hole in the middle of the table like weeds. Several white cardboard boxes marked "for IRS" were on the table. There were four cushioned chairs, two on each side of the table. Two windows looked out onto Broad Street.

"Sit wherever. Make yourselves comfortable. Or try to anyway in here. Heh." Prim left.

"All those boxes for us?" Keisha asked.

"Think of it as a buffet. Take as much as you want but make sure you finish what you take."

"Now that you mention it, I'm hungry now. I left the house without eating and without my coffee, which I do have in the mornings by the way."

The door opened abruptly with Frederick and Brad ushering themselves in.

"You haven't changed a bit, Ivan," Frederick said giving Ivan a firm hand-shake. "Still looking good with that ponytail."

"I thought you never liked it," Ivan said with a smile.

"Mr. Anderson and Mr. Benson won't be joining us today. Sorry," said Brad.

Ivan stared at Frederick. "You told me yesterday they'd be here."

"Yeah, well, something came up. They can't be here. Probably tomorrow. But the good news is we gathered up all the records you asked for, as you can see. It's all in those boxes. Anyone want coffee? We also have donuts. You must be Keisha," Frederick said offering his hand to her.

"Yes, and yes I will have coffee and a donut. If that's alright."

"Of course it is. That's why I offered it. How do you like your coffee?"

"Black, one Splenda if you have it. Touch of milk."

"You, Ivan?"

"I'm fine. I assume we can plug in here?" Ivan indicated the cords erupting from mid table.

"That's what they're there for. All for you. I'll have Prim get your coffee and donut. And I'm in the room next door and Brad is down the hall, so if you need, anything just step right in and let me or Brad know."

"How about a room with a better view?" said Keisha. "Just kidding."

*   *   *

Whenever Ivan is asked what it's like being a tax auditor, most people snort at his answer: "It's like being an archeologist." Those with intellectual stretching capacity nod. Others just stare at him. Ivan always explains that, just as an archaeologist digs through artifacts for history, so does the tax auditor dig for meaning behind the numbers, the secret stories told by receipts and canceled checks; the truth underneath the vouchers and authorizations that gives life to the numbers, weighing business trips with actual time spent on business; matching the names of the business attendees with the names on boarding passes. All this and more could tell a very different story than the layers of ledgers and bloated balance sheets. The parsing of paper could present something other than what appears to be transparent and clearly recorded.

This was Ivan's job, to reveal the hidden story. But to get to the prize he had to go through the seemingly endless drudgery of listing, counting, tallying, footing, and calculating. After it's all over, in many cases, there is no treasure to be found, nothing known that wasn't already known. That's the shame of it; all that work and for what?

There were moments – and it's those moments he lived for—when something enlightening popped up, similar to an archeologist finding a new civilization among stones and rotting wood. That's how it was for Ivan when he audited Frederick's luncheonette client and found it impossible to reconcile how the luncheonette made all that money when their cost of supplies and food purchases didn't validate it. That small finding, in an audit of a hole-in-the-wall greasy spoon diner led to the downfall of mobster Eddie Malano.

But what did he have here? A major city newspaper practically in bankruptcy. Could it have anything to do with Sandra's murder? Ivan decided it could not, as the audit was planned well before she went missing. Ivan tapped his fingers on the desk as he went through Anderson's travel expenses.

"Excuse me, Ivan?" Keisha was standing right next to him. Ivan wondered for how long.

"Sorry, what?"

"Don't mean to interrupt your concentration but I was just noticing, I was doing the advertising like you said I should do, and I was just noticing the advertising sales in last year's records were a lot higher than the year before."

"Okay."

"You know I'm from Philadelphia, right? And not that I'm a big shopper but I do know most of the stores in Philly, especially the bigger ones?"

"If you say so."

"And I was doing what you told me to do, poking at some of the advertisers and I see there's a lot of new advertisers in last year's records that's not in the prior year. I mean like it was their first time advertising and they were paying for big ads. Thing is, I never even heard of these stores. And some of them sound bizarre."

"Bizarre like what for instance?"

"So take this one: There's an invoice from Longwidth Clothes. That's the name of the store. I looked them up on the internet. Nothing comes up."

"What about the address on the invoice?" Ivan asked.

"It's a Delaware address that doesn't exist. I called the phone number on the invoice. I get a those beeps you know, and the recording 'the number you are trying to reach is not in service.'"

Ivan looked at the boxes of documents on the table.

"Just that one?"

"No, that's just it. I found ten like that so far. I checked the addresses, called some numbers, nothing, like it's some alternate universe."

Ivan tapped his fingers on the edge of the keyboard, something he did when in deep thought.

"Tell you what. Go to Brad. Tell him you'd like an unread, untouched copy of last year's Thanksgiving Sunday *Times* and an unread, untouched copy of the prior year's Thanksgiving Sunday *Times* as well. Stress unread, undisturbed copies. He'll probably say what for, but you say, why? is that a problem? Tell him you'll wait for him to bring them to you. And then wait. When you get them, bring them here."

"You'll think he'll just do that?"

"He won't like it, but he has to."

These are the steps Ivan relished the most. The ones outside the box; the requests that take the audited by surprise. You're asking for what? Whatever for? Won't know until I get it. If it's nothing, you have nothing to worry about. Do you have something to worry about? If so, tell me now. Get in front of it. But whether it turns out to be nothing or something, what matters right now, Brad, is that we're asking for it. You not providing it tells us there's something you're worried about. He wondered how the exchange between Brad and Keisha would go down—her with her cocoa-butter smile and soft brown eyes sweetly asking for something Brad has to physically get up and get.

A half hour later Keisha came back carrying two copies of Thanksgiving Sunday *Times* as if they were two ancient stones unearthed from the dark and damp, rarely visited stacks room. It would disclose a bit of history that perhaps no one foresaw. Keisha carried them like a tray with an overloaded sundae, careful not to spill any of the heaped-on chocolate sauce. Even before she placed them on the table, Ivan noticed the disparity between the two issues.

"How did he respond to your request?" Ivan asked.

"Annoyed. Perplexed. Resistant. Take your pick."

"All of the above?"

"Yeah. But here they are."

"Let's put them side by side."

"Okay, what are we looking for?"

"Size."

"Size matters? Just kidding."

"One Sunday *Times* is about an inch bigger than the other. Which one is bigger?"

Keisha looked at the dates. "The one from two years ago is bigger."

"And which year did you say reported more advertising income?"

"The one from one year ago. By about five point five million dollars."

"So why isn't the one from last year bigger? Shouldn't it be?

"Maybe there are more articles?" Keisha suggested.

"No, the *Times* is not going to spend more money on paper for articles. It's the ads. So why does the thinner paper earn more advertising income?"

"Well, I don't know, but they are reporting it on their tax return as taxable income. So we don't have a tax adjustment there."

"What do we have?"

"Beats me."

"We have less ads in the year they received more advertising income. Doesn't that seem odd to you?"

"It does. Why is that?"

"That's what we need to find out. Here's what I want you to do. From last year's advertisement sales ledger, I want you to put together a list of the advertisers in order of largest sales to lower sales. From full page ads to quarter page ads. Follow?"

"Yeah."

"Then do you know what I want you to do next?"

"I sure don't."

"I want you to find those ads in last year's newspaper. You can start with the ten you already identified."

"You mean like physically go through that newspaper and look for the actual advertisement and get my hands all dirty from the newsprint?"

"Exactly. Start with the big advertising section. It's a whole section. Do you know why I'm asking you to do this?"

"Yeah. To see if the ads really exist. And if they don't, then what are all these advertisement sales all about?"

"Why are we doing this audit? Both Frederick and Brad said there's net operating losses going back several years and that we're wasting our time looking for a tax adjustment. You noticed this yourself. We're not looking for a tax adjustment."

"Then what are we looking for?"

"Pornography. We'll know it when we find it. And maybe, Keisha, you found it."

"So why would an advertiser pay for an advertisement when he's not putting in an advertisement?"

"We need to find out where these fake ad monies are coming from. Who's paying for them? From what bank are the checks being drawn from? We need copies of them, electronic or otherwise. Then we'll contact the payers and ask them if they're happy with the results of their ad in the *Times*. Note their response. See if they say yes. Are we having fun now?"

"Sounds like a great idea. I'm excited to do it. What are you up to, by the way? Are you having fun?"

"As a matter of fact, maybe."

"So what's maybe?"

"Anderson's travel. Michigan, Florida, California, England. Why does Anderson need to go to England?"

"What does it say there?"

"International Convention of Editors."

"Sounds legit."

"Too legit. We'll need to ask him about it."

"We?"

"I mean you. Okay, now let's get back to work."

"I thought we were working."

"I mean the tedious part of the work."

"Gotcha." She headed back to her chair.

"And Keisha?"

"Yeah?"

"Picking up on the advertisements, great find."

Chapter Twenty-Eight

The shelter Sandra Wolf had found for Abisha Sallaz occupied a four-story cement block building in a residential section of North Philadelphia. With windows lined up like carefully spaced dominos, its bulky front appeared punched in the middle to allow an entranceway large enough for a school bus to park, ideal for taking children to the Philadelphia Zoo or the Franklin Institute. The doorway was shielded by two heavy columns on each side and an overhead cement mast forming a rectangular arch. Abisha had lived there since escaping from her violent husband, and it was where she was now employed.

After parking the pickup, Gregg and Liz walked across the street to the building. From the second floor, the curious faces of children randomly popped in the windows. Liz rang the doorbell and was immediately buzzed in through the heavily secured front door. Abisha greeted them with a bright smile and a bright green hijab. She wore blue jeans and a loose sweatshirt.

"Liz, you must be," Abisha said as they shook hands.

"I am."

"And you must be?" Abisha asked turning to Gregg.

"I must be Gregg. I have no choice." Gregg grinned.

Abisha smiled back, her face lighting up. "Come on in and follow me. I have an office. Well, not really an office, just a space."

"That's cool," Gregg said as they followed Abisha. "I just got a truck."

"And don't mind the kids, they just curious."

Liz took Abisha's choice of apparel as a sign of freedom from her previous restrictive life and her comfort of living here on her own terms as a Muslim.

Walking through a wide hallway of threadbare carpet, they passed rooms filled with kids passing the time; toddlers tumbling over soft Gymboree slides, oversized balls and cushioned circular tunnels; teenagers in a room ignoring one another, engrossed in texting and games. In another room, a girl and boy were playing Connect4. One girl sat alone on a couch reading a book. None seemed at all curious about the visitors walking through.

"Here's me," Abisha said stepping around her desk. "What I call home. Might not look like much of one but it's a life saver for me. How you like my fish?"

Behind her desk on a shelf sat a small fish tank filled with polka dotted, striped, purple, yellow, and green fish. And goldfish.

"I love their colors!" Liz said. "Did you choose the fish?"

"Actually, I made it a project with the kids. We all went to the pet shop—Petco, ya know? They got some great fish over there. And the kids had a great old time picking out the fish. Each kid was allowed to choose a fish, so it was like their own, know what I mean? Their own personal fish."

"What a great idea!" Liz exclaimed.

"Yeah, I thought so too. Ownership, know what I mean? So they come here, my office, to take a look at their fish, their personal fish to see how they doing. Feed them and all. Their own personal fish."

"I never did have fish," Gregg said. "We did have a dog though."

"We can't have no dogs. Against the rules."

"I can understand that," Liz said.

"Too high maintenance, too messy and really too friendly to be here. Just the way it is."

Abisha sighed, sat back, and then something broke in her. She began to sob. "So Sandra. My poor Sandra. I just cry and cry whenever I think about it. Like I'm trying not to do now. I almost fainted when I heard it was her on the TV. She was everything to me. She gave me my life back. I owe her my life, that's how I literally feel. Wasn't for her, I don't know, maybe I'd be dead."

"I know exactly what you mean, Abisha," said Liz. "I was her friend too. She was my teacher at Temple. Tell me how you two met."

"You know how she found me?"

"No. Tell us."

"At the police station. I was there registering a complaint against my husband. I finally got the nerve to do that. Took guts, if I don't say so. And she was there, Sandra, she happened to be there and she heard me talking to the police about why I was there and everything with my husband and she wanted to talk to me. So that's how it all got started. Told her all about what was going on with me. And she wanted to know if this happened to other Muslim women and I said some, it was not just with me, I told her but other Muslim women too. I didn't want her writing about me though and she said she wouldn't unless I gave her the okay, which I did eventually. So we spoke a few times, and I was telling her what was going on with me and she said she would find me a place to stay, a shelter but I said I wasn't ready for that. But then I finally was ready. My husband hit me so hard, it was like, I was dizzy and all, and I fell to the floor, I couldn't see straight. Couldn't think straight. I just crawled out the door and got up and took off. I didn't know where I was going to. All I knows is I gotta get outta there. And it was night, ya know. And I didn't realize at the time but my nose was broke. I was scared.

"I didn't know where to go, what to do, nothing. Didn't want to go back to my folks again, 'cause they just tell me to go back home again. I had no friends 'cause all our friends was his friends. So what do I do? I call Sandra. 'Cause we had just spoke the other day and she gave me her number. So she says, she tells me I should come over to her house in Society Hill. I tell her I got no money. She tells me I should take a cab and she's paying for it. So I grab a cab and I can see the cabdriver don't want to take me 'cause of how I was, how I looked and he asked me do I have money for the cab and I say 'course I do, but I don't. So I give him the address in Society Hill and I see him shaking his head but we go and when we get there, there is Sandra, waving a twenty in her hand. I stay with her for a few days until she finds me this shelter where I move in with my kids. And here I be."

"That's an amazing story, Abisha," Liz said. "Amazing how things worked out for you here. Sandra was an extremely resourceful and good-hearted person."

"Don't I know it. So you was her student at Temple?"

"Yes. She taught journalism and I was taking her class. We were very close. More than just student-teacher. We were friends. And, you don't know, but I was there when they found her."

"You was? Oh man, I would just go crazy. How you deal with all that?"

"Not easy. Still having trouble. And the police still don't have a suspect."

"So yeah, what's with that?"

"Have they spoken with you?"

"No. They suppose to?"

"I don't know. I thought they might have. But Gregg and I are just doing our own thing, trying to put the pieces together and taking a shot here and there and looking at the whole picture, looking at motive. Did she have enemies? If she did, who were they? Did your husband know you were staying with Sandra in her house?"

Abisha looked at Liz as if she had told her the fish in the tank behind her had turned into sharks.

"Tarek, yes he do, but he never met Sandra; doesn't know who she is. He don't read the papers neither, he don't know what's going on in the world. He don't vote, he don't have the brains to even figure out how to murder someone let alone get away with it, if that's what you want to know, and he's a coward. 'Cept when it comes to hitting his wife half his size. So as much as I hate him and want to see him behind bars, I'd say no, don't waste your time on him."

Liz remained silent. What could she have been thinking, she asked herself.

"We know we're not detectives," Gregg stepped in. "We just thought we'd run the idea past you to see if the police should be looking in his direction. We just wanted to get your take on that. I'm sure you want the murderer found just as much as we do."

"I sure do. But it ain't him. If I thought it be him I'd tell you in a split second. I'd tell the police already. But it ain't."

A small voice came from a long curly haired black girl of about five years old. "Can I feed Sparkly?"

"Sure Mazy, come in now. These are my friends, Liz and Gregg."

Mazy waved her hand at Liz and Gregg but didn't look at them. She focused on the fish.

"Which one is Sparkly?" Liz asked.

"The purple one," Mazy said, pointing.

"Why do you call him Sparkly?" Gregg asked.

"Because he sparkles when he moves," said Mazy. "You see? Watch, he changes color."

Liz and Gregg looked closer at the purple fish but neither noticed any sparkling or any color change. Abisha leaned back in her swivel chair as if she was the proud mother of both the little girl and the fish.

"Where's the fish food?" Gregg asked looking for it in the vicinity of the fish tank.

"I got it right here." Abisha opened the bottom drawer of her desk. She pulled out the food and winked at Gregg.

"So they don't keep grabbling at the food and feeding them," she said to Gregg as if sharing a secret.

"Here ya go," Abisha said, handing the small canister to Mazy. Mazy opened the jar, looked for her purple fish and shook the food directly on Sparkly.

"Not too much," Abisha reminded her.

"Can the other fish have some of Sparkly's food too?" Gregg asked.

"Nothing's stopping 'em," Mazy answered in a way that showed the ridiculousness of Gregg's question.

They all watched Mazy as she tried to follow the darting purple fish with the fish food, giving it a one-shake when Sparkly stopped for a breather.

"Okay, that's it," said Abisha. "Don't want to overdo it now. Need to save some for the rest of our fish owners."

Masy did one more push-the-envelope shake before handing the canister back to Abisha. She then ran back to jump on the Gymboree.

"Well let me ask you then," Liz said. "do you remember Sandra ever talk about anybody who might have it in for her, maybe because of something she wrote?"

"Like who?"

"Anybody. Anybody who she might be having a problem with. Would she share something like that with you?"

"With me, no, no one like that. The only thing she said was, she didn't know when the article would come out on account of she still had to convince her boss."

"What exactly did she say about that, having to convince her boss?" asks Liz.

"Just what I said, that's it. Said she had to convince her boss. I don't know nothing else."

"Did she say why?" asked Gregg.

"Not really. Just that sometimes he could be a hardass, is all. I don't know."

"Well, we don't want to take up any more of your time, Abisha. Looks like you're doing a great job with these kids."

"I try."

"You're succeeding. Great idea on the fish!"

"Yeah, well, like I said, if it weren't for Sandra, I don't know what."

As they walked across the street to the pickup, Liz thought how wrong she was to think she was the one who'd come up with the suspect, and that suspect would be Abisha's husband. Michael Banks put the idea in her head and the more the idea made its way through the circuitry of her brain the more true and clear it became to her, like an archer's target. She pictured Abisha's husband crouched in hiding on her street, ready to pounce just as Sandra turned her key to open the front door. After strangling her, he would walk out, locking the door behind him and disappear. But no, that scene was only in her mind, and it didn't even fit the evidence, and now it was quashed.

"So what's your take?" Gregg asked after closing the driver side door.

"Sounds to me she just laid another layer of speculation on Anderson. What do you think?"

"We got nothing. Being a hardass doesn't make you a murderer."

Liz sighed, reaching for her seat belt. Gregg was right. They had nothing.

Gregg started the engine. "Where to now?"

"I don't know. Take me anywhere. Surprise me."

"Ok!" Greggs said, revving the engine. "Surprise coming up!"

Chapter Twenty-Nine

Ivan made sure the conference room door was closed before calling Sabrina.

"Say this to me again because I'm not quite understanding," said Sabrina. Ivan imagined her switching the phone from one ear to the next as if one ear was smarter than the other.

"We're not sure if we understand either," said Ivan, "but we do know what we found. In one case a company called "Longwidth," supposedly a clothing store for big and tall men in Delaware, paid $10,000 for a one-time quarter-page ad in the Thanksgiving issue. Keisha called them. The number was disconnected. A Google map search for the address shows a vacant lot."

"How many did you say you found like this?" Sabrina asked.

"Ten. We did a sampling of the Thanksgiving issue, the biggest spending weekend of the year. Some of the invoices actually say "Thanksgiving issue." All payments were made electronically. I think what we need to do is trace those payments to the bank they come from, find out who owns the accounts and who authorized the payments. Can the FBI do that?"

"I would think they should be able to," Sabrina said. "Have you brought this to the accountants' attention?"

"I'm holding off on that."

Ivan pictured Sabrina's fingers lacing through her braids; what she does when she's thinking things through.

"Yeah, hold off. I'll call the FBI. See what they can do."

"If they refuse, we pack up and go home."

"What do you mean?"

"We're on a fishing expedition here and just caught something big. If we have to throw it back, there's no point continuing this audit."

The next call Ivan got was from a guy named Spencer, a special technical analyst at Langley. Surprised but impressed at how quickly the call came, Ivan told him about Longwidth.

"What would you like me to do?" Spencer asked.

"Trace these wire transfers to the bank they came from, find out who opened the bank account, the name of the account owner and the source of the deposits into the account. Can you do that?"

"Give it a shot. Call you back in a bit."

Ivan assumed that meant an hour, but was again surprised when Spencer called back in minutes.

"Check your email," Spencer told him.

With Keisha looking on, Ivan opened Spencer's email.

"What we're seeing here, Spencer," Ivan said, "is that Longwidth has a bank account at the Bank of Delaware and the funds going into this account were wired from Rabobank in Saudi Arabia. Am I seeing that right?"

"Yuppers," Spencer answered as if he saw this every day. "The name of the person who opened the account is Walid Zair."

"Does that name mean anything to you?" Ivan asked him.

"Nope."

"I'm going to email you the nine other payments we found. Can you look into those too?"

"Yep. Will come right back at ya in a bit."

And in a bit, Spencer did.

"It's all the same," Ivan observed. "All these advertisement payments for these fake advertisers come from separate accounts in the Bank of Delaware, and all monies coming into those Bank of Delaware accounts come from wire transfers originating from Saudi Arabia. All supposedly owned by Walid Zair. What's your takeaway on this, Spencer?"

"Don't have one. I'm just the messenger."

"I thought you're an analyst."

"Fancy for techy. Want fries with that?"

Ivan and Keisha heard a soft knock on the door followed by Frederick walking in.

"Don't mean to barge in. How are you guys doing here?"

"Good. Thanks for your concern," Ivan answered, adjusting his computer screen towards him.

"Just want to let you know if you need anything else from me, it's best you let me know in real time, as opposed to waiting at the end of the day and handing me a pile of asks. That'll make it easier on me and Brad."

"Good to know." Ivan kept his eyes on the monitor.

"Do you have anything for me right now?"

"Nope."

"How long do you plan to stay today?"

"Oh, we were thinking of spending the night. Got a lot of boxes to get to."

"Well, I'm leaving at five. Just so you know."

"Now I know."

Frederick closed the door behind him shaking his head.

"You still there, Spence?"

"We didn't say good-bye."

"Anything else for Spence, Keisha?"

"I? I don't know," said a bewildered Keisha. "Do I?"

"Nothing for now, Spence. Can I call you back if I need you?"

"Emailing you my work number. I'm always here. You guys have fun in Saudi Arabia."

"We need to do some brainstorming here." Ivan said to Keisha after hanging up with Spencer. "The first question, why is Saudi Arabia giving the *Times* money and why is the *Times* taking Saudi money under the guise of advertising sales?"

"That's two questions, but yeah. And who's in on it?"

"Write these questions down. And how long has this been going on, another question."

"I only looked at one year. And I'm not even finished with that."

"But you came up with over five million dollars' worth of fake advertising sales. Know what I think?"

"Am I supposed to?'

"I think the *Times* is taking money from Saudi Arabia because it can't find any more real advertisers or investors willing to prop them up. The question is, why Saudi Arabia?"

"And who contacted whom first?" Keisha offered.

"Put that down too. Let's assume for the moment Saudi Arabia made the first contact. They knew the *Times* was in financial trouble. They offered to help. But the *Times* doesn't want anyone to know they're taking Saudi money, so they launder it as advertising sales. But what's in it for Saudi Arabia? What does the *Times* have to offer Saudi Arabia?"

"What?" Keisha asked.

"Only one thing. Media coverage. Positive media coverage."

"Even if they do something bad?" Keisha asked.

"Especially then. It's how you spin it."

"You think Frederick and Brad know? You think that's why Fred walked in just when we were on the phone with the FBI? Perfect timing or what."

"I don't know. I doubt it. Frederick was the accountant on a case I had several years ago where the mob was laundering money through a luncheonette. Went right over his head. If he didn't pick up on that, I doubt he knows anything about this."

"What about Brad? Wouldn't their own controller pick up on that up if he wasn't in on it?"

"Doubtful. It's on the books, its being recorded; there's an invoice, a vendor, an address, a payment, it's included in taxable income. That's all he's looking at. Brad has no reason to look for the actual ads."

"Gotcha. That leaves Anderson and Benson."

"Benson is the publisher, Anderson controls the spin. And something else just occurred to me."

"What?"

"The reason Anderson didn't publish Sandra Wolf's stories."

"Are we going to be asking them these questions tomorrow? Are we going to be pointing out to Frederick and Brad today what we found out?"

"No. Not today. Let's see how our interviews go with Anderson and Benson tomorrow."

Ivan's cell rang. "Sabrina?"

"You sure did trigger some excitement over there. The FBI wants to meet with us first thing tomorrow morning in their office."

"We're scheduled to interview Anderson and Benson tomorrow morning."

"Move it to the afternoon. You and Keisha in my office tomorrow morning and we'll all go up together. Eight thirty. See you then."

"We must have hit a nerve," Ivan told Keisha. "Tomorrow morning we're meeting with the FBI."

"Oh wow."

"Let's wrap up here for now. Put the items that we're in the middle of looking at in a separate box. I'll go speak to Fred."

Ivan knocked on Fred's door and walked in. "We'll be back tomorrow late morning or early afternoon. Meantime I have a list for you." Ivan handed Frederick a sheet of paper.

"Travel receipts, no surprise there," said Fred said. "Legal fees, art items? What art items?"

"The ones on the wall."

"Are you kidding? They've been there for ages."

"Just the ones purchased in the last two years."

"Are you looking for anything in particular?"

"Yes, the art expenses in the last two years."

"Do you think we'll be able to wrap this up tomorrow? Because what you're asking for is nuts."

"Depends on what tomorrow brings."

Keisha waited for Ivan outside Frederick's office, her computer over her shoulder and Ivan's computer in her hands.

"Here you go," she said handing him his computer.

"Thank you," Ivan took his computer. "Let's say goodbye to Prim."

Chapter Thirty

The eighth floor of the federal building was off-limits to everyone except the FBI. Sabrina was given a temporary card so that she, Ivan, and Keisha could enter.

Agent Jed's office was meant to look over the Delaware River but six city streets' worth of tall buildings got in the way. There was another reason they couldn't see the river; Jed's portly partner Marcus was sitting on the windowsill.

Jed was in his early thirties with a receding hairline beginning to turn gray. He wore a close-fitted dark suit and leaned forward in his swivel chair to emphasis the points he was making.

"What you found could be pivotal. It could be what we were looking for." His question was directed at Ivan and Keisha, but mostly at Ivan.

"I have some questions," Ivan said.

"Of course, but wait until I finish," Jed said. His voice was full of authority and expertise. "After I'm finished, your questions may be answered."

"Jed," said Marcus, "maybe we should start with some backstory," He had short brown hair parted in the middle and a thin brown mustache. He looked to be in his early forties.

"Okay, you tell them Marcus."

Marcus got off the windowsill and began to speak as if from a podium, remembering to look at audience members individually.

"Ever since 9/11, our main concern, and what I mean by our main concern is the FBI, Homeland Security and ICE, has been combating domestic terrorism. We've been tracking pockets of domestic terrorism in various parts of the country. A focus of our monitoring is on various sects of Islamic communities. Now I don't want you to get us wrong. It's only some, not all, sects that we're looking at, the dangerous sects because it's our job to identify them in order to protect our country. Now you heard of Al Qaida, and ISIS, right? Have any of you heard of the Deobandi branch of Islam?" He ended the question resting his eyes on Keisha.

"Are you asking me? No. I mean I'm Muslim but that whole scene is foreign to me."

"I don't mean to put you on the spot. What about either of you?" Marcus looked at Ivan and Sabrina individually.

"Can't say I have," said Ivan.

"Me too. I don't know anything about it." said Sabrina.

"So I'll tell you. You heard of the Muslim Brotherhood, right?"

"Heard the term," Sabrina answered.

"The Deobandi branch of Islam comes from a city in India, called Deobandi, starting way back in the 1860s when India was all of Pakistan and Kashmir and Bangladesh and modern India. And just like the Muslim Brotherhood, which, by the way didn't come into being until 1928 in Egypt, the Deobandi allied itself with the Wahhabi Saudi Arabia form of Islam which is a pretty radical form of Islam. Having all that oil money Saudi Arabia funded much of the Deobandi enterprises to the tune of about 100 million dollars annually.

"You should also know that in the Deobandi world a Muslim's first loyalty is to his religion and then to the country in which he lives. But even within the Deobandi there are different groups. One of them is called Tablighi Jamaat. There are 75 to 125 million members of Tablighi Jamaat in the world. Another group is called Lashkar-e-Taiba, and we know about that because of the Mumbai massacre in India, you know about that, right?"

"I do," said Ivan.

"Me too," said Sabrina.

"And there's another one that we've all heard of called the Taliban. And here's where it gets even bigger. The groups that we know of, like ISIS and Hamas and so on, formed an alliance with the Central Asian Deobandi group. And do you know what it's called? Al-Qaida, led by Osama bin Laden."

"And so, the question is," Jed picked up, "the question we're all about is this; are they here in America in some form or another? And the answer is, I'm sorry to say, is yes. We all saw them on the day of the San Bernardino massacre. The perpetrator of that terrorism was a Deobandi Tablighi Jamaat. So was his wife. Her father worked in Saudi Arabia. Remember the Pulse nightclub shooting in Florida? The terrorist who committed that attack attended a mosque in Fort Pierce, which was directly connected to the mosque in San Bernardino. Scary right? Well, our job is to connect the dots, and unfortunately they've seeped into the structure of the Islamic community here in the United States. These groups are almost invisible, but that doesn't mean they don't exist. Our job is to flush them out."

"So," Marcus took over, "now you're wondering how do you fit into all this? Where do you come in, right?"

"I'm afraid to find out," Keisha said.

"As we said, our job is to keep our country safe, and that includes safe from domestic terrorism," Marcus continued, "One day we're told that one of the radicals we've been monitoring in England, who is from Saudi Arabia and has ties to Deobandi radicals in our country makes contact with, are you ready for this? The editor of the *Philadelphia Times*, Alexander Anderson. We have no idea why. Our intelligence seemed pretty certain that something was going on between those two, but we couldn't figure what."

"So we decided," Jed took over, "to look in a different direction. We came up with the idea of looking at the *Times* itself."

"And that's when we came to you," Marcus jumped in. "To see what, if anything you could discover through a tax audit of the *Times*. And you did."

For a moment everyone paused. Ivan broke the silence. "Do you mean to say that Alexander Anderson made a deal for the *Times* to get funds from a radical extremist from Saudi Arabia?"

"That may be exactly what you discovered," said Jed.

"Is that a crime?" Sabrina asked.

"In fact, it is!" said Marcus like a carnival barker to a contestant who just won a Kewpie doll. "Failure to disclose foreign investment is a violation of the requirements established by the Bureau of Economic Analysis. We're talking thousands of dollars of penalties. The question is, why is this Saudi radical funneling money to the *Times*?"

"Is that what you're asking us to find out?" asked Ivan.

"It's what we need to find out," Marcus said.

"We were planning to ask Anderson about those advertisements today," said Keisha. She then looked at Ivan, thinking maybe that wasn't for her to say.

"We want you to hold off on that," said Jed. "Now that we know what's going on, we want to continue monitoring the money."

"Ivan, didn't you already bring the advertisement discrepancy to the *Times'* attention?" Sabrina asked.

"They gave us actual copies of the Thanksgiving issues. They don't know why we asked for them."

"Do what you normally do but don't give away what you stumbled upon," said Jed. "Anything else you find, run it by us first and we'll let you know if it's something we want to pursue or drop."

"You did a great job, by the way," added Marcus.

"You certainly did," added Jed. "You did great."

"Thanks," said Keisha. Ivan said nothing.

"Any more questions?" Marcus asked. "Ivan, did we answer all your questions?"

"All the ones I care to ask."

"You have more?"

"No."

"You sure?"

"Sure."

"Well, that's it for now. Let me give you all our cards. Again, if you see anything I should know about, you'll let me know asap, ok?"

"You can count on us, gentlemen," said Sabrina.

At the elevator Ivan turned to Sabrina. "Are we working for them now?"

"What do you mean?"

"It's one thing for us to do our jobs and report back. It's quite another for them to tell us what to do and how to do it."

"Like how do you mean?"

"Telling us not to raise the advertising issue with them."

"It's their show. We should just cooperate here."

"We told the *Times* we'd be there late morning and it's about that now," said Keisha. "We should probably go."

"Ivan, I'm counting on you," Sabrina said as she got off her floor, leaving Ivan and Keisha in the elevator.

Chapter Thirty-One

The first thing Ivan and Keisha noticed upon their return to the *Times* were crumpled pink tissues around the legs of Prim's chair. It reminded Ivan of petals tossed by a flower girl at a wedding. Keisha saw a hygienic mess.

"I'm guessing you're not having a good day," Ivan said to Prim. He was dressed in a blue business suit and tie, ready to meet the executives. Keisha was smartly dressed in a blue skirt and blazer and beige hijab—for this meeting, she had apparently eschewed her normal bright colors. Their laptops were strapped over their shoulders.

"Try horrible. My deadbeat ex screwed me again and it's making me literally sick. As you can see. This whole thing came down last night and I'm going nuts. Sorry." Prim bent down to pick up the fallen tissues, her uncombed blue and yellow hair looking like a feather brush. "Maybe I will give you guys his social security number after all." She pulled out another tissue, wiped her nose and stuffed the tissue in her tight jean pocket. "By the way, they're pissed at you."

Ivan lifted his shoulders in a questioning gesture. "How so?"

"You're late. They don't like late. Believe me, I know they don't like late."

"Except we're not. We told them yesterday we'd be here about noon," Ivan said, checking his watch. "And it's before noon."

"Doesn't matter. As far as they're concerned, you're late and they're pissed." Prim picked up the phone and buzzed. "They're here. Yes, finally. Got it." She hung up and sniffed while attempting a smile.

"You can go back to the same room as yesterday. They'll meet you there."

"Feel better," Keisha said with a smile as she passed.

"Yeah, not happening." Prim pulled out another tissue.

Ivan noticed the journalists watching them as they made their way back to the conference room. At this point, Ivan believed they all knew who they were and why they were there.

Ivan scanned the conference room for any indication of intrusion: anything not where they left it, folders shuffled, papers disordered, a chair relocated. Nothing. Everything right in place. He'd been doing these mental maps surveys his entire career, and he was certain he'd missed nothing.

Brad appeared at the door, holding a folder. "Benson left," he said to Ivan's back. "He couldn't wait. He had another appointment."

Ivan turned towards Brad and frowned. "What about Anderson?"

"He's here but perturbed. You're screwing up his schedule."

"Nonsense. I told Fred we'd be here by twelve. I also gave him a list of things I needed. Is that it?"

Brad handed Ivan the folder. "Truth be told, I actually needed the extra time to gather it all. Alex would like to get this over with as quickly as possible, so as soon as you're ready he'll come in."

"Bring him in now." Ivan said. "Fred too."

"Will do."

When Brad left Ivan said to Keisha, "I know we were talking about you doing the interview, but after what we found out last night and this morning I'd think I should do the asking."

"No argument from me. In fact, I'm glad you said that. I was actually nervous and I think I'll learn more from watching you than from screwing this up."

"We'll both learn. I'll sit here, you sit next to me so we're both facing the door as they come in. And let's put these newspapers on the table in front of me. At some point, I'll be handing them to you and you'll give them to Brad. Placement is everything."

"Everything?"

"I hate having my back to the door."

The door opened with Brad entering first followed by Fred, and a moment later, making a deliberately slow entrance like a king, Anderson swaggered in. His body and breath seemed to take ownership of the conference room. He was taller and heavier than Ivan had expected, his thick, wavy gray hair stridently combed back, his burly, neatly trimmed goatee blasting out his persona to the world. His small gray eyes pierced through Ivan, telling him with silent certainty he considered him an unworthy adversary.

Ivan stood and offered his hand. Anderson was wearing a Jerry Garcia tie, an oddly avant-garde addition to his conservative suit. "Thanks for making time for us, Mr. Anderson. I know your time is valuable."

"It is that." Anderson took Ivan's hand firmly without a smile, without a nod. Ivan gave Anderson a bright smile and a grip that took Anderson ever so slightly aback.

"I'm doing my patriotic duty showing up here today. I trust you feds appreciate that. And we can dispense with formalities. Call me Alex."

"No problem, Alex, I'm Ivan, and my partner here is Keisha."

Keisha rose and offered her hand. "Good to meet you Mr. Anderson, I mean Alex."

"Now you got it. Pleasure's mine," Alex smiled at Keisha, taking her hand gently. "Let me know if anybody gives you any trouble."

"Oh? Why would that be?" Keisha asked, eyebrows raised in confusion.

"You never know. Are you from Philly?"

"West Philly, yeah."

"And you, Ivan?"

"I grew up in the Northeast," Ivan answered.

"Did you attend Northeast High?"

"I went to Central."

"Of course you did. You're a smart guy, Ivan. So we're all Philly people here. We're all family. And like all families we may have our squabbles, but we all love each other. Isn't that right, Brad?"

"Ah, yeah, sure," Brad said, sounding like he was not expecting to be thrust in the middle.

"Speaking of family," Ivan said. "Why don't we start by having you tell us a little about the *Times* family. We all know you're the patriarch. What's a typical day like for you?"

Anderson looked at Ivan as if he'd just been asked to explain a Philly soft pretzel. Then he chuckled. "I can understand why you ask that question, Ivan. I imagine for you, all days are all the same. Ledgers, trial balances, bank statements. But if you know anything about the newspaper business, and I would hope you know something, maybe you saw the film "The Front Page?" You'd know there's no such thing as a typical day here at the *Times*. So I really don't know how to begin to answer your question, Ivan. But to get this thing going and get you out of my hair as quickly as possible so I can go on with my atypical day, I'll tell you what you want to hear. But let me start off by saying this, and I'm saying this to everybody in this room. And maybe you heard me saying this before. Maybe not Frederick over here but certainly you, Brad."

He leaned over and gazed intently into Ivan's eyes. "Nothing matters more in our democracy than local journalism. I think we can all agree on that, right? And I think we can all agree that we should hold our leaders accountable. And when I say leaders, I'm not just talking about the corrupt politicians, but our jaded judges, our untrustworthy police, the fallen-from-grace clergy, the rotten and underfunded school systems that are failing our youth. You all know what I'm talking about, right? Ah, but Ivan, you're lucky you went to Central. But what about the rest? The city schools are producing a generation of illiterates. And it's our job to shout about this from the rooftops. If people in power screw up, they need to know we, us, the *Times* will let the whole world know. That's what we do. This paper is the heart of the city. Everything else is the skin and bones. Isn't that right Brad?"

"Oh…. yes. Of course, yes."

"You bet it is." Alex got up and began walking around the long rectangular table. Frederick opened one of the bottles of water Prim had put in the center of the table earlier that morning. Keisha sat up straight, her eyes following Anderson around the table, though she shielded them from the sun when he paced in front of the window.

"So what do I do every morning of a typical day, you want to know? Ivan? I hold meetings with my staff editors several times a week. We talk about what we think is newsworthy, we decide what's going on the front page, and who's going to write the lead story. We come up with deadlines. I take lots of calls. Calls from stakeholders of all stripes; from government officials to civil administration officials, sometimes the mayor. Did you know that, Ivan? Did you know I take calls from the mayor?"

Ivan was in the middle of twisting open the cover of a water bottle. He didn't answer immediately, just took a long swallow which everyone around the table heard going down his throat. Keisha did her best to suppress a giggle.

"I do now."

"I'm sure Brad knew that," Anderson said pausing from his walk around the table, his eyes affixed on Ivan. "Didn't you, Brad?"

"Of course I did. You know I did."

Anderson continued walking around the table. "Police chiefs, chairman of the school board, union leaders, clergy, sanitation people, and our own board of directors. They're going to want to know about this meeting, by the way. We also survey the wires like AP – Associated Press in case you didn't know what AP is, Reuters too, and decide what international news goes in, what's not in. And of course I write my own editorials. Does that answer your question, Ivan?"

"Sounds like you're an expert in time management," Ivan replied.

"A lot more than you might think, I'm sure. Do you even read the *Times*? Do you read my editorials, Ivan?"

"When they're on a topic that interests me."

"What topics interest you, Ivan?"

"Sports, food, taxes. But our talk today isn't about me, it's about you."

"Ask me anything you want. I'm done with my speech." Anderson sat back down clasping his hands behind his head. "I'm an open book. That's the thing about being in the spotlight. Everyone sees what you're doing. Everyone reads what you say and they know what you think. Your life is not your own. When I speak at public affairs, I'm asked all sorts of question; about the election; about the next SEPTA strike. They think I know everything, and you know what? They're right. Isn't that right Brad?"

"That is right, I must say," Brad dutifully answered.

"Life's been pretty damn good to me, I can't complain. I mean I complain all the time, don't get me wrong. Do you know how long I've held this job, Ivan?"

"Twenty years?" Ivan guessed.

"Try thirty. And I plan to be here another thirty. 'It's good to be the king.' Anybody here see that Mel Brooks movie, 'History of the World Part I'? Keisha, do you know what I'm talking about?"

"I sure don't. But I don't see a lot of movies, though. Sorry."

"Why are you sorry? Why do people say sorry when there's nothing for them to be sorry about? Never quite understood that. What about you, Ivan?"

"Actually, that's a good segue to my next question," Ivan continued. "You said you do quite a few speaking engagements. Where do you speak?"

"All over. When people ask me to speak, I make the time to go. Networking with the people, especially in Philadelphia, is paramount."

"Anywhere else?"

"Lots of other places. Are you asking me about something specific?"

"Florida, California?"

"Both places. In Miami there was the 'Computation plus Journalism Symposium'. About finding new ways to use data and algorithms to find news stories. Combining the talents of computer scientists to exchange ideas about industry and internet and academia. Sounded kinda nutty to me but they asked me to speak and I went."

"What did you speak about?"

"How I decide what stories to write about in Philadelphia. Told them it's simple; just follow the sounds of gunshots."

"And California?"

"That was more normal. A workshop for college professors of journalism. More my speed. Talked about the human-interest side of the story. Anything else, Ivan? Make it quick. I have an important phone call in a few minutes."

"Just one more. The trip that you took to London."

Ivan saw it. He saw it in Anderson' eyes, a sudden calmness of breath, an unsettling motionlessness. There was a pause in his confidence. It lasted a nanosecond but it was there.

"Conference of International Newspaper Editors. Come on Ivan, how long is this going to go on? I have a paper to run."

"You spoke at that conference too?"

"That's right."

"Because I'm looking at the itinerary and I don't see your name on the speaker's list." Ivan tossed the conference brochure across the table. Anderson ignored it.

"I was an add-on. A last-minute entry."

"What did you speak about?"

"About America's first free press and how it interrelates with the international media. Really? This is what your job is about? Because if I had your job, I'd kill myself. Anybody know what movie that line is from?"

"Oh, I know that line," said Keisha like a proud, knowledgeable student. "It's from 'A League of Their Own,' right?"

"It was a three-day conference," Ivan noted. "You were in London for two weeks. What were you doing for two weeks?"

"I combined it with vacation. Are we done?"

"As long as the vacation part was paid by you personally," Ivan continued. "But I have here numerous expenses over the two-week period paid by the *Times*. Hotels in Oxford, Liverpool, Churchill Museum, shows."

"You must be desperate, Ivan. If you must know, and I guess you must, I reimbursed the *Times* for that. It's all there."

"Where?"

"There. Wherever."

"Well maybe Fred or Brad can show us where because Keisha and I couldn't find it."

"Ivan," Fred started up, "I wish you would have asked for that yesterday. We could have had it ready for you."

"You know," said Ivan, "before we get into that let me just give these newspapers back to Brad, get it off the desk so we have more room. Here you go,

Brad." Ivan picked up the newspapers, handed it to Keisha sitting next to him who in turn dutifully handed it to Brad. Brad shook his head in annoyance.

Keeping Alex in the corner of his eye, Ivan said. "Oh, just one thing, Brad, when you get a chance, please find the advertisement for Longwidth in those newspapers, will you? We couldn't find it."

"Are you saying we didn't report the advertising income?" Brad asked.

"I didn't say that."

"So what's the problem?"

"We couldn't find the ad so we're asking you to find it for us. That shouldn't be a problem, should it?"

"Yeah, it is. I have a lot more important things to do than flip through newspaper pages. You're basically asking me to do your job. You really want me to do that? If you really want me to do that, its gonna have to wait until I find time."

"That's okay," Ivan said. "We'll just keep the audit open until we get it."

Throughout this exchange Ivan noticed Anderson licking his bottom lip, tapping his fingers on his goatee.

"I have an idea," Frederick chimed in. "Why don't we ask Prim to look for it? She can do that. That'll save us all time. Are you okay with that, Ivan?"

"So long as we get it," Ivan said, and casually looked over at Anderson, who stared back with the intimidating gaze of a prizefighter.

"I'll call her," Frederick took out his cell phone. "Meanwhile, do you have any more questions for Alex? As he told you, he has a newspaper to get out."

"The Florida and California trips. They were all three-day conferences too, but you were at both places for two weeks on the company credit card. Did your wife go with you?"

"Hey, you know what?" Anderson said, rising from his seat. "It's obviously you're playing a trial-and-error game with me. And I won't stand for it. Fred, you deal with this bullshit. That's what we pay you for."

And just then the door opened with Prim standing there, brightening up the room with her colorful hair. But the brightness lasted only for a moment when two other people pushed their way in after her.

"They wouldn't let me call you. I tried."

Barging in right behind Prim and flashing their badges were Detectives Moss and Lopez and two uniform police officers. Both looked briefly at Ivan with surprise, but none of them gave any indication of recognition.

"Alexander Anderson," Detective Moss began, "You're under arrest for the murder of Sandra Wolf. You have the right to remain silent, but anything you say may be used against you. You have a right to an attorney. If you can't afford one, the city will provide one for you. We could do this the easy way or the hard way. But you need to come with us now."

Ivan's mind shuffled the pieces; FBI's involvement, money from Saudi banks, Sandra's articles, Sandra's mom saying Anderson was the only male companion she knew about the whole time she lived in Philadelphia.

"What the fuck is this?" Anderson bellowed.

"Guess you want it the hard way." Lopez pushed Anderson's head down on the table, grabbed his wrists and cuffed him. "Now we drag you out of your castle in cuffs."

"You're out of your minds! You're both nuts. Typical stupid Philadelphia police. I know what this is about," Anderson bellowed loud enough for most employees in the proximity of the conference room to hear. "Payback for exposing the corruption and sexual harassment on the police force. Something you should be thanking me for."

"You can explain all that to the judge." Moss said, opening the door wider. "I'm sure he'll love to hear all that. But right now we have a police car waiting for you outside."

"Let's go, big guy." Lopez led him through the main corridor of his kingdom, where a thousand eyes stood agape at the spectacle. Everyone was motionless and mystified, with one exception. Doug picked up his phone.

Ivan stood next to Frederick, witnessing what he knew was the destruction of a reputation beyond repair. Keisha put her arm around a stunned Prim, who took a step closer to her. Ivan knew, between the arrest and the monies from Saudi Arabia, Anderson's life would never be the same. Soon the world would know it, too.

Stupefied, Frederick turned to Ivan. "I assume you'll we'll be putting this audit on hold for a while?"

"I don't think so, Fred. Will the *Times* be putting its publication on hold for a while?" Anderson disappeared through the front doors.

Frederick stared at Ivan.

Ivan said, "I don't mean to add to your troubles, but when you get the chance, you can tell Anderson or you can tell his personal accountant, if that's not you, that we're expanding the audit to include his personal tax returns for the last three years."

"Are you out of your mind?' Frederick glared at Ivan.

"I assume he files jointly, so you can also spring the good news on his wife."

Chapter Thirty-Two

With Anderson in tow, Detectives Moss and Lopez went outside, where *Times* reporters shouted questions and shoved microphones in their faces. Uniformed officers moved the crowd away. Cameras and cellphone cameras captured the fury in Anderson's furrowed forehead. Moss and Lopez ignored the questions. Anderson glared at the reporters, his reporters, with icy anger. Lopez pushed Anderson's head down and shoved him into the back seat of the police car.

At police headquarters, a horde had already gathered. More pictures were snapped, more questions fired at them. The look on Anderson's face was no longer anger but fear. Minutes later it appeared on the *Times* digital front page with the headline *"Times* Editor Arrested for Murder."

Inside police headquarters, Lopez handed Anderson a sign that read "4" and pushed him into the lineup room.

"What is this?" Anderson ground out.

"You're a smart guy, what does it look like to you?" Lopez answered.

Moss watched from the one-way window room. With her was Tommy 'Angel' McGinnis.

Moss spoke into the microphone. "Everyone face forward."

"That's the asshole right there!" McGinnis barked, pointing at Anderson.

"Take a good look, Mr. McGinnis," Moss said. "It's very important you get it right."

"I'm looking good. Number four is the asshole I saw outside her house that night who almost crashed his fucking car door into me when I was riding my bike. That's the asshole."

"Number four, step forward," Moss said into the microphone, then turned it off. "Thank you very much, Mr. McGinnis. That's what we needed to hear from you. This could go a bunch of ways at this point. We may need to call you again if this goes to trial."

"No sweat. Nail the bastard."

Anderson sat in the interrogation room, his eyes intensely narrowed and full of indignation. He focused his gaze first at Moss, then Lopez, then back to Moss.

"Mr. Anderson," Moss began. "You know you have a right to an attorney, and you don't need to say anything to us without an attorney present. But we just want to let you know the evidence we have against you is overwhelming. The man who identified you is sure he saw you going to Sandra Wolf's house the night of her death. She was recognized leaving the DoubleTree Hotel where you had a package from Victoria's Secret delivered to the penthouse room that was booked in your name. In the ashtray of that room, we discovered a remnant of a marijuana cigarette with both your and Sandra Wolf's DNA. At her house, where her body was found, she was wearing the lingerie you purchased. Your fingerprints were lifted from the lingerie, as well as from a tie similar to what you're wearing now, which we believe was used to strangle Ms. Wolf. Do you have anything you'd like to say?"

Anderson face looked like a balloon about to pop.

"You idiots sew loose pieces of dangling threads and call it evidence. But let me tell you something. You're just like that auditor. You're all the same, the government, the police. You all got a bug up your ass about me. You don't have squat. Yeah. I want my lawyer. I need to get out of here."

Lopez brought a landline phone into the room, plugged it in and handed it to Anderson. Anderson dialed Jack Finch.

"Come down and get me out of here."

"I already spoke to the DA and the judge," said Finch. "They're not allowing bail just yet."

"What do you mean! What kind of bullshit is that?" Anderson yelled.

"At least until the arraignment, which will be in a day or two."

"A day or two? Finch, do your job. All this crap they call evidence is nothing but bullshit. You have to get me out of here now. I didn't kill her!"

"Benson is here. I'm putting him on."

"Alex, it's Conrad. We're with you a hundred and twenty percent. We're going to get you out of there as soon as possible. We all know you're innocent, a hundred and twenty percent. But looks like what you need right now is a criminal lawyer."

The sound of Benson's words made Anderson feel as if his life has been pushed into a different realm, never to return to the world as he once knew it.

"Jack is not a criminal lawyer, but we have good news for you. Vernon Carlson offered to defend you."

"Are you out of your mind? He's a mob lawyer. His clients are hit men."

"He gets them off. And he'll get you off too, Alex. He's putting his personal reputation on the line."

"His reputation? What about mine? He's not even part of a law firm. He's by himself."

"Which is why he'll spend all his time on you. You'll get more than your money's worth. But to be honest, Alex, we did make calls to other criminal law firms in Philadelphia. All said they'll get back to us."

Anderson swallowed hard. "Why is that?"

"This is just my opinion, and I could be wrong, but over the thirty years you worked here, you pissed a lot of people off."

Anderson looked down on the floor and shook his head. "All I did, all I ever did is write the truth. I'm hated for that?"

"Alex," Benson said, "this is an injustice. We're all on your side. We all know you could not have killed Sandra. It's an absurd, malicious accusation. What do you want me to tell Vernon?"

Anderson continued to stare at the floor and imagined it forming into a whirlpool with himself sucked in, unable to see the bottom.

"Tell him to get me out of here," Alex said.

"Calling him as soon as we get off. And the first thing we'll tell him we want him to do is to get you out so you can get back to work. You're going to be in good hands."

Lopez took the phone from Anderson and gripped his arm. "Come on, big guy. I'll show you to your suite."

Chapter Thirty-Three

Convalescence was not something Harold Samuels was good at. Nor was he good at acknowledging his mistakes. Or relying on others, including family. But here he was, wearing a green Land's End robe with his son's initials, IRS, embroidered on the front, sitting in a cushiony recliner with a hospital-supplied walker by his side like a loyal puppy. Liz had put on the big-screen TV for him but not to the channel he watched in Miami, so after she went back to the kitchen, he put it on mute. She told him they were concocting something heart-healthy, which he figured meant bland.

Harold took the moment to reflect on the past few weeks: how it began with celebration and ended in near death. Should he go back to Diana? His heart wanted to, but his head was telling him no. What had been clear to others was now becoming clear to him. Staring at the soundless screen, he shuffled options in his head. Would he need a caregiver? For a moment he thought he would have been better off had he never made it out of Belize. He needed to come up with a next step.

"Here I come with hot soup. Chicken vegetable. I made it. Alice is on the sautéed vegetables and fish. Dad the salad."

"Thanks, but you don't need to go through all this nonsense for me."

"Oh, we're not doing this for you," Liz said as she swung the table on wheels high enough to straddle the armrests over Harold's chair. "It's for us. You just happen to be here, so we pulled out another bowl. No trouble at all."

"You're just trying to make me feel good. Well, it won't work. I'm determined to feel bad."

"Let's see who wins."

"I hear you're learning to be a journalist?"

"Maybe. Think that's a good choice?"

"No."

"No? Why not?"

"Where I live, we have the *Miami Herald*, the *Miami Times*, *Miami Today*, *Miami Hurricane*, The *Sun Sentinel*. All my neighbors get at least one of them, maybe two. Know how I know? Because when I visit them, they're all piled up in the recycling can, unread. I can think of much better ways to throw money away. Slot machines, horse races, a game of poker. Even two hundred and fifty channels on cable television. At least you get some pleasure out of those things. But to take the newspaper off the step only to reposition it in a recycling bin, what's the pleasure in that? Waste of money, waste of paper, waste of trees. And when I heard you were going to be a journalist, I just started thinking about you spending all that hard work writing, only to be tossed in the trash. That's why I say no. What about pharmacy?"

"Wow. Never thought of all that," said Liz. "But I don't know anything about pharmacy."

"Neither did I until I learned. Hell, if I can learn it surely you can. You're a lot smarter than me. With pharmacy, people don't throw away the things they buy. They swallow them whole."

"Funny, that's what a lot of the newspaper readership does. I guess we have the same clientele."

"See, I told you you're smarter than me."

"Here's salad." Ivan put the big bowl and tongs on the big coffee table between his father and the couch and saw the remote on his father's lap. He glanced at the silent TV.

"Grandpa was just telling me I should forget journalism and become a pharmacist. What do you think, Dad?"

"Pharmacy is boring. Journalism is dangerous."

"So I'm back to square one. Should I be an accountant?"

"Now there's a fun job," Ivan said, filling Harold's salad bowl.

"Hey Alice," Liz raised her voice just a tad. "Should I be a lawyer?"

"I think," Alice walked in with the bowl of sautéed vegetables, "you make great soup. You should be a cook. Where's the remote?"

"I got it here," said Harold, "Why?"

"Turn it up. Quickly please."

"What's the fuss?" Harold reached down to fish out the remote that had slipped through his legs. He aimed it at the red dot under the screen, where the face of defense attorney Vernon Carlson loomed large and confident and adamant, making an opening remark for the press swarm, trying to give equal face time to the crowd and the camera. Harold turned up the volume.

"We just left Judge Griswald's courtroom for the arraignment of my innocent client, Alexander Anderson. The Commonwealth has charged my client, the distinguished long-time editor of the *Philadelphia Times,* with an unsubstantiated and ludicrous charge of first-degree murder. We have entered a plea of not guilty, of course. He did not kill journalist Sandra Wolf, God rest her soul. In fact, his heart weeps for her and her family."

A reporter yelled out, "The city says they have the evidence to prove Anderson is guilty, and the grand jury agrees. What do you say to that?"

Carlson addressed the entire crowd. "I've seen their evidence and I can tell you it's flimsy, highly questionable, and entirely circumstantial. The state needed a suspect and targeted my client. They do this all the time, believe me, I know. And just like all the other times, they will fall flat on their collective faces."

"Isn't it true Anderson was having an affair with Sandra Wolf?" a woman reporter asked.

"An affair? No."

"Well, if he was having an affair with her," said the same reporter, "isn't it possible he may have killed her in a fit of rage?"

"As you very well know, Margie, murder convictions are not decided on possibilities. They're decided on overwhelming evidence, the kind the state is completely lacking."

"What about the witness who ID'd him at Ms. Wolf's house the night of the murder?" shouted a young male reporter.

"Well, there's a good question. Tell me, Jay, what exact night did the murder take place? Was it even at night? Do the police know the answer to that question? Does anyone know the answer to that question? The police don't know. The prosecutor sure doesn't know. Does anybody know? I don't know. My client surely doesn't know because he wasn't there. No one knows. Their case is all guesswork."

"Then why isn't Anderson out on bail?" another reporter shouted. "Does the judge consider him a flight risk?"

"Now that sounds pretty ridiculous, don't you think? He's the editor of the biggest newspaper in Philadelphia. Where could he possibly go? He's recognized everywhere. Do you know where he would go? He'd go back to his office at the Times building to serve his readership. To serve all of you as he's been diligently doing for over thirty years. I'm confident bail will be set shortly.

"But I would like to make a plea. Whoever did kill Sandra Wolf, I ask you to come forward, give yourself up, and let this innocent man go back to his family, his wife, to the job he loves, to the city he cherishes, for the people who live in this city of brotherly love."

The image switched back to the anchor. "Action News asked some Philadelphians what they think of the arrest of Alexander Anderson for murder of journalist Sandra Wolf. Here's what some had to say:

"Do I think he killed her?" said a man in his twenties in Center City, wearing an Eagles T-shirt and a backwards baseball cap. "Yeah, I think he's capable. Everybody is capable of doing' crazy s**t when they get mad. You know what I'm saying'?"

"My question is," said a middle-aged man, pausing from mowing his lawn in the suburbs, "why would he kill her? What was the motive? That's what I want to know. That's the key. Maybe they got into an argument? I'm not saying getting into an argument is a motivation but if that's what happened, I'm not a lawyer but I think then we're looking at manslaughter. Or in this case woman slaughter. I mean I don't want to sound sexist."

"You're innocent until proven guilty, right?" said a middle-aged woman in Mount Airy. "So first they need to prove him guilty, and then nail his ass."

"Looks like Vernon Carlson is using the trial-in-the-public-arena trick," Alice said at the end of the news clip as she spooned steamy vegetables on her plate. "It's risky and makes it difficult to find jurors. I love his 'God rest her soul' line. Neat touch coming from an atheist."

"How do you know he's an atheist?" Liz asked, taking a seat on the couch with a plate of food.

"He told me. Actually, I believe he told me he's an agnostic. Which makes his comment even more ironic."

"When did you speak to him?" Ivan asked, standing while he sipped soup.

"At the Eddie Malano trial. Carlson was his lawyer. He told me this when he was trying to hit on me."

"Oh yes. I remember you telling me that," Ivan said. "But Malano is in prison."

"For extortion, drugs, and running prostitution. Not murder. Carlson got him off for murder. I can certainly understand why Carlson wants to represent Anderson. New type of clientele. Almost respectable. Unless he's really a murderer."

"I think," Liz added, "the fact that he's using a criminal lawyer that gets gangster murderers off tells you he's guilty and needs the best representation to prove reasonable doubt."

"My granddaughter's got a point. The guy is guilty as hell."

"What do you think, Alice?" Ivan asked.

"As you heard him say, you need overwhelming evidence for a murder conviction. That's why he's attacking the evidence as flawed and insufficient."

"Didn't he say something about the grand jury?" Liz asked. "That it agreed with the district attorney? Doesn't that tell you the prosecutor has a strong case?"

"I'm actually surprised they went to the grand jury. It's not necessary in Pennsylvania."

"Why not?' Harold asked chewing on his salad. "What's different about Pennsylvania?"

"We don't have an indicting grand jury like other states do. We got rid of that in the early 1990s. What we have is something called an investigating grand jury that makes a presentation to the judge about whether there's sufficient evidence to recommend that a case should go to trial. Usually, the District Attorney would only make a request for a grand jury if he believes there may be witness intimidation or there are too many possible defendants. We don't have either one here. My guess is that because this is such a high-profile case the District Attorney wanted the grand jury's concurrence. And now that he has it, he feels comfortable going forward with indictment."

"Meaning he's probably guilty and this Carlson guy will get him off like he does his mob murderers," Liz said putting her plate down on the coffee table. "And they'll be no justice for Sandra Wolf."

"Let's not jump the gun," said Alice. "There's a whole trial yet to go, a real trial, not our own little trial here in the dining room."

"Well, I'm done. Everything was terrific," Harold said, wiping his mouth and hands on a napkin. "Compliments to the chefs."

Alice took Harold's plate and headed to the kitchen, feeling what she thought was Harold's used napkin between the plate and her hand. But in the kitchen, she saw it was a folded-up piece of paper. She unfolded it. It was a check made out to Alice with a note written in the memo line: 'hospital plane—thanks.'

Chapter Thirty-Four

One of the wonders of Philadelphia was the ten-mile bicycle path on Kelly Drive that stretched along the bank of the Schuylkill River, passed Boathouse Row, the Art Museum and continued down to the Penn's Landing Dog Park.

On Saturday morning, Ivan parked his car a few hundred feet from the City Ave entrance to Kelly Drive. He pulled his bike off the bike rack and, with his graying ponytail tied tight, he slipped on his red and blue bike helmet, put on his wire-rimmed sunglasses with lens that viewed the world in twilight and started on the trail.

He passed street vendors selling water ice, soft pretzels and ice cream, zigzagged his way through the crowded corners and down a hill under a bridge where he picked up speed to give himself a seamless momentum to the upswing climb. At the end of the path was a sign promising more bike path coming soon. He'd been seeing that sign for the last three years, but so far there were no signs of further construction.

Ivan took a break near one of the grassy knolls by a wooden bench tucked in a cul-de-sac of bushes melded to a slab of concrete. He removed his helmet, sat on the bench, and sipped from his water bottle. He watched the cars crossing the bridge above as the noon sun reflected off his sunglasses. On the bench where he sat, there was a small medal memorial tag on the backrest paying homage to Rob Stuart, a Schuylkill River trail advocate who died suddenly at the age of forty nine. Another young death. A man noted for engaging in hard negotiations with city politicians over budgets and designs, he fought to make this shared corner of the world a better place. Now, years later, he was memorialized by a tiny tin on a park bench, barely visible and easily unnoticeable.

Ivan couldn't help but ponder the similarities of these young lost lives; Stuart, dedicated to improving the park; his wife Nancy, dedicated to helping the sick; Sandra Wolf, whose writings and warnings may have led to her murder. What is it about God that takes away so many of the good and leaves us with so many of the bad?' More religiously and philosophically capable people than he asked the same questions and came up with unsatisfying answers. So why bother?

Ivan's attention was drawn to a wobbly cyclist who seemed to be staring at him as he rode his bike. It was one of those Blue Cross rental bikes scattered throughout the park and various places in the city. They had weirdly covered wheels like stationary bikes. Ivan thought that renting this Blue Cross bike could not have been on this man's mind when he got dressed this morning; he wore black leather shoes, long dark pants, and a blue button-down shirt. The man veered awkwardly off the path and headed towards Ivan applying the pedal breaks just before he was about to crash into the Robert Stuart bench.

"Sorry about that. Been a while since I rode a bike."

"The clothes you're wearing don't help," Ivan said, instinctively moving his legs out of danger.

Straddling the bike, the man reached for the water bottle. "Yeah, I seem to have a problem with appropriate apparel. You should see what I wear at the Phillies games. You're Ivan Samuels?"

Ivan took a closer look at the man and realized who he was. "I plead the Fifth."

"I'm Vernon Carlson. I'm the attorney defending Alexander Anderson, the man charged with the murder of Sandra Wolf." He offered his hand. He was a bit younger than Ivan, neat hair, dorky black sunglasses resting on his forehead. But his voice, his eyes, and his hand—which Ivan took—embodied all the confidence of a Philadelphia attorney who knew what he was doing, even though he knew what he was doing may be the morally wrong thing.

"Anybody who watches the news knows who you are."

Ivan remembered seeing him years back on the six o'clock news discussing why his client, a mid-level mobster accused of murdering another mobster, pled not guilty. "The evidence is just not there to find my client guilty," Carlson bellowed. "And I will prove him innocent." Indeed, he did just that. When his client was acquitted, there he was again on the Eleven O'clock News: "I applaud the jury for doing their job, for doing the right thing." Ivan remembered one reporter from the *Philadelphia Times* shouted a statement that contorted into a question. "But that doesn't necessarily mean he didn't kill him."

"It most certainly does," was Carlson's quick and resolute response.

On TV, Vernon Carlson looked large and in charge. The bobble-headed reporters with their microphones swirling around him gave him the aura of a rock star. Ivan remembered Alice noticing the space between his shirt collar and his suit collar, pointing out his suits were not tailored.

"Mind if I sit down?"

"You know, Mr. Carlson, this spot on the Schuylkill trail is not exactly where one would randomly meet someone. You were looking for me."

Carlson swung his leg off the bike, pushed the kickstand down and sat next to Ivan. Ivan moved over.

"Ah, that's better. The seat on this rental bike is so small and hard and pointy, I don't mind telling you, it was killing my ass. Look, I have my people. We all do. It's all part of the job, finding things, finding people. Staying a step ahead. Knowledge is power, and when it's in the hand of the lawyer defending you, well, it could be the difference between life imprisonment and acquittal. I don't mind saying, I've been pretty good lately at acquittals."

"Not so good at getting your client out on bail, though," Ivan said.

"The main thing is, Ivan, it's just you and me in this little corner behind these bushes. Me the defense attorney, you, the agent in charge of the tax audit of the *Philadelphia Times*."

Ivan took a sip of water.

"Regarding bail, that was retribution for Anderson taking pot shots at the judge for how he handled a police brutality case seven years ago. Some people carry grudges to their grave. But if they can find a way to screw you, they will."

"You believe your client is innocent?" Ivan asked.

"My usual answer to that question is that it really doesn't matter what I believe. What matters is doing the best job I possibly can in order to get my client off. But in this particular case—" He shrugged, looking a little surprised. "Yes."

"Whatever it is you want from me, I'm sure it's not something I can give you."

Vernon took a sip of his Dasani. "I would never ask you to do anything you're uncomfortable doing."

"You've already done that. Asking if you could sit down."

"I get it. I'm an unexpected, unwanted add-on to your day today. I'm an intrusion. I am that guy. You're not the only person I've cornered like this, and you won't be the last. This is my life. I don't know what you think of Alex Anderson as a person or as an editor or what you think of the *Philadelphia Times* itself – I have no idea nor do I care. I wouldn't read the newspaper either, but I have no choice. Maybe I'll pick up a case when I read it. Even when I'm not working, I'm working. Like now. Like when I'm having a drink at my favorite bar McCrossen's to contemplate my strategies. Do you know that bar?"

"I do."

"I never see you there."

"I didn't say I go there. I just said I know it."

"You'd make a good lawyer. Why didn't you become a lawyer?"

"Now you're starting to sound like my mother."

Vernon sat back and looked over the river. "I think you and I have a lot in common."

"I doubt that."

"You want me to be brutally honest?"

Ivan turned to look at this guy sitting next to him. He had never met Vernon Carlson before but now he was challenging him to turn his soul inside out. What was with this guy?

"Shoot," Ivan said.

"Vernon took another sip of his water. "God, I wish this was Bud and not water. But my PI warned against it."

"What's a PI?"

"Private investigator. I use him for tracking people down. You, for instance. I'm on my own, Ivan. I have a secretary who is also my office manager and my bookkeeper and keeps my life on course. Without her I'd be in shambles. I can't do it all. So I use a PI."

"You had me followed?"

"Don't sweat it. I needed to know the best time to catch you. Where nobody would see us."

Ivan looked around and saw two women in their thirties jogging. Their sweat-stained sleeveless exercise tops were printed with the words 'I love her' with arrows pointing at each other. They had mermaid tattoos on their arms and legs —all illustrating how serious they take their run, their art, and each other. Vernon saw them too.

"Not anybody who matters anyway."

"I can't help you, Vernon."

"What if I told you, you could? You're not going to change 'can't' to 'won't' are you? Which brings me back to telling you how much we have in common. For one, we both only use part of our brain for thinking seriously. The other part we use for cynicism. Why? Because we're both sort of pissed, yet we'd do anything for the people we love. I don't have anyone I particularly love right now so that makes us different. We both share a contempt for the idiots we've worked for, yet for some odd genetic reason we're underachievers. You're a CPA with a capped income. Me, I'm a lawyer with a messy little office in a walk-up on Chestnut Street overlooking a McDonalds. At some point, could be sooner or later, preferably later, between walking up those stairs and eating those hamburgers, I'm going to have a heart attack."

"Looks to me like everybody loves you. You're sought after every time you leave the courtroom."

"Publicity doesn't translate to love. Nor is it necessarily lucrative, I'm sorry to say."

Ivan flips the lip of his water bottle, looked out at the rowers on Delaware River and took a sip.

"There's lots of big law firms in Philly. If you went with one of them, you'd probably be a partner by now."

Vernon nodded his head. "I'm not what they wanted. Not exactly their type. I wish I could change that. Change my type. But to tell you the truth, Ivan, I don't know what exactly my type is."

Ivan looked him over. "Looks to me like you're the *Philadelphia Times* type."

"That's actually pretty accurate and pretty funny. And there's two reasons for that. One, the *Times* is in perpetual bankruptcy, but they know how to get a damn good lawyer at a bargain price; a lot less than any of the high-powered Philadelphia suits, lord knows we have a barrel full of them in this city. That's our city—brotherly love; that is if you can find a brother you can love or trust. I never could. And two, those firms don't like to lose. They believe he's guilty."

"Why don't you?"

"Because I've seen the evidence, I heard the prosecutors' rendition of what they think are damning facts. But all they have is speculation."

"From what I'm reading in the papers they have quite a bit and everything points to Anderson; DNA, fingerprints, no forced entry, that bicyclist IDing him in front of her house the night of the murder, him being the last person seen at her house, his tie being the murder weapon. How do you overcome all that?"

"How did you know about the tie?"

Ivan blinked. "I thought I read about it in the papers."

"No, that was not publicly revealed. Sounds to me you know more about this case than I thought you did, or at least more than you should. You're hiding something."

Ivan took a deep breath. "Not from anyone who matters."

Vernon leaned back and took a long, slow look at Ivan. "Well, isn't this interesting. I could have you subpoenaed. Or you can just tell me now."

Ivan took a sip of water and looked out over the river.

"Is there anything else, Mr. Carlson?"

"The biker never saw him actually go into the house. He's also not the type to commit murder over a story. Yeah, he has a temper, but in the end he's a newspaper editor. He fights with words; he fights a bad story with his own lousy story. Not by strangling a journalist with his Jerry Garcia necktie. Why does an IRS tax auditor know about the alleged murder weapon?"

"Maybe you should get your PI on it."

"There's the cynical side of your brain kicking in."

"You forgot to throw into your mix the so-called alleged affair Anderson was having with Sandra. I know you denied it on the news. Here's how most of the public see it: Anderson demanded she not publish those pieces but she refused. They got into a heated argument and things got out of hand. He has a history of arrests and a tendency toward violence. He could have killed her in a moment of rage for exercising her First Amendment rights. At the very least he'd be looking at manslaughter."

Vernon cocked his head, looking at Ivan with a sudden revelation. "So it is true what they say about the IRS. Guilty until proven innocent."

Ivan took a long last swig of his water, picked up his hot-rod red bike helmet, stood up and strapped it snugly on his head.

"I see why you're on your own, Mr. Carlson."

"I will do what I need to do to keep my client from going to prison. Sorry about the IRS crack. That's just my crude attempt at being whimsical. But you have a problem now Ivan. You need to tell me what you know."

"If you think Anderson is innocent, don't you think the best way to prove that is to find the person whose guilty?"

"Anderson told me you might possibly found something during the audit. Something he's concerned about. Whatever it is you find, he's asking that you tell me about it first."

"Really, now. Why would I do that?"

"For one, he's still the editor. And it might help find the person that did murder Sandra Wolf."

"Wouldn't I first go to the police with that information?"

"They wouldn't know how to use it. My client would. Do we have an agreement? We're talking about an innocent man's life."

Ivan hopped on his extra cushioned bike seat. "You need to invest in a real bike, Vernon. Riding that rental, you look like a dork."

"Doesn't matter to me. Keep me informed, I'll hold off on the subpoena. We have a deal?"

Ivan clicked on his helmet. As he pushed back onto the trail, he said. "I'll think about it."

Chapter Thirty-Five

Ivan and Keisha drove through morning rush-hour traffic west on the I-76 Schuylkill Expressway, squeezing into a bottleneck of three converging lanes. Ivan veered into the right lane. It was bordered by overgrown shrubbery that hid the exit sign to Old Gulph Road, his exit of course, so it took only a few moments to find the quiet suburban neighborhood where his quarry lived. At the end of Old Monk Place stood one large, lonely colonial-style house surrounded by a meticulously cropped lawn and exotic flower landscape. Considering the controversies his work got him into, Ivan was not surprised to see that Alex and his wife Sonia secluded themselves from the city.

Ivan pulled into a circular driveway and parked behind a BMW. In front of the BMW was a Lexus.

"That's probably Louie Vargas' car, their accountant," Ivan noted. "They want us to go around the back."

"Oh really?' Keisha said. "Why is that?"

"He didn't say, I didn't ask."

Strolling to the back was like taking a self-walking tour of a miniature Longwood Gardens. Flourishing green, red, and yellow flowers edged with hearty green plants were artfully arranged along the side of the house and at the edges of the spacious trimmed lawn.

"This is why the back," Keisha said. "To show off."

Ivan knocked on the one of the six rectangular panes of the glass back door.

"It's open," Ivan heard Louie's quick voice called out. Ivan and Keisha entered and were immediately accosted by two bear-sized shaggy-haired dogs.

"Whoa," Keisha stepped back. "Are we being attacked? Definitely not up for this." The dogs were inquisitive, nosing them up and down but surprisingly quiet.

"Don't mind them," Louie called from the next room. "They're just making sure you're not from the IRS. They'll leave you alone once they had enough of smelling you. Which is more than I can say for myself. Come in here."

"Where's here?" Ivan called back.

"You need a GPS?"

When the dogs backed away, wagging, Ivan and Keisha walked through a doorless entryway to the dining room, where neat piles of paper sat on the spacious table. At the head sat Louie, gray hair combed back over a large square head, thick gray mustache, and piercing big blue eyes shielded by thick-lensed microscope-like glasses. He wore a maroon shirt unbuttoned at the top, proudly exposing gray chest hair and a gold necklace. Quite the contrast from how Ivan and Keisha dressed in their business best.

"Don't mind me if I don't get up," he said without looking up from jotting something down. "I'm a little tired after drudging up all the damned documents you wanted. Now that they're here, knock yourself out. You said you wanted to talk to Sonia? Well, she has something she wants to say to you too. And so do I."

Sonia Anderson emerged from the kitchen like a ghost and on cue. She was tall, poised, and dressed smartly in a light green pants outfit. Her shoulder-length black hair perfectly framed her high forehead and cheekbones, bright green eyes, narrow nose and questioning lips with just a touch of makeup. She's capable, Ivan thought, of smiling and perhaps even laughing, but probably not lately and certainly not today. Today she gave a no-nonsense look to Ivan, then eyeballed Keisha suspiciously. Ivan's attention, however, was drawn to the artwork hanging on the wall behind her.

"Before I sit down and answer your questions," Sonia said, standing behind one of the dining room chairs, her hands gently placed on top of its cushioned back. "There is something I want to say."

"Please do, Mrs. Anderson," Ivan said giving her his full attention.

"I want you both to know that I think what you're doing is a disgrace. And when I say you, I don't mean just the United States government, but I mean you two personally. Government doesn't function without individual people behind it. My husband is sitting in jail, falsely charged, I'm here alone and vulnerable as you can see, and you come into my house, taking advantage of his absence, taking advantage of me, of my situation. You have absolutely no compassion. I was going to have my lawyer present, mind you, but Louie, who I trust, persuaded me not to, at least not right now, so I am taking his advice, for the moment. But I reserve the right to have my lawyer present in the future, depending on how this, this interrogation goes. Louie says I need to cooperate so I'm cooperating. But you should know I have a meeting with the Arboretum Association of Montgomery County in just an hour and it will take me twenty minutes to get there. So I hope we understand each other, or rather at least I hope you understand me, which is really all I care about. Now, I am going to sit down."

Sonia kept her eyes on the chair as she pulled it out even though she didn't need to.

"And you should know one more thing at the get-go," Louie added. "We consider this audit Alex's audit, Alex's problem, not Sonia's. I can save you a lot of time and trouble and tell you that Sonia didn't know and had no reason to know any of the shenanigans that Alex may have been up to, what monies from the *Times* Alex was using personally, if any, because that still has not been established. But I'm just telling you now she's innocent. She's an innocent spouse. I want to make that clear from the get-go. We clear, Mr. Samuels?"

"Mrs. Anderson," Ivan began, facing her and ignoring Louie, "if you want to have your lawyer present you certainly have the right to do."

"As I said, you have less than an hour of my time."

"Is it okay if we call you Sonia?" Ivan asked.

"Doesn't matter to me. Just make this quick."

"Let me assure you, Sonia, we're not here with any predisposition. We're here to conduct an audit. We let the facts speak for themselves. You'll be afforded the opportunity to dispute our findings, and you have a right to file an innocent spouse claim, as Louie mentioned, if you believe you didn't know or had any reason to be responsible for any transaction made by your spouse."

"Alex," Sonia says. "My spouse has a name."

"He most certainly does," Ivan continued. "His name and yours are on numerous business travel documents that became personal pleasure travel. For instance, travel to Yosemite, The Grand Tetons, Zion National Park, Key West, and England. You do recall going to these places with your husband? With your husband Alex?"

"Of course I do. They weren't so long ago, and I'm not so old that I can't remember."

"I also want to establish that you don't work for the *Times*, is that correct?"

Sonia sighed. "What kind of question is that?"

"So as far as your part goes, these trips were all pleasure."

"Pleasure but not all pleasurable."

"Meaning?" Ivan inquired.

"Not every place you go is a pleasure. Haven't you traveled? Do you really need to know this for a tax audit?"

"I need to know this. I need to know if you were aware of any compensation that Alex received that was not reported on the tax return."

"What on earth are you talking about?" Sonia scowled.

"The answer to that question," Louie piped up. "Is no. An emphatic no."

"The reason I ask is that Keisha and I are going to conduct what we call an indirect method to discern any unreported income. Part of what that means is we look at all the deposits that went into you bank accounts, weed out any that would not be taxable, like gifts or loans, and once we do that, what's left should be the taxable income, such as Alex's salary, investment income, rent from your shore property. Is there any other income that you know of that I haven't mentioned?"

"I can't think of any. Louie?"

"No, I can't. But if you find anything like that, I can assure you Sonia is not aware of it, not part of it, and completely innocent of it."

Sonia looked at her watch.

"I have one more question," Ivan said.

"Go ahead, as long as it's pertinent. Time's a-wasting."

"I couldn't help noticing that artwork you have hanging on the wall behind you. What can you tell me about it?"

The other thing Ivan couldn't help noticing was Sonia's blinking. The only time she blinked since she walked into the dining room.

"You like it?" Sonia bounced back. "It's Islamic art. Keisha, you must know something about Islamic art. Don't you?"

"As a matter of fact, I do. I paint, when I'm not doing tax audits."

"The reason I ask," Ivan continued, "is because there is a painting very similar to yours hanging on a wall at the *Philadelphia Times*. Did the *Times* purchase the one on your wall?"

"Oh, I see where this is going. No, Mr. Samuels, I purchased that one myself. The artist is local and both the *Times* – Alex and I like to support local artists. The *Times* paid for its art on their wall, I bought mine with my own funds."

"Yours and Alex's together?"

"My own funds, as I just got finished telling you." Sonia checked her watch. "Any more questions? Because I need to leave."

Keisha checked her own watch. "I thought you said an hour. It's only been fifteen minutes."

Sonia stared coldly at Keisha. "Do you have any more questions?"

"When did you purchase it?" Ivan asked.

Sonia turned to Ivan. "When did I purchase it? I don't remember, why?"

"A year ago, two years ago?"

"Perhaps. It's all in that pile of crap you made Louie drag up."

"Thank you, Sonia," said Ivan. "You enjoy the rest of your day at the Arboretum Association of Montgomery County. If we do come across something we need to ask you about we'll let Louie here know and you can get back to us."

With overstated delicacy Sonia pushed back from the table, got up, and turned to go. Then she turned back.

"Mr. Samuels, you say that with a snicker of cynicism in your voice. But you need to understand the value to one's equilibrium to keep a semblance of continuity during troubling days such as these. Keeping a normal routine is imperative to keep anxiety under control. That's what my therap— that's what my friends tell me. I'm going through a perplexing time but I'm going to enjoy this day outdoors with flowers and friends. So you all here have a pleasant day shuffling through these piles of papers. Because that's what you do. While I go out with my friends. Because that's what I do." She turned to go, then turned back again and smiled. "If you haven't been to the Arboretum, Mr. Samuels, I would suggest you plan to do so and learn to appreciate the beauty this world has to offer."

"Nice meeting you too, Mrs. Anderson," Keisha said to Sonia's back as she walked away without replying.

"One thing about Sonia." Louie noted when the front door closed, "she got her priorities straight. Anyway, all the records for the last three years are here. I'll be in the kitchen doing my own work. And speaking of kitchen, Sonia may come off cold and harsh, but she did have her maid fix you up a couple of sandwiches for lunch. What do you think of that?"

"Wow, that was very kind of her," exclaimed Keisha.

"Kind of Sonia or her maid?" Louie chuckled. "When you're ready I'll tell Juanita, I think that's her name, and she'll bring it out."

As they had discussed, Keisha tackled the tax deductions and Ivan dove into the indirect determination of income. Through the humming of the refrigerator and the occasional chirping of birds, the only sounds for hours were the tapping of three keyboards and the shuffling of papers. At noon Juanita brought out tuna and egg salad sandwiches on whole wheat along with a pitcher of nana iced tea.

An hour after lunch, Ivan stepped outside for fresh air and pulled out his cell phone. Then he went to see Louie in the kitchen.

"Keisha and I are about to take off."

"Oh, good. Everything in order, I take it?"

"Here's where we stand. All the personal travel Alex charged to the *Times* will be added to the Anderson's income for each of the three years. Sonia went on those trips, and she knew they were business trips. If you want to make an innocent spouse claim that's your right but I'll tell you right now I'll deny it. You can appeal my decision if you want to, that's your prerogative."

"So you're gonna play hardball. We can play hardball too. What else?"

"Here's a list of deductions Keisha put together that we're disallowing unless you can show documentation to prove otherwise. A lot of charitable deductions."

Louie took the list, glanced at it, and said, "No problem. We can prove all that, I'm sure."

"I thought everything pertaining to the years we're auditing was in those boxes you gave us. Why weren't the documents pertaining to the charitable deductions there?"

"Maybe we overlooked it. We're human, you know."

"And here's another list. My indirect method to reconcile the income reported on the return. It's off by a hundred thousand each year. Could you think of any explanation for that?"

"Yeah. Your indirect method is bullshit."

"We're looking at a tax deficiency of between forty and fifty thousand dollars each year. That doesn't include interest and penalties."

"You must feel very proud of yourselves."

"I know we planned to make this a two-day audit, but we'll give you and Mrs. Anderson some time to look over what I gave you and see if you have any explanation for the discrepancy. I'll call you to schedule the next meeting."

"Sonia is a busy woman. You're lucky she was able to see you today. She'll have to see how she can fit you in to her schedule of civic duties."

"Oh, and one last thing," Ivan said as he turned to go. "I don't suppose Sonia gave the artist from whom she bought the painting a 1099 form, did she?"

Louie looks straight at Ivan then started to laugh. "That's a joke, right?"

"It's actually a serious question but I can see why you think it's funny."

"You planning on penalizing her for that? For not issuing a 1099?"

"Depends. Do we need to go out the back door or can we use the front where my car is parked?"

"The back. Always the back for you."

Chapter Thirty-Six

On the drive back Ivan said to Keisha, "Mind if we stop for coffee? There's something I want to show you."

"We're still on the clock right, right?"

"We are. Have you ever been to Valerio Coffee Roasters in Manayunk?"

"No but I like the sound of it. 'Roasters in Manayunk'. Sounds aromatic."

"A change of pace from Starbucks. Good pastries too."

Ivan got off the expressway at Belmont Avenue and soon arrived at the coffee shop. Two elegant, tall semi-circular glass storefront walls sandwiched a wooden entrance door with a mosaic tile floor. Ivan and Keisha walked into a coffee-fragrant café with wooden plank floors and a ceiling of swinging light bulbs hooked onto several wires that looked like a mini zipline. Ivan ordered a chemex slow pour, Keisha the cortado, and they agreed to split a blueberry muffin.

They took a table in a semi-secluded corner of the café. Ivan cut the muffin with a plastic fork and gave Keisha the bigger piece. "What's your gut feeling about Sonia Anderson?" Ivan asked.

"Husband's in jail and she goes out with her friends looking at flowers. Odd."

"And what do you think of Louie's chances of prevailing on the innocent spouse claim?"

"Well, you already told him you're denying it, which I agree with. I mean, how can she not know? And where is that additional income coming from?"

"Most of the deposits are going into an account in Alex's name only and I wouldn't be surprised if these deposits are from Rabobank, the same foreign bank where the deposits for the fake advertising income came from. We need to look further into that when we're at the office.

"So now you're saying Sonia may be innocent?"

"Let me show you something else," Ivan reached into in his inside jacket pocket, pulled out an envelope and took out a canceled check. He placed it on the table.

"This check was written to Ian Jefferies, the artist who did the Islamic art painting. Drawn from the *Times* bank account."

Keisha scrutinized the check. "Ian Jeffreys, five hundred dollars. Dated last year. Not sure I would pay that much."

"Look at the back."

"His endorsement and oh wow, deposited in Rabobank. You think he's part of this scheme?

"It's certainly possible."

"I mean, I know it's not your typical PNC but that doesn't mean lots of people don't have an account there, right?" Keisha asked.

"Very few ordinary people in America have accounts there. Now let me show you something else."

Ivan took out three checks and laid them on the table in front of Keisha. "These checks are payable to Ian Jefferies and signed by Sonia Anderson," Ivan explained. "Anything catch your attention besides the red azalea background design?"

"Egads!" Keisha almost choked on her muffin. "The amounts! Two for nine thousand dollars, one for seven thousand!"

"The memo line says 'art'," Ivan pointed out.

"How many pieces did she buy?"

"I only saw one."

"Did you show this to Louie?"

"Not yet. Wanted to mull it over a bit. Noticed how Sonia tightened up when I asked about the painting?"

"I did notice."

"See how she scurried out of her house, earlier than she needed to? Three checks all under ten thousand dollars. What does that say to you?"

"Of course. A currency transaction report is sent to the IRS from a bank when there's a deposit over ten thousand dollars."

"Three checks under ten thousand dollars totaling twenty-five thousand dollars for a painting you just told me you wouldn't pay $500 for. You said you know something about Islamic art. What can you tell me about that painting we saw on the wall?"

"Oh, well, I don't know a lot, really. I've always dabbled in art when I was young and still do a bit. My mother thought I had talent, so she made me take a summer class at the Moore's Summer Art & Design Institute."

"But what can you tell me about the Ian Jeffries paintings? We saw one at the *Times* office and now on Anderson's dining room wall."

"Well, the main thing I know about Islamic art, it's supposed to illustrate harmony with Allah. The art is part calligraphy, arabesque patterns, geometric patterns, and floral patterns. When you have all that, you have creative harmony. And when you have Allah in your life you have harmony. So all Islamic art is a reflection of having Allah in your life. Does that make sense?"

"From an artistic, religious point of view, yes," Ivan took a bite of blueberry muffin.

"The painting at the Anderson house and on the wall at the *Times* office, from what I saw, they both have those four components I just mentioned. I gotta say this though; the artist, this Ian Jeffries, or whatever his real name is, he knows what he's doing."

"Do you mind if I ask you something?" Ivan said, taking a sip of his chemex.

"Go ahead," Keisha answered.

"This idea of harmony and balance in Islamic art that you're telling me about; that's all fine and good as far as art goes, but if that's what Islam is about, harmony and balance, then how do things like 9/11 and San Bernardino happen?"

"Yeah, well, there's a lot to know about Islam. Just so you know, that's not my Islam. I think I mentioned I'm with the Ahmediyya mosque."

"Yeah, I don't think I ever heard of it."

"Probably not, and neither did I until I went. It's different from the Islam you hear and read about in the media. You hear about Sunnis, Shia, maybe Salafists. In terms of Islam, it's relatively new, like the late eighteen hundreds. It actually began as a revival movement within Islam, emphasizing peace, love, justice, and sanctity of life. Not violence. It rejects violence outright. And where it's really different? You probably heard Islam believes that Mohammad was the last prophet, right?"

"Okay."

"Well, we don't believe that. We believe he was a prophet but not the last prophet. Ahamdiyya believes somebody else was."

"Who would that be?' Ivan asked.

"A man named Mirza Ghulam Ahmed of Qadian, India. Never heard of him, right?"

Ivan shook his head. "Should I?"

"I know. Most people when they think of Islam and Muslims think Muhammad. But believe it or not, this sect, the Ahamdiyya, has about twenty million followers all over the world."

"So why haven't I ever heard of them?"

"Maybe because they don't do terrorism. They're peaceful. This Mirza Ghulam Ahmed wrote books and gave talks about changing radical views. And the part that also spoke to me is that he accepts the teachings of other religions —not just Mohammad but Jesus and Abraham and Moses and Buddha and lots of others. I'm not saying it all makes sense, but it makes the most sense, and I feel comfortable there. And do you know what port they came to when they first came to this country?

"I'm going to say Philadelphia."

"That's right! Brotherly love!"

"Getting back to our artist. The fact that he does Islamic art and knows what he's doing, can you tell from that whether he's one of you or one of them?"

"As far as art is concerned, all Islamic art is pretty much the same. So," Keisha took her last bit of muffin, "where do we go from here?"

Ivan took his last sip of his chemex. "Did I tell you I saw his artwork one other place besides the *Times* and the Anderson home?"

"I don't think you did."

"I saw it hanging on a wall at a mosque in south Philly. Not one of your mosques, though. Would you like to pay them a visit with me?"

"For what purpose?"

"When I went outside for a breather during our lunch break, I had the office do an inquiry on the name Ian Jeffries. Nothing came up. Off the grid. He was paid over twenty-five thousand dollars for artwork that we know of and no record of him filing a tax return. I think that's worth a visit, don't you?"

"Can we do that? I mean, I can see we expand our audit to Alex Anderson personally because he's part of the *Times*. But this Ian Jeffries?"

"Ordinarily I would agree. But this case we're working, with FBI involvement? This situation is anything but ordinary. If you don't feel comfortable coming with me, it's totally understandable."

"No, we're a team. I'm coming with."

Chapter Thirty-Seven

Her confidence beefed up after interviewing Michael Banks, Liz called the *Times* for an interview with Conrad Benson. When she told him Sandra Wolf was her instructor at Temple, he agreed to give her 45 minutes.

She read over her notes on the SEPTA bus to the *Times* office and wondered if her questions would cause the powerful publisher to throw her out of his office. If he did, it would mean she was asking the right questions.

At the front desk, the secretary Prim put her hand over her cell phone. "Be a sec." Liz smiled and stood there, listening to Prim's side of the conversation. "I'm the wrong person to ask what to do. I have enough damn problems of my own with Tommy. What are you sorry about? What does your sorry butt do for me? Gotta go, ma."

Turning her scowl to a smile she said to Liz, "Hi, sorry."

"Oh, no problem. Love your hair! I have an appointment with Mr. Conrad Benson. I'm Liz Samuels with the Temple News."

Prim cocked her head and examined Liz. "You're the second Samuels in a week. And before that, never in my whole life met a Samuels. Huh. Follow me."

Liz followed Prim through a door that led to a bustling newsroom filled with energetic chatter. Reporters stood at desks wearing headphones and talking into microphones; others urgently pounded keyboards as if they were in a race against Mother Nature and Time itself. Noise traffic, foot traffic, and Liz wanted nothing more at that moment than to merge into it, be a part of the flow as she followed Prim through the lefts and rights of the hallway. She completely forgot to ask if the other Samuels was an older man with a ponytail.

"Your two-thirty is here," Prim said at the entrance to Benson's office.

"Come. Sit. Won't be a minute." Benson was focused on his desktop monitor and tapping away. "Prim, get her a bottle of water."

"Oh, no thanks, brought my own bottle," Liz pulled it out of her bag as she sat on the green leather guest chair across Benson's table.

"Finishing up here, won't be a second. "When you told me Sandra Wolf was your instructor at Temple I thought the least I could do to pay homage to our blessed Sandra is grant an interview to her student." Benson turned the monitor aside. "You did say journalism is your major?"

"Yes, and I was very fortunate to have her as an instructor. She was incredible."

"Tell me in what way?"

"Oh, in every way: how to craft an article, ask the right questions, how to get to the real story. She gave great constructive criticism. Do you mind?" Liz showed Benson her tape recorder.

"Did you know she came from Ohio?" Benson asked.

"I did."

"A quick study, though. Picked up on the city's faults and strength in no time. Not everybody loved her, but everyone respected her. That too is an achievement. And now you tell me she was a good journalism instructor as well. Let's find out if that was true, shall we?"

"Yeah, okay," Liz put the tape recorder on Benson's desk and turned it on.

"You should ask before you put on a tape recorder. I would think Sandra would have told you that."

Liz was taken aback but didn't let Benson's comment unnerve her. She turned it off but kept her finger on the button and looked at him. "Sandra told me I should always use a recorder when I can to make sure the interviewee is quoted correctly."

"Good advice. Go ahead," he said with an I'm-testing-you sort of smile. Liz pushed the button and moved her chair closer to Benson's desk.

"It seems to me the *Times* has really had its world rocked recently. The shocking and sudden death of Sandra, the arrest of editor Alexander Anderson accused of her murder. How are the *Times* and you handling it all?"

Benson sat back. "You captured our situation precisely, Liz. The sadness of Sandra's death, the inconceivable murder charge against Alex. It's all been, how should I put it?" Bensen paused and looked out the window. "Surreal. First, and primarily, our hearts, our collective hearts, go out to Sandra's family. We've been in close contact, and they know we are there for them for whatever they need. So yes, we are in mourning. But none of this has stopped us from publishing our paper. I'm proud to say we haven't missed a single issue. We put in place an interim executive editor, Nathan Schmidt, who's doing a terrific job under the circumstances; We have no plans of letting down our readership. We're reeling but we're resilient. And I think our readers realize that too. Believe it or not, circulation is up."

"You said 'the inconceivable murder charge against Alex Anderson.' Why do you say 'inconceivable'?"

"Because it's inconceivable that he would do such a thing. I've known Alex for decades and he's not a man that would commit murder. It's beyond comprehension. The police are under pressure to make an arrest so they think they could put bits of evidence together and make the charges stick. It's absurd. And when it's proven in court that he's innocent, the police and the district attorney, the whole lot of them will hang their heads in shame. Make sure you print that."

"Word for word, sir. You mention bits of evidence. But what are your thoughts about the witness who spotted Anderson at Sandra's house that night? Does that make you hesitate?"

Benson shook his head in exasperation. "It's ridiculous. Sandra and Alex conferred with each other about stories all the time, both in the office and outside the office. That's the job. In fact, that afternoon she interviewed the leader of the teacher's union about a possible strike. Nothing unusual about them working together outside the office, and I'm sure his lawyer, Vernon Carlson, will render that testimony worthless."

"Then let me ask you this." Liz felt her stomach flutter, but pushed on. "You said they conferred on stories. If that's the case, then how did those last three articles she wrote end up being published in the *Philadelphia Chronicle*?"

"Poor judgment on Sandra's part, I have to say. We told Sandra we weren't ready to publish those stories. We needed to do more fact checking. She was making a serious accusation about a prominent citizen of Philadelphia. You don't make those kinds of accusations unless they can be air-tight verified. But Sandra was anxious. She took the matter into her own hands. That was not the right thing to do. And the *Chronicle*, a paper that obviously has no scruples, went ahead and published them, which was unethical."

"Why unethical?"

"Two reasons. They knew Sandra was legally bound to the *Times*. She had a contract. They enabled her to breach that contract. They were enablers, thus unethical."

"Were you going to fire Sandra? Were you going to sue her?"

"Legally we could have done both. But we decided we weren't going to do either. We decided we were going to give her another chance; We were going to have a conversation with her, to lay down in no uncertain terms what she did was not in keeping with the *Times* code of conduct, and if it happened again there would be consequences. But of course, we never did have that conversation."

"What parts of those articles were factually incorrect?"

Benson moved his chair closer to his desk and looked squarely at Liz "The parts about James Warren. If you want more specific details, you'd have to get that from Alex Anderson. I rely on Alex, I rely on my staff."

Liz stared back. "So you personally don't know what was factually incorrect."

"I already answered that question."

"After that article about James Warren was published, there were several letters to the editor agreeing with the main point; that James Warren, now Jamil

Abdullah Hakim, was creating a Muslim-only community in parts of south Philadelphia. Is that the part the *Times* is saying was not factually accurate?"

"Let me tell you something about James Warren," Benson said, pointing his finger at Liz. "I've known him for years. He has a big heart. He's put his own money into the neighborhood where he grew up. He built affordable housing for the community, created jobs, schools, medical facilities, and recreational facilities. Have you been there? You should go down there and look for yourself. It's thriving, thanks to him. People make a big deal about him converting to Islam like it's a crime. So he established a mosque in the neighborhood. Is that any different than an Italian neighborhood building a church or a Jewish neighborhood building a synagogue? James Warren, or rather Jamil Abdullah Hakim, is doing a great service for the city of Philadelphia. He should get a medal."

"Here's a verified fact. A quote from Warren about his foundation. I quote: "Hoops Housing Foundation is here for the people, and the people are here for Islam." What do you make of that?"

"Tells me he's proud of his religion," Benson countered without skipping a beat.

"I also found this: Warren is a member of an organization called the Muslim Alliance in North America. I did some fact-checking myself and found that this organization is part of the Muslim Brotherhood organization committed to creating an Islamic State in America. And sure enough, the name Jamil Abdullah Hakim shows up on the Muslim Alliance board of directors. What do you make of that?"

"I'll tell you what I make of it. It's Islamophobic. It's scare tactics. It's ignorance. It's boarders on slander of accusing a proud American citizen of treason. I'm sorry to say Sandra taught you bad habits."

The fluttery feeling had turned to excitement – there really was something here! "There's something else I found that I'd like you to comment on. I found, on the internet, yes, that Islam forbids the killing of journalists, but with this caveat 'if they are honest.' But then it says that when Islamists do kill journalists, it is because they believe the journalists are spreading propaganda. I can send you the link. My question is, since you don't believe Anderson is guilty of killing Sandra Wolf, do you think it's possible she was killed because of what she was writing about James Warren?"

"So now you're accusing James Warren of murdering Sandra Wolf?" Benson raised his voice. "Is that what this is all about? Let me tell you something else about James Warren that you won't find on the internet. Before James Warren came along, that neighborhood was full of drug dealers and prostitutes and criminals. A very unsafe place to walk through, let alone live in. A very depressed neighborhood. But James was committed to doing something about it. He was determined to put an end to the crime. He found out who the criminal elements were. He found out it was all controlled by mobster Eddie Malano. Heard of him?"

"Who hasn't?"

"Warren put together a group of young, strong, respectful men. They were dressed in black suits and bowties, and they did two things. They went around the neighborhood in groups of five or six and told the drug dealers to leave. Then they brought the junkies to rehab centers. When Malano got wind of what was going on he sent in his lieutenant Mack Casselette and five of his thugs into the neighbor to give Warren a warning. But Warren was ready. He surrounded himself with twenty of these men dressed in suits and bowties. Yes, they were black, yes they were Muslim. Cassellette looked them over and began like he always did. He said, 'You know who I am, right?' And Warren said, 'I know exactly who you are and I know exactly what you do. And I'm not gonna tell you what to do or what not to do. But I am telling you this. You can't do it here. Do we understand each other?' Well, after that conversation, the drug dealers and prostitutes disappeared. Warren told me the whole story but asked that we not write about it, and we honored his request. I believe that was the beginning of the end of Eddie Malano."

Her dad had a little bit to do with that, Liz thought. She went on, "That is quite a story, Mr. Benson. But don't you think that it supports the points Sandra made in her articles? That Islam has kind of taken ownership of the neighborhood?"

"Haven't you heard of the Community Watch program? Don't you have it where you live? Many communities have them. Italian, Irish, and Muslim."

"If I could," Liz flipped her note pad. "I want to turn to something else. The last article Sandra published in the *Chronicle* was about Abisha, a Muslim woman who was abused by her husband. Sandra actually helped her escape from him."

"Domestic violence is something we take seriously, no matter who does it."

"Then why didn't the *Times* publish that piece?"

He sighed heavily. "It was all part of the package. Again, something you need to ask Alex. I don't interfere with the details of what goes in or when."

"Abisha said that her husband was following the teachings of Islam." Liz felt her heart beating as she was about to ask her next question." Did the *Times* avoid publishing Abisha's story because it might make Islam look bad?"

"You know what, we're done here. Turn off the tape recorder."

Liz didn't move.

"I said turn it off," Benson shouted.

Slowly Liz moved to turn it off.

Benson stared at Liz, forehead bunched up. "If this is how Sandra taught you to conduct an interview then I'm sorry to say you had the wrong teacher. Was it your intention to get me to say I think James Warren was behind Sandra's murder? Was it your intention to say the *Times* is insensitive to domestic abuse in the Muslim community?"

"Just trying to get to the truth Mr. Benson." She met his gaze with her own. "I'm just trying to understand why the *Times* didn't publish those articles. And I still don't understand."

"You have a lot to learn about this city, Miss Liz."

"If you don't think Anderson killed Sandra, then who do you think did?"

"I have no idea. But it's irresponsible of you to make accusations about a prominent and respected citizen of the city based on something you read on the internet."

"If the *Times* is convinced that Anderson is innocent, then why wouldn't the *Times* pursue every angle to prove it? Am I mistaken about that?" Liz put the tape recorder in her bag.

"I'll call Prim to lead you out."

"No need to. I can find my way." Liz picked up her bag. "Would you like me to send you the article before it goes to print?"

"Don't bother."

Liz walked through the office hallway, avoiding eyeing the reporters' active desks to keep her heart at bay. She felt her chances of ever working here or at any other major news desk were gone. But then her attention was drawn to a picture on the wall on the other side of room. She walked over to it for a closer look. She scrutinized the Islamic design, the brush strokes and recognizes the Islamic art design as one similar in design to the one in the mosque she visited with her dad, the one in James Warren's neighborhood. She saw, tucked tiny in the right-hand corner the initials IJ and something in her mind clicked.

Michael Banks was right. There was more to the relationship between the *Times* and Warren's neighborhood. That's what Sandra had discovered, and that's why the *Times* refused to publish her articles. But what exactly? She looked over the vibrant room, a place she knew she would never work. She looked beyond to Benson's office where he was on the phone and wondered if he was talking to someone about her.

On her way out she stopped at Prim's desk to ask more about the other Samuels. But as she was about to ask, Prim, now looking up Liz with a half-smile, she realized that if it was her dad on official business, disclosing their relationship would not be a good idea. Instead, she swapped the words in her mouth to "Hope everything goes well with your mom."

Prim's half-smile was cut in half again. "She's a mess. You want her?"

Liz was about to tell her she's lucky to have a mother, that she would do anything to have the comfort and joy to have her own mother back. But from the hard look on Prim's face, it was clear her mother gave her only pain. Not knowing what to say, because there was really nothing she could say that would make a difference, Liz gave her a nod and walked out.

A SEPTA bus was right there, and she hopped on. She focused on the article she was about to write about how the *Times* ducked hard questions and feared finding out the truth behind Sandra Wolf's murder. Even though she knew publishing it would be the last nail in her not-yet-begun career's coffin.

Chapter Thirty-Eight

Imam Ahmed was about to kneel for the afternoon prayer of duhr when he spotted Ivan and a young black woman in a hijab and business suit entering his mosque. Remembering his last meeting with Ivan did not end well, he wondered if bringing this woman showed a change of heart, a readiness to turn towards Allah. Not wanting to miss a dawah opportunity, Imam Ahmed stood up and approached them.

"Good to see you again, Ivan, and once again your timing is impeccable." Turning to Keisha he asked, "And you are?"

"Keisha Lamont."

"Keisha, if you are here to worship, as you see, the sisters gather in that corner."

"I can see, but we're here on official business." She showed him her IRS credentials. Ivan did the same. Imam Ahmed's eyebrows twisted like a roller-coaster.

"Internal Revenue Service? Ivan, you didn't show me your credentials the last time you were here."

"That wasn't official business. And truly, I didn't know official business would bring me here again. But we're not here for you. We're here to speak with Ian Jeffreys."

"Who?"

"The artist you introduced me to last time I was here. Remember?"

"You mean Ishmael Jihad. He's not here."

"Do you expect him for duhr?" Keisha asked.

"No."

"Then where can we find him?" Keisha asked.

Iman Ahmed looked at Keisha as if he's just been insulted.

"Why?"

"A tax matter. Obviously," said Ivan. "Do you know where he lives?"

"I don't give out personal information about our congregants. Sorry."

"Who here would?" Ivan insisted.

"No one here would. Everyone here is here to pray. In fact, we were about to begin when you walked in. You can stay if you like, and we can speak more…."

But Ivan was looking past him, past the shoes, the faded rugs. He looked towards the back wall, where stood a tall, well-postured man, thick dark beard, hands at his sides, dressed in a dark dishdasha and a square taqiyah on his head, giving him a look with eyes that, if they were hoses, would be gushing full-force through the barred windows.

"Thank you, Ahmed, but I think we'll speak with your boss."

Ivan walked passed Ahmed and Keisha followed him towards Jamil Abdullah Hakim, who beckoned them to follow him to his office.

On the walls of his office were photographs of him in his 76ers jersey with Mayor Wilson Goode, with Mayor John Street. Several basketball trophies adorned the shelves. There were pictures of him in Muslim garb with other Muslims. Ivan recognized one of them, Louis Farrakhan, leader of the Nation of Islam. There was a portrait of Malcolm X. And there was one Islamic painting with the initials in the lower right corner, IJ. An open Koran lay on the desk.

"Please sit," Hakim said in a calm, deep voice that displayed confidence and control. There were two cushioned folding chairs across from his desk. Hakim was already seated.

"The last time I saw you," Ivan said as he sat down, "was at Corestates Arena. You and I were both wearing Sixers jerseys and both taking shots. You, on the court against the Lakers, me in the mezzanine with Yuengling."

"Did we win?" Hakim said as he put a bookmark in his Koran.

"We did. You had a thirty-point game that night. You made us proud."

Hakim nodded, low enough to see the whole top of his taqiyah. "I was proud doing what I was doing then, absolutely. But I'm even prouder doing what I'm doing now. What we did here didn't happen overnight. You must know that. It took sweat. But I'm used to sweat. Now tell me, who am I talking to?"

"This will tell you," Keisha reached out and showed him her credentials. Ivan did the same.

Hakim looked closely at the credentials with the intensity he'd always brought to taking a foul shot. Then looked up at them. "You two make quite the diversity team. Now why are you here?"

"A member of your mosque, Ian Jeffreys, the artist," said Ivan. "We need to speak with him."

"I see."

"Do you have his address?"

Hakim smiled. "Don't you?"

Ivan smiled back. "Let me ask you this question. When does a basketball player take a three-point shot from center court?"

"When all is lost. Which is why you never saw me ever take that shot."

"The thing is," Ivan continued, "there's always that chance that shot could be a game changer. We're taking that shot coming to see you."

"There's no chance of that. Not today."

"And why would that be, Mr. Hakim?" asked Keisha.

"The man you're talking about. The one who did all the nice paintings? That man is not the same man he was."

"You mean he's no longer an artist or no longer a Muslim?" Ivan offered.

"A few months back he went on the Hajj to Mecca, Saudi Arabia. Like all good Muslims are supposed to. From there he went to Pakistan. When he returned, he was different, his whole countenance shifted. He looked at you but not really looking at you. Hearing you but not really listening to you. Talking lots of foolish talk. We can't have that. We put a lot of money and prayer to make this neighborhood a place of peace. It's important for you to know, you personally and the Internal Revenue Service, that we are committed to a safe, clean neighborhood. Especially now with all them lies about me in the newspaper, making me look bad. I don't need no thanks. I give thanks to Allah. But I all I get are attacks in the Islamophobic media. So that's it. He ain't here."

"He was here the other day when I came by," Ivan said.

"Well, he's not today."

"What kind of foolish talk?" Keisha asked.

"What?"

"You said he was talking a lot of foolish talk."

"The kind that best be left unsaid."

"Mr. Hakim," said Keisha. "From what you're saying about Ian Jeffreys, all the more reason you should give us his address before he gets himself into trouble."

Hakim sat back in his chair and smiled sardonically.

"Sister, you know what the holy Koran says? 'Do not enter any houses except your own homes unless you are sure of their occupants' consent.' I don't have his consent. You don't have his consent."

"The Koran also says," Keisha responded, "'And do not kill one another, for God is indeed merciful unto you.' That's verse four twenty-nine. You have more than enough reason to tell where he lives."

"I don't give out personal information to anyone who just walks in here. I don't care who you are. We can chit chat about the Koran, we can chit chat about basketball or the Eagles or whatever. You're my guest. You can stay as long as you like, hear what Imam Ahmed has to say today. Always enlightening. Always good to learn something new about the ways of Allah. But that's all you're getting from me."

""Here's my card," Keisha put her card on the desk. "When you do speak to him, please tell him to call us. Always best to get in front of it. As a basketball player, I'm sure you know that."

Hakim picked up Keisha's card. "I don't want you to get the wrong impression, sister. You can have this back."

"Keep it. You never know when you might need it." Keisha stood up and walked out, ignoring Hakim's outstretched arm holding the card. That was when everything about James Warren changed for Ivan. Even in his brown dishdasha and olive colored kufi, Ivan saw the legend. Telling the story of his neighborhood, reciting Koran verse with pictures of Malcolm X on the wall behind him, Ivan still saw the Seventy Sixers team player. But seeing him reject Keisha's card, Ivan saw what Sandra Wolf had seen: Jamil Abdullah Hakim rejecting America.

Chapter Thirty-Nine

The next day Ivan, Keisha and Sabrina sat in FBI agent Marcus's office. "You're sure? You're sure he said Pakistan?"

"Keisha and I both heard him, Marcus," said Ivan, irritated by the second guessing.

"I'm looking him up now," said Jed, his laptop open on his lap. "Ian Jeffreys, Ah, we got him."

"You got him in custody?" Ivan asked.

"No. I mean, he's in our system."

"He wasn't in our system," said Sabrina.

"He has a passport," Jed answered. "He made a trip to Saudi Arabia and yes, Pakistan. He's a handling code four 4."

"Meaning?" Sabrina asked.

"He's a person of interest," Marcus explained, his desk messy with folders, rubber bands and paper clips. "Code four is the lowest. But that could change."

"So he could be a terrorist?" Keisha asked.

"Let me explain what's going on here," Marcus said moving up to the lip of his swivel chair, putting his elbows on the table and clasping his hands together like a model tower. With every sentence he looked at a different member of his audience. "We get intel from all over the world all the time. We review it. If we think it's worthy, we hold it; if not, we scrap it. In this case we got intel about Americans cavorting with radical elements in Middle Eastern countries. That's all we got. No names, no ID, but we held onto it. We took note of every American returning to United States from the Middle East and designated them a person of interest. Code four. This Ian Jeffreys was one of them."

"If I remember correctly," Ivan interjected, "and I'm sure I am, some of the 9/11 terrorists were put on your Watch List about a month before 9/11."

"That's a fact, yes." Marcus said, looking down at his desk as if doing so would make that fact go away.

"And one received a status of pilot trainee by the Immigration and Naturalization Services a year after 9/11." Ivan added. "I am right?"

Marcus took a rubber band and fidgeted with it. "Not proud moments, Ivan. Which is why I am determined not to allow screw ups like that ever to happen on my watch. You said James Warren was uncooperative?"

"He made it sound like it was a religious obligation not to give us Ian Jeffrey's address," Ivan said.

Jed looked up from his laptop. "I say we need to pay Mr. Warren a visit."

"I agree," said Marcus. "Ivan, why don't you come with us. He knows you. He might feel more comfortable if he sees you with us. It's up to you."

Ivan looked at Keisha, then at Sabrina.

"Keisha too?" Ivan asked.

"Ah, thanks, but no thanks. I had my fill of Mr. Hakim." Keisha said.

* * *

Marcus, Jed and Ivan took the elevator to the basement garage and got into a gray government Chevy. As they drove out Ivan asked said. "You mentioned Jeffreys may have been cavorting with 'radicalized elements.' What exactly did you mean by that?"

"Damn good question, Ivan." Jed said, rolling up the window and lowering the volume of KYW 1060 to inaudible. "And you're asking the right person. It just so happens I've been working with other agents and the New York Police Department on a project to figure out this whole process of radicalization. What we've come up with is that radicalization comes in stages. We believe it starts with Islamist leaders who target young vulnerable Muslims. What I mean by that is Muslims who feel isolated, outcasts, needing to belong to something, anything. These leaders teach them that to be a true Muslim, you must be a Salafi Muslim, which they say is the purest type of Sunni Muslim. They make it seem that being a Salafi is a badge of honor. They build a big brother relationship and convince these youth that non-Muslims and Muslim who don't follow the teachings of Salafist Islamic belief, are infidels who either need to convert or be killed. I'm serious. They get indoctrinated. They're made to believe they were chosen by God. Allah. They accept violence as part of their religion. The hard-core ones become jihadist terrorists. They get trained for a specific purpose. Like the 9/11 terrorists."

Marcus added, "When you told us this guy just returned from Saudi Arabia and Pakistan, and changed his name to Jihad, you got our attention."

Jed parked across the street from the mosque. Ivan got to the door first, but Jed went to read the bulletin board and Marcus peeked into the window of the shed adjacent to the building. Ivan's phone rang.

"I just spoke to Liz about having dinner with her and Gregg tonight," Alice said. "What do you say?"

"I'm busy right now."

"Liz says Gregg is working downtown near the Liberty Bell today, so maybe you two can come together?"

"I don't know right now."

"I'll text you his cell. When you know, give him a call."

"Fine."

Inside the mosque Ivan saw pockets of people reading and reciting, and several others sitting together discussing a passage in the Koran. Ivan noticed

Imam Ahmed and Jamil Abdullah Hakim at the back. They appeared to be arguing. They stopped when they saw Ivan with two other men. Hakim came over with a look saying that this time, Ivan was not welcome.

"Now what do we have here?" Hakim said eyeing Marcus and Jed up and down.

"FBI," Marcus and Jed showed their badges. Hakim bent down to give the badges a closer look.

"Oh, I can see that now. FBI, IRS, what's next, INA, then ICE and next the CIA? Why don't you just arrest me now and get it over with?"

"We hope that won't be necessary," said Marcus. "Ivan here tells us you have the home address of Ian Jeffreys. We need the address, as it could be a matter of national security."

"How's that?"

"Let me put it this way, Mr. Warren. If you don't give us the address and Ian Jeffreys commits a crime, you will be arrested as an accomplice. And this mosque? Shut down. Cooperate, and there will be no trouble at all. You make it easy for us, we make it easy for you. Simple as that."

All the murmurs, all the readings, all the reciting ceased. All eyes were on the silent standoff between the mosque leaders and the government. Both sides stood like bricks. Hakim turned to Imam Ahmed who was now standing by his side and nodded. The imam went to the office.

"Did you speak to Jeffreys after I left last time, Mr. Warren?" Ivan asked.

"As I told you the other day, I want no part of him. He needs to take care of his own business." Imam Ahmed returned with a folded paper and gave it to Hakim. He read it and handed it to Marcus. "Are we done?"

Marcus unfolded the paper and read Jeffery's address. "We are. For now. Appreciate your cooperation, Mr. Warren," said Marcus.

"My name is Jamil Abudullah Hakim."

"Whatever." Marcus pulled out his cellphone and called ahead for a search warrant.

Chapter Forty

Ishmael Jihad sat cross legged on the hard wood floor of his Germantown apartment, bending over a leaf of cotton rag paper, putting the finishing touches of his carbon pencil sketching of Independence Hall. His tongue protruded slightly to the side, his show of concentration. His sleeves were smudged with black, but he wasn't concerned, as he planned to change into his brown body-length dishdasha and light brown kufi head covering before going out. Satisfied he got it right, he put the drawing aside on top of his pile of other Philadelphia scenes. He smirked at the thought of selling them on the sidewalk alongside other desperate artists. That was him once, hustling his art to patriotic tourists before he found the truth, before finding the path to Allah, before the falling out with his mother, his father, and his siblings. He had no regrets. He remembered what his imam mentor in Pakistan told him. "O you who believe! Stand firmly for justice, as witnesses to Allah, even if against yourselves, or your parents, or your relatives."

He recalled with consternation the last conversation he had with his roommate, who had refused to believe what he told him about being a good Muslim; that Sharia law should be imposed wherever Muslims live and by any means. He told him the words of scholar Ibn al-Qayyim, that the messenger of Allah is that he would fight those until they accept his religion; that jihad is simply a means to a greater end; that fighting to raise the word of Allah is the way of Allah. He tried to impress upon his friend that under Islamic law, a just war is protecting access to Islam for all humanity.

He friend's response astonished him and confused him. He said if that is what a true Muslim is, then perhaps he is not. On one hand, he had convinced his friend of the truth of Islam, but instead of embracing it, his friend rejected it and moved out. The experience underscored the teachings of his Pakistani mentors; that his enemies were everywhere; infidels and Muslims who pretend to have faith. Both must be eliminated.

He would do his part. He had planned for the most opportune time. He planned to do it on a weekend when the streets were bustling with tourists. But the phone call from brother Jamil Abdullah Hakim was a message from Allah telling him the time was now.

* * *

Marcus, Jed, and Ivan arrived at Ian Jeffrey's first-floor corner apartment in a dilapidated row house duplex. The wooden steps were wobbly and several wooden slats on the porch were broken. Ivan walked gingerly around the porch to peer into the windows between two dangling shutters. He saw no one inside.

Jed knocked. He then tried the doorknob. The door opened.

"Stay outside and away from the doorway," Marcus told Ivan as he and Jed drew their guns. Ivan stepped away and faced the street, his back against the house. He saw people slowing their pace, looking inquisitively in his direction. Kids braked their bikes, teenagers in tank tops stopped walking but continued bouncing their basketballs, women in hijabs picked up their pacing pushing their baby strollers. At one alley, several young men in sunglasses took slow drags on their joints while leaning on a dumpy car. Across the street, Ivan saw older folks glued to their porch chairs as if waiting for a movie to begin.

"All clear," Marcus called out.

Ivan entered. He saw a couple of beat-up chairs and a stained couch. A mid-size flat-screen TV stood in the corner with a DVD player underneath. DVDs were scattered on the floor. On the couch was a shirt with sleeves rolled at the elbows and pants with holes at the knee. Opened art books and Popular Mechanics magazines sprawled out on a glass coffee table. Dirty dishes in the sink begged to be washed like a cat waiting to be fed. On the kitchen table were several glasses with beverage stains at the bottom, clearly accustomed to being forgotten.

Ivan joined Marcus and Jed in the bedroom in the back where they were packing Ian's laptop, flash drives, a cell phone and several labeled CDs in a huge vinyl bag they had brought with them.

"You were right, Ivan." Marcus said. "The last call on the cell phone was from Jamil Abdullah Hakim. And I want to show you something else." He opened the bottom drawer of the desk. Inside were several handguns and what appeared to be the beginning of a home-made bomb.

"What's this?" Ivan said picking up cotton rag papers hiding under the desk. He laid the drawings out on the desk crowded with art materials.

"Drawings of the Art Museum, Independence Hall, the Liberty Bell," Ivan said, answering his own question.

"It's more than that," Marcus said as he quickly took out his cellphone. "FBI Agent Marcus. Send police with back up to Independence Hall and the Art Museum. Possible imminent terrorist attack at either one or both of those locations."

Remembering Alice's phone call, Ivan searched for her text of Gregg's number. The kid was working too close to Independence Hall today for him to rest easy.

* * *

Ishmael Jihad sat on a bench across the street from Independence Hall on Chestnut Street, near the Liberty Bell. He had arrived just as a tourist group was entering the Hall where the Declaration of Independence had been written, then read aloud publicly for the first time in the open square behind the two-story red brick façade. The building was topped by a Thomas Stretch clock, a bell tower and a steeple, like a layered soft ice cream cone. He figured the tourist group was in the room where the windows remained shut in the summer of 1787, back when the Constitution was being written. He remembered being told that on a class trip: that sweaty men bickered over words on parchment that would guide the American people forever. Thomas Jefferson should have known better. He read the Koran. Yet he chose the Constitution over Sharia. Ishmael reached inside the hidden slit he had carefully made on his dishdasha to make reaching his weapon easy. He rehearsed in his mind what he was about to do.

The tour group came out with happy and proud faces. They had just learned where America all began. Well, Ishmael thought, this will be where it will end. He got up, looked up and down the block and was pleased to see more people coming from both directions. He walked across the street and saw the elderly security guard eyeball him. He reached into the slit of his dishdasha, pulled out an AK-47 and shouted.

"Allahu akbar!"

He shot the guard, the gun recoiling pleasantly in his grip. The crowd shrieked in terror and ran in different directions. Ishmael fired randomly into the running crowd. He shot aimlessly down and up the streets and between the three brick arch entrances leading to the inner courtyard of Independence Hall. People ducked. Some put themselves between the shooter and their children. Ishmael twirled like a protractor and fired again. He was filled with the fire of Allah, and he felt his face shine like that of an angel. Birds flew from their perches, cars stopped and honked horns. Bullets ricocheted off the brick façade. People fell.

Something crashed into him. He went numb.

*   *   *

The shooting stopped.

People were crying and screaming. Some people peeked from behind their hiding places. Ishmael lay on the ground, his gun nestled against his chest. The people looked around expecting to see a police officer, but didn't see any.

"He's faking," someone said. "It's just a ploy," said another after taking a quick look. No one moved from their hiding places. One woman peeked from behind the arch. "I see blood around him. He's bleeding."

"Look up there!" a tourist yelled out.

For all his precise planning and precautions, Ishmael did not anticipate everything, nor did he pay any attention to the guy high up in the cherry picker replacing the bulb of a fifty-foot streetlight, a guy who was still pointing his fired 9-millimeter Glock at Ishmael in one hand, his other hand holding a cell phone to his ear.

It was Gregg.

Chapter Forty-One

As Frank Lopez was leaving the police station he turned to Valerie Moss and said, "Don't forget to go home, Val."

"Are you watching this?" Moss was watching from her desk the six o'clock news on the office TV that hung from the station ceiling.

Frank joined Valerie. They both watched how the afternoon shooting unfolded.

"Anybody killed?" Frank asked. The camera showed bleeding people on stretchers loaded onto ambulances. The commentator pointed to blood on the ground as he described how and where the shooter was shot.

"Don't know yet. Several in serious condition. The shooter was taken out by a guy in cherry picker."

"What guy?"

"An electrician, they said. He was fixing a street light."

"Really! Who is he?" Frank asked. An inane joke popped into his head: how many light-bulb changers does it take to shoot a terrorist?

"They didn't give his name yet," Moss said reaching for an opened bag of chips on her desk. "He was taken to Jefferson. As were the wounded. Frank?"

"I'm right here."

"Just asking, you don't have to tell me. Have you ever shot at anyone?" Valerie's eyes were still on the TV as she chewed.

"Once. It was either him or me. I decided when I first became a cop it was never gonna be me. It was in an alley and there was a fence. There was no place for him to go. I told him to put his gun down, but he turned to me with the gun still in his hand. Again, I told him to put it down. He didn't. So I shot him. Caught him in the leg. What about you?"

"A couple of times. Like you said, I had no choice."

"What happened?"

"First time it was in North Philly. He was behind a car. I told him to drop it. He shot at me and missed. I shot back and he fell."

"You killed him?"

"He survived, in the end. Then he went to prison for thirty years. But that was some time ago. When was the last time you were at the gun range?"

"Been awhile. Maybe now that we both got some time we should go."

The phone rang on Moss's desk. Without taking her eyes off the TV screen where the camera showed viewers the height of the streetlight, she picked up. "Detective Moss."

"Good evening detective. It's Gupta. I see you haven't left for the day yet."

"No, you have something for me?"

"We have a hiccup."

"Meaning what?"

"You remember the skin particles and hair under Miss Wolf's nails?"

"What about them?"

"We did the DNA. I need to tell you it does not belong to Alexander Anderson."

Moss turned to Frank. She put her phone on speaker. "What do you mean not Anderson's?" Frank moved closer.

"Just as I said."

"That can't be, Gupta. That just doesn't make any sense." Moss scratched hard lines on the pad next to the phone.

"Let me talk to him," Frank raised his voice a bit. "Listen, Gupta, you guys are making some mistake over there. As you know, all the evidence we got shows Anderson…"

"Detective Lopez, I don't mean to interrupt, but the mistake is that you have the wrong man in custody."

"That's no way possible. What are you trying to do, Gupta? There is no other man." Lopez slammed his other hand on the Valerie's desk. "He was ID'd in a line up. His DNA was all over the place."

"I'm not here to argue, just to tell you what we found. I know this news is distressing. For us too. But we must face it. We stand by our work."

Moss interjected. "As Frank was saying, that contradicts all the other evidence. All the other DNA results, all the fingerprints that point to Anderson. I agree with Frank. Something is not right. I ask that you please look at it again." Moss and Frank heard Gupta taking a deep breath, as if he were readying himself for a deep dive into a ten-foot swimming pool.

"It doesn't contradict the other evidence. It supplements it."

"Oh, that's rich," Frank said. "Well tell me, Gupta, who does that other damn DNA belong to?"

"Ah, Detective Lopez, if we knew the answer to that, we'd have the murderer, wouldn't we?"

Moss hung up. Lopez paced the floor. On the news, a witness was being interviewed. "I mean, he came out of nowhere, just started shooting and shouting like Muslim terrorists do."

"So now what?" Lopez asked.

Moss crumpled her bag of chips and threw it in the trash can besides her. "We find out who belongs to that DNA."

Chapter Forty-Two

After answering all the police questions, assuring them he wasn't a threat to society, after all the questioning by the city psychiatrist to assure her he was not a menace to himself, Gregg was handed back his Glock and offered a ride home. It was clear that there had been some competition to determine which officer was going to have that honor.

"Go easy on him. He's a hero," said a grinning policeman when Liz opened the door. "You should be very proud of him." Liz thanked the officers and threw her arms Gregg.

"Oh, God, we are so," Liz said, squeezing him. "...so, so I don't know what.... worried, scared, proud." She let go and stepped back to look at him from head to toe. "Mostly relieved you're here." She hugged him again.

"Do I hear we have a hero in the house?" Harold called out from the comfortable chair in the living room. "Bring him back here. He needs a drink. What kind of drink do you want, a scotch, a bourbon?"

"I think both." Gregg said as Liz led him in, holding tightly to his hand.

"You deserve it," said Harold.

Liz brought him to dining room where Alice greeted him with a hug and Ivan held out a Yuengling. "How about this for starters, hero," Ivan said.

"That'll work too." Gregg took the bottle, and then took several gulps.

"What you did," Ivan said clinking his bottle with Gregg's. "We're awestruck. We all owe you. I mean the entire city."

"I'm sure your mind is spinning in all different directions," Alice put her hand on his arm. "How are you handling all this? Seriously. Will you be okay?"

"I think," Gregg said, turning to look at everyone. "Yeah, I think okay."

"You need anything, Gregg, I mean anything, you let me know," Alice said. "Okay?"

"Yeah, Okay."

"I'm sure you're starved," Alice said. "Let's all sit."

"You know I'm staying right here in front of the TV," said Harold.

"We know," said Liz. "We didn't forget you."

Ivan passed the salad bowl to Gregg. "What questions did they ask you at the police station?"

"Everything," Gregg said, taking a mouthful of cucumber and tomato. "Everything they could think of. Who am I, why was I there, did I know this was going to happen, did I know the guy, why do you carry a gun, where did I learn to shoot, did I practice taking that shot? Do I want a drink of water? And the more they kept asking me these questions, the more I asked myself, was it really me who did that? Like, I saw what was going on down there, this guy going nuts shooting everybody with an AK-47 and I was like, oh my God, I gotta do something. When I reached for my gun, it was like, I wasn't doing this, I was making someone else do it. Like I was having some out of body experience. Do you know what I mean?"

"I know exactly," said Alice.

Gregg put down his fork and looked down at his plate. "You know, I've been going to that gun range for years. And I get bullseyes all the time, so at one point I asked myself, do I really need to keep practicing? But then I say to myself, yeah, I go so I don't get rusty. Chances of me ever using a gun are practically nil, but you never know, right? Considering the neighborhoods I go to. So I was up there, in the cherry picker, the least likely place I would need a gun, right? No one coming up from behind, no one getting in my face. I'm all alone up there in the air. Doing my job. Changing the bulb. I'm looking up the block, I see that soft ice cream store and I think that as soon as I'm done here, I'm gonna pop over there and get myself a chocolate vanilla swirl cone.

"But then my phone rings and I pick up and it's Ivan. I mean I'm shocked because Ivan never calls me, I didn't even know he had my number. Why would he? And all you said was," he turned to Ivan, "what did you say? To tell you the truth I wasn't sure what you said. I heard you say something about wanting to give me a heads up. So I turned my head literally and looked down and I see this guy suddenly shooting with what looks like an AK-47. And I'm telling you, I'm not a religious person you know, but I, I just felt, right just then something, a message coming right into my head, saying you, you, Gregg, you are the only one who can do something about this. The crazy nut is shooting at everybody, but he doesn't know you're up here. It was like God telling me I put you up there, up in that cherry picker just now for a reason, I made you decide to continue going to the gun range for a reason, and this is the reason, to stop this clown from killing everyone."

Gregg took a deep breath, and another drink. "And then I just did what I practiced doing so many times; I reached for my gun behind my back, aimed, held my breath, and fired. Like all in one movement. And I hit him. I saw him fall and everything suddenly got quiet. For a minute. Well maybe not a minute, I didn't even know how long, I mean, it took a minute for me to register that I hit him. But I kept my gun pointing at him in case he got up and started shooting again. His gun was still in his arms. And then I got scared. I got scared because I just realized, or I thought I just killed someone. But it turned out I didn't kill him. Does any of this make sense?"

"It all makes sense," said Liz. "And you didn't kill anybody. You saved people. You saved people's lives."

"Yeah, I guess, I guess I did."

"You did the right thing, Gregg," Ivan said. "Stay with that."

"But how did you know?" Gregg turned again to Ivan.

"It was on the news."

"No, I mean to call me right then?"

"What do you mean?"

"How did you know to call me right then?"

"Oh, Alice gave me your number earlier. She told me you were working down there and thought…."

"No, I mean how did you know to call me to give me the heads up?"

"The news is on," Harold shouted from the living room. They're talking about you, Gregg. Better get in here."

Ivan was the first to get up and head to the living room, saved from answering Gregg's question.

On the large flat-screen TV, an anchorman stood in front of a taped off area in front of Independence Hall. He walked as he talked into his microphone.

"Earlier this afternoon at busy Independence Hall packed with tourists in downtown Philadelphia, a man fired what police say appeared to be an AK-47 into a crowd of tourists, sending them running for cover in all different directions. When it was all over one man was killed and seven seriously injured, including the shooter. Witnesses said they saw a man up in a cherry picker by this streetlight (the anchor walked over to streetlight) on this corner of Sixth and Chestnut. Police confirmed it was the man in the cherry picker who fired the shot at the shooter, wounding him in the shoulder. The man in the cherry picker is an electrician hired by the City of Philadelphia. His name is being withheld by police for security reasons. Police say had he not acted, there would have been more injuries and perhaps more fatalities. His gun was legally registered, and he is not being charged with any crime.

"Police confirm the name of the shooter is Ian Jeffreys. He is also known as Ishmael Jihad. He is from the Wynnefield section of Philadelphia. He has no previous police record. Action News contacted the family of Mr. Jeffreys. A spokesperson for the family said they are sorry for what Ian did and pray for the well-being of the victims. Their hearts go out to the family of Chuck Moreno, the security guard at Independence Hall who was killed. Action News discovered Jeffreys attended the Masjid Center of Philadelphia. Imam Ahmed of the Masjid Center told Action News that Ishmael Jihad had been a member of that mosque but had not been seen there for quite some time. At a press conference this afternoon, the police commissioner and the mayor had this to say."

The camera went to the police commissioner.

"We have Mr. Ian Jeffreys, also known as Ishmael Jihad, in custody. He is being treated in the hospital. What we know is that people heard him call out "Allahu akbar" before he went on his rampage. We did manage to speak to him briefly. What he said to us was 'America needs to change and the change needs to start where America began.' As soon as he's discharged from the hospital, he'll be taken into police custody and held without bail."

The camera shifted to the mayor of Philadelphia standing at the podium with self-assurance.

"Let me say first and foremost that our hearts go out to the family of Chuck Moreno and the people who were senselessly injured. We pray for their speedy recovery. This type of violence has no place in our city. This crime was done by a sick and cruel individual and justice will be done, I can promise you that. But the people of Philadelphia need to know," the mayor looked straight into the camera, "that this barbaric, cowardly act has nothing to do with Islam."

Ivan's cell phone rang. He frowned at the name on the screen.

"Sabrina?"

"Yeah, hey, don't mean to disturb you at this time but those two FBI agents, Marcus and Jed, want to see you and me right now."

"Right now? Are you kidding?"

"Sorry, now. Would I be calling you at this time of night and telling you this if I was kidding? At my office."

"Did they say why?"

"They never say why. I'm leaving now. See you in thirty minutes."

Chapter Forty-Three

Ivan deliberately rang the front doorbell. The subsequent wait for an answer, he knew, was just as deliberate. It lasted two minutes. Then the door opened.

"You can't follow simple instructions, always the back door. We told you this last time." Louie wore a black button-down shirt with gray pants. Despite his rant, he held the door open.

"This is Mary Thomas," Ivan said as Louie closed the door and looked her over. "She'll be assisting me today."

"What happened to the other one with the, you know." Louie circled his finger around his head.

"Family emergency," Ivan answered. "Is Sonia here?"

"She's doing you a big favor, she wants you to know. She had you down for next week."

"And we very much appreciate the accommodation, Louie. Did you discuss the tax adjustments with Sonia?"

"I went over it with her and she's disgusted. But it doesn't matter. Like I told you. She'll be filing an innocent spouse claim. If you had just waited the week, I would have handed you the claim form and written you out a brilliant treatise. But no."

"Again, appreciate the flexibility," Ivan said.

"Like before, take a seat in there." Louie nodded in the direction of the dining room. "I'll summon Mrs. Anderson."

The two went to the dining room. Ivan pointed out the painting on the wall. "This is the painting I told you about."

"Very interesting."

"Gets more interesting," Ivan answered.

Sonia Anderson entered the room like a queen indulging peasants with a moment of her precious time. She was wearing heels, and a dark brown pants suit. Her nails were perfectly manicured and her hair was pinned up, not a strand out of place. She looked glossy.

"I am here. And once again you caught me between appointments, but Louie said you had questions only I could answer and would only take a few minutes. But I believe he already told you what our answer will be, no matter the question. Nevertheless I agree to endure the question for the sake of bureaucracy. I see you have a new assistant. Who are you?

"Mary Thomas."

"No matter. I don't even know why I bothered asking. So what's your question? Or do you have questions? Plural."

"First we want to say we appreciate you agreeing to change the appointment," Ivan began. "Care to sit down?"

"No. I'll stand."

Nobody sat.

"Well then, we'll get right to it. Our question pertains to these checks." Ivan pulled out from his inside jacket pocket the three checks made payable to Ian Jeffreys and placed them on the table. Sonia eyed them like they were dead bugs.

"What about them?"

"We'd like you to tell us about them."

Sonia shrugged her shoulders. "It's no secret I'm a lover of the arts. I have been all my life. Did you know I studied art in college? No, of course you didn't, how could you. I was an art history major. I realized, though, that I didn't possess the raw talent to produce serious art. What I did have, and still have, is an eye to recognize talent. Especially young talent. I saw potential in Ian and I chose to be his patron. It's not the first time I've done this. You can ask Louie. He knows. Louie, do you remember Bonnie?"

"Bonnie? Oh yes, of course, Bonnie. Very talented, Bonnie," Louie answered.

"From Yardley. Now there was a talent. She really understood the combining of texture with color. Such vivacious colors she had, such richness! She was not afraid of taking chances with her brush and I took my chances with her. She needed large canvases. That was her style. Just thinking of her canvases gives me goosebumps. Her parents, bless their hearts, didn't have much money, so I helped fund her schooling at Philadelphia College of Art. You can ask her. We're still in touch. Want her number? And so it is the same with Ian. I recognized his talent, how his art invokes his culture and tells a story. So once again I committed myself to fostering his talent. Those checks are for tuition at the Moore College of Art. Anything else I can help you with, Mr. Auditor?"

"Why didn't you pay the Moore College of Art directly?

"I wanted to give him the responsibility to pay the college directly. To give him confidence."

"The checks are made payable to him and note 'for art" in the corner. Not art school," Ivan said.

"He knows what the money was for."

"But why three checks? Why three checks dated in three sequential weeks?

"I have a budget too, you know. I'm sure you can understand that."

"No, actually. You inherited a substantial trust fund from your parents. Twenty-five thousand isn't even a drop from that bucket. I'm thinking you kept it under $10 thousand per check to keep the IRS at bay."

"Yes, of course you'd think that. I'm not surprised. But it really doesn't matter what you think, does it now?"

"In fact, it does. Using your own funds so extensively would show that you may not have benefited from your husband's undisclosed and unreported income. That might qualify you for innocent spouse relief."

"Well then, there you go, and I thank you for telling me. So that clears the matter up then?"

"I have one more question," Ivan said.

"Better be a quick one," Sonia looked at her watch.

"I want to show you something," Ivan said and took something out of his other inside jacket pocket.

"This is Ian's cellphone with a text message which I'd like you to read." Ivan held the cellphone to Sonia's face.

"I'm sorry, what? What am I looking at here?" Sonia took the cellphone in both hands and held it at arm's length. Ivan didn't let go, forcing Sonia to hold Ivan's hand. She looked it with a condescending frown. "'Now is the time.'"

"It's your text message to him. Remember texting it?"

"You're being ridiculous. Of course not."

"Well, Ian does. He remembers very well. He told the police 'the only thing better than killing an Islamophobic infidel is being paid to do it. Especially when the infidel is a lying journalist.'"

Sonia maintained her haughty posture, but her face paled. "What on earth are you talking about? Louie, do something!"

Ivan continued. "He told us this text was your go-ahead to enter the house with the key you took from your husband Alex's spare key ring. I guess your husband never thought you'd know what those keys were for. Never thought you'd ever figure out it belonged to Sandra's townhouse. He underestimated you. But you outsmarted him."

"He always underestimated me. I mean…"

"And you underestimated us, Mrs. Anderson," said Detective Moss, showing her badge. "You're under arrest for the murder of Sandra Wolf. You have the right to remain silent. Anything you say may be held against you. Turn around." Detective Moss took out her handcuffs and locked them around Sonia's wrists. There was no Mary Thomas.

"This is preposterous! Louie, do something!"

"This is entrapment!" Louie bellowed. "A cheap IRS trick. Don't worry Sonia, I'm calling your lawyer right away."

"You can tell him to meet us at Philadelphia Police Station Roundhouse downtown," Detective Moss told him. "We have a car waiting for you outside, Mrs. Anderson."

In the driveway, a policeman and a policewoman stood at either side of the police car. When they saw Sonia come out in handcuffs, the policeman opened the back door. A blurry-eyed and disheveled Alex Anderson stepped out.

"Sonia, what's going on?" Alex called out to his wife as she was led in handcuffs to the other side of the backseat. "Sonia, where are they taking you?"

"Fuck you, Alex!" Sonia screamed as the policewoman fingered her head like a bowling ball, pushing her down into the seat Alex had warmed.

Chapter Forty-Four

Alice picked up a newspaper from the kiosk in the lobby of her Center City Philadelphia office building and put it in her handbag.

"Getting the *Philadelphia Chronicle* this morning, Mel." The blind man held his hand out from behind the kiosk and felt Alice putting two quarters into his palm.

"You're looking pretty this morning, Alice. I can tell by the perfume."

"You always know what you're talking about, Mel, so who am I to argue?"

"A lawyer?" Mel smiled, showing a missing front tooth.

"See what I mean?" Alice responded.

"Your elevator is here, have a good day."

Alice got off at the ninth floor and headed to her corner office overlooking the crowded corner of Walnut and Sixteenth.

"Oh, good morning, Alice," greeted Lucy the office secretary as Alice walked passed her. "Stephanie Malano returned your call. I told her to call back in a half hour."

"Thanks Lucy." Alice closed her door and put her bag down by her desk. She sat down in her black, high back leather swivel chair, pulled opened the *Philadelphia Chronicle* and put it on her mahogany desk.

Philadelphia Chronicle

Anderson Out of Jail But Not Out of Trouble

By Liz Samuels

June 20 — While all charges against Alexander Anderson for the murder of journalist Sandra Wolf have been dropped, he has nevertheless been fired from his job as executive editor of the *Philadelphia Times*, a position he held with a tight fist for over thirty years. He also faces a lawsuit from his former employer.

Wanting to clear the air and his name, Anderson agreed to talk to the *Chronicle* about his arrest, his firing and his plans for the future.

Liz: First, thank you for granting the *Chronicle* the opportunity to get your side of this very troubling ongoing story. You spent almost two weeks in jail. Why were you charged in the first place?

Anderson: Easy. The police, the mayor and the district attorney targeted me as their scapegoat. They're vengeful people and wanted my head for writing the truth about them all these years. They saw an opportunity to get back at me and they took it.

Liz: To be fair, the city did come up with evidence pointing in your direction.

Anderson: It's all in the spin, my dear. You ought to know that; you're a journalist. They found my DNA and Sandra's DNA on an item picked up in the hotel room; they found my fingerprints on a tie they determined to be the murder weapon. They put these pieces together and pinned the murder on me like a tail on a donkey.

Liz: How do you explain your fingerprints on the tie?

Anderson: It was my tie; of course it would have my fingerprints all over it. I'm still trying to get my head around how my wife schemed it all.

The phone rang. Alice picked it up. "Alice Dyckman."

"Alice. It's Stephanie. There's no one at the counter now so I got maybe a minute. So what's the verdict?"

"I'm sorry, Stephanie. Judge Whitney denied your innocent spouse claim."

"Shit, so now what?" Stephanie stepped away from a browsing customer. "They gonna take away my paycheck again? I'm working for nothing now? I mean shit, how am I supposed to live?" She put her cell to her other ear. "I mean what the hell!"

"They're not going to garnish your salary again, Stephanie. They're going to leave you alone."

"What do you mean? You just said the judge said I was guilty."

"On your innocent spouse claim. You still owe the tax, yes. But the IRS is not going to take any further enforcement against you, at this point."

"So, I don't get it. Does that mean then for all intents and purposes I am innocent?"

"That's one way of spinning it," Alice said.

* * *

Harold spilled Monday's pills onto the kitchen table and poured himself a glass of Poland Springs water. He swallowed three pills in one gulp, then went back to reading the newspaper article his granddaughter opened for him before she left with Gregg that morning.

Liz: How do you explain the witness who saw you at her house that night?

Anderson: He saw me because I was there.

Liz: That's not what you told the police when they first interviewed you.

Anderson: When the police first interviewed me, all I cared about was keeping my relationship with Sandra a secret. I knew I had nothing to do with her murder.

Liz: Okay, so you were there. Then what?

Anderson: I got out of my car. I walked up the steps to her house to ring the bell. But by then the effects of our earlier intoxication was wearing off. I realized there was no undoing the argument we had at the hotel. I realized what I wanted wasn't going to happen. It was a turning point, literally and figuratively. I got back in my car and drove home.

Liz: Tell us about the argument.

Harold's phone rang. "Yes, hello, who is this?"

"Mr. Samuels?"

"Yes, who is this speaking please?"

"Kathy Kelly from Kelly Realtors. You called me about the condo for sale at Green Hill Condos. I can meet you there this afternoon if you like. Will that work for you?"

"Oh, yes, this afternoon, but I have a problem. I have no way of getting there. I just had surgery, everyone's out and the doctor doesn't want me to drive and there's no one here to take me."

"No worries, sugar. I'll come personally to pick you up, and then bring you back home. But I can guarantee once you set your eyes on this gorgeous condo overlooking the swimming pool you're not ever going to want to leave. Say two o'clock?"

* * *

Ivan sat on the train on his way to work, smiling with pride as he read his daughter's article.

Anderson: It was about her article, the one that appeared in the *Chronicle* the next day. I gave her the impression we were going to publish it the next morning, and then I let it slip that we weren't. Thinking back on it, I should have just lied and told her what she wanted to hear, that it would be out the next morning. Had I done that, had I lied, she wouldn't have run out and she'd be alive today. And for that I'm sorry. I'm sorry I didn't lie.

Liz: Your publisher, though, Conrad Benson, said the article needed fact checking.

Anderson: That was just an excuse. The truth is, I was never going to publish it.

Liz: And why was that?

Anderson: There was too much at stake.

Liz: Like what?

Anderson: Very few people in Philadelphia take on responsibilities like I do. Or did. Not even the mayor. You have to understand that the *Times* was—is—in bankruptcy, on the verge of collapse. Investors were drying up. If things continued the way they were going, we'd be out of business in six months. I found a way to keep the paper afloat. I found a way to infuse it with cash. When the board found out what I was doing, instead of being grateful, instead of thanking me, what do they do? They fired me.

Liz: In their statement, published in the *Times*, it said you were fired for financial impropriety. That you received funds from, quote, undisclosed and questionable sources, end of quote. Could you tell us about that?

Anderson: If I did, it would no longer be undisclosed, would it now? Besides, I'm under strict orders from my lawyers not to discuss it. I've already told you too much.

Liz: You seem to be implying that this undisclosed source had something to do with why you didn't publish Sandra's piece.

Anderson: Let's just say that everything comes with a price. As far as I was concerned, not publishing Sandra's piece was a small price to pay.

Liz: It wasn't a small price for Sandra.

Anderson: My wife murdered Sandra. She and that terrorist artist.

Liz: Did you know him? Ian Jeffreys, or Ishmael Jihad. The *Times* has some of his art on the office walls.

Anderson: As an artist I knew him. Not as a terrorist. My wife took an interest in his art, got to know him, got to know him pretty damn well apparently, and convinced him to murder Sandra. He didn't need much convincing. Sonia showed him some of Sandra's past articles about Muslim terrorism, gave him money. That's all it took. She found Sandra's house key on my key ring, made a copy, gave him my tie, instructed him what do and how to do it. I'd say that's as pre-meditated as it gets.

Liz: How are you handling all this, Mr. Anderson?

Anderson: Under the circumstances, I think pretty well. Probably better than most people would.

Liz: So what's next for Alexander Anderson?

Anderson: I'll take some time off. I think I'm entitled. Then, I'm thinking of starting my own newspaper. Online only. No hardcopy.

Liz: Interesting! How will it be different from the *Times* or the *Chronicle*?

Anderson: It will cover the stories that the other two don't tell. It'll ask the questions that aren't being asked and should be asked.

Liz: Interesting! Do you have a name yet for you new endeavor?

Anderson: "*The Philadelphia Gap.* What other outlets let fall, we fill the gap. What do you think?"

Liz: Sounds perfect.

Anderson: Want a job?

Liz: Will you pay my health insurance?

Anderson: Jerry Maguire!

When he got to his office, Ivan saw written messages, new case files and the red light blinking on his phone telling him he had 16 voicemail messages.

"Welcome back," said Hector. "As you can tell, you were sorely missed."

"Had I never returned, all this would belong to you." Ivan waved his hand over the entire surface of his desk.

"Oh, I'm not deserving of all that. But Keisha, you should will it all to her."

"Knock knock," Tina stood at the threshold of Ivan's cubicle. "Your appointment is here."

Ivan looked at his watch. "Wait, I don't have any appointments. I just got back. Look at my desk."

"You don't have to explain it to me. But the guy out there asked for you." Tina says. "What do you want me to tell him?"

Ivan sighed. "Who is it?"

"Same guy as last time," said Tina.

"Told you," said Hector. "Sorely missed."

"Here," Ivan handed Hector the *Chronicle* as he walked passed him. "My daughter's article on the front page."

Hector unfolded the paper, looked it over and pointed to her byline. "Cool beans, man. You must've done something right for once."

Ivan opened the door to the reception area and saw Leslie Glassman sitting there, clutching a manila envelope, one leg twitching up and down like a runaway hose, one eye aglow like a red onion, a band aid on his nose. When he saw Ivan, he stood up.

"Mr. Samuels, I decided to take your advice and divorce my wife. But I need your help."

* * *

Liz turned down the music in Gregg's truck as they parked. They looked up in silence at the 93-foot open-air concrete tower standing lonely on a mound amidst a wide lush green field surrounded by a thick forest. They'd been driving for four hours.

Arm in arm, they walked towards the tower. It encased forty long aluminum tubes that swayed and chimed with even the slightest breeze. They represented forty distinct voices. Liz closed her eyes, and imaged them talking all at once, as they most likely had on that grim day.

After a few minutes of listening, they took the path leading to the wall with the forty names etched in. Behind the wall was the spot where the forty heroes, strangers hours before they perished in the little-known town of Shanksville Pennsylvania, refused to allow Al Qaeda terrorists reach their deadly destination of crashing their plane into the nation's Capitol Building. Leaning on

Gregg's arm and reading each name, Liz wondered what Sandra would say about being here. She imagined her face getting up close to each name, as if doing so would allow her to get to know the person better. She saw Sandra curling her lip as she did when she got serious.

"You're like them, Gregg," She looked up at him.

Gregg shook his head. "What do you mean?"

"Heroic. Just like them, you stopped carnage from happening. You're my next exclusive."

"Oh, I don't need the publicity."

"Well, the thing is, it wouldn't be about you."

"Then that's fine. Write about me without it being about me. I can go along with that. Whatever that means."

"It would be about ordinary people stepping up."

"Hmm. One minute I'm an exclusive, and the next I'm ordinary. I get it."

Liz playfully hit him on the belly. "I know you get it."

"Tell you what," Gregg said reaching into his pocket. "I'll make you a deal. I'll be your exclusive if you'll be my exclusive." He took out a small velvet box and offered it to her. Liz stared at it for a second, looked up at Gregg, then took it with both hands.

"Oh my. Oh, my God." She opened the box. Inside was a diamond ring, sparkling in the afternoon sun. The random glittering brought to mind the intermittent chimes of the tower she heard a moment ago.

"Gregg, I'm... I'm ... I don't know what to say." Liz looked into his eyes. He returned the look and smiled nervously.

"I know it's a weird place to do this, but the moment just grabbed me."

"This place is about bravery and positivity and selflessness," Liz said. "It's the right place. It's the perfect place for us."

Gregg looked intently into Liz's eyes. "That's just what I was thinking."

###

About the Author

Leonard Getz, CPA, is a retiree from the Internal Revenue Service. After retiring he was a writer and researcher for the Middle East Forum. He's published numerous articles for the Philadelphia Bulletin, the American Thinker, New English Review, PJ Media, Daily Wire, Jewish News Syndicate, Lifestyles Magazine, Nostalgia Magazine, Lock Haven Express. He's the author of the film book "From Broadway to the Bowery," and he was a video interviewer for Steven Spielberg's Survivors of the Shoah Foundation, interviewing Holocaust survivors about their experiences. This is his first novel.

Made in the USA
Middletown, DE
11 November 2022

14736811R00201